THIS HOMEWARD JOURNEY

THE MOUNTAIN SERIES ~ BOOK 10

MISTY M. BELLER

Unless otherwise indicated, all Scripture quotations are taken from the Holy Bible, Kings James Version.

ISBN-13 Trade Paperback: 978-0-9997012-7-0

ISBN-13 Large Print Paperback: 978-1-954810-31-0

ISBN-13 Casebound Hardback: 978-1-954810-32-7

To my sweet mother-in-law, Barbara.
The way you pour out your love on our family is a legacy we'll always treasure.

Remember ye not the former things, neither consider the things of old.
Behold, I will do a new thing; now it shall spring forth; shall ye not know it?
I will even make a way in the wilderness, and rivers in the desert.

Isaiah 43:18-19 (KJV)

CHAPTER 1

Only a final massive obstacle lies between us and a new life. I can push through the last of this journey. I must.
~ Rachel

June, 1869
Fort Benton, Montana Territory

Rachel Gray straightened her shoulders as she scanned the dim interior of Fort Benton's trade store. The high brick ceiling made the room feel less hemmed-in than she'd expected, but her vision still spotted with remnants of the bright afternoon outside.

Men's laughter echoed from a back room, tugging the knot in her middle. She'd come into this tiny trade room tucked inside fort walls because she'd hoped to avoid all the raucous men sloshing down the streets of the town. Through the week she and her son had camped outside the town, she'd had her fill of mountaineers sated from an afternoon of drinking and gambling.

It seemed when the men stumbled from their bedrolls late each morning, they headed straight for the gambling tables. Not that a man could help his addictions once the demon was planted inside him. But these were a sorry lot. Maybe they'd come west hungry for gold or to escape their lawless past. She worried some were even running from a hangman's noose. But all they'd found was drink and cards. The sights and sounds of their den still churned her stomach into a tight wad.

"Howdy, ma'am. Need help with somethin'?"

She spun to face the man who strode toward her from beside a large hearth. His buckskins and overgrown beard made him a perfect match to most of the others she'd observed around the town, though his manner seemed proficient enough. Like a worker in the course of his duties.

He strode behind the wooden counter, bent to peer at a lower shelf she couldn't see, then straightened. After spreading his hands across the worn wooden surface, he peered up at her as though eyeing her over spectacles. He wore none, but the look was telling, as was the indention across the narrow part of his nose.

She pulled her gaze upward to his assessing eyes. "I've a question about the trail northward. Is there a guide here who knows it well? All the way to the Canadian territories? I need someone to tell me the best route through the mountains."

His graying eyebrows shot upward. "You aimin' to go through the mountains? It's a sight easier through flat land."

Maybe he thought women the weaker vessel, but he'd not traveled with her the last two and a half months. She and her son had managed quite well trekking across the territories alongside the Missouri River.

Without the help of a man. And they could continue north alone, too, as long as they had a map to guide them. Finding the trail through the mountains would be much harder than following the Missouri River as they'd done to this point.

Of course, Andy tried to fill the role of a man, but at twelve, he carried only the good qualities of the male species. None of the weaknesses.

And she'd keep him that way as long as she had breath in her body. Thus, the need for their journey northward.

Ignoring the shopkeeper's question, she proffered one of her own. "Have you a map or sketch of the best route through the mountains?"

His mouth pinched as he studied her. "The best route is to the east, through the prairieland alongside the mountains. You be goin' to Fort Hamilton?"

Apparently, he did know the northern country. A sliver of satisfaction filtered through her. "I'd rather go through the mountains. I prefer that terrain to the flatlands."

His brows hiked up again, nearly brushing his thinning hairline. "You musta ain't seen those cliffs yet. You'll go twice as fast an' stand a sight better chance gettin' where yer goin' if you stay on the prairieland."

She let his words slide past her. His statement may have been true, but she'd also seen the two trains of freight wagons heading on that same eastern route just this week, filled with supplies from the two steamboats docked beside the levee. She'd not spend the next weeks in the company—or rather avoiding the company—of a stream of vice-ridden freighters.

But she also didn't plan to pick a verbal skirmish with this man. "Perhaps you could provide me with a map for both routes. Have you such? Or is there someone nearby who could sketch the trails?"

Obtaining actual maps might be too much to hope, but she didn't want to have to ask directions at each settlement she passed. Entering every town would require rubbing elbows with too many strangers.

And leaving Andy alone each time.

The man ran a hand over his greasy hair as his look turned thoughtful. "I could probably draw up something that showed the milestones I know of." His focus turned sharp again. "Can you give me a day or two?"

The relief sinking through her almost brought a smile. "I can." A day or two would allow their horses more time to rest before they had to take on the rough terrain they'd encounter next.

He nodded, then his expression eased into something hopeful. "I don't suppose you have a way to pay for my efforts?"

She wasn't sure whether to be incensed that he would think she'd consider taking goods without paying for them or weighed down by the fact that she'd have to part with their hard-earned animal pelts. She settled for a displeased expression. "I have furs to trade." After hoisting her bundle to the counter, she unfastened the cloth wrapping the skins and unrolled them. "I need cornmeal, beans, salt, and any kind of horse feed you have. How much will you offer for these?"

The way he perused the stack made it clear he knew his wares. And she had nothing to be ashamed of in these. Every animal Andy brought down for their food had been carefully skinned, and she'd spent long hours readying these hides. She and her son may not have had two nickels to spare, but out here in the frontier, they wouldn't need coin anyway. Trading was the expected means of obtaining supplies.

For the rest of the journey to find Henry, they could barter for whatever they needed. *Thank you, Lord.* The idea of having enough food seemed almost too good to trust. As was the hope of finding her brother in this wilderness, but she had to try.

After examining the furs, the man leveled a long, and thankfully sober, gaze on her. She tensed for the insulting offer that would come next.

But the deal he proposed was slightly better than she'd been hoping for. Had she misjudged the price of supplies in this western fort? Or maybe the value of furs was higher than she'd estimated.

Either way, she couldn't afford to miss even one pound of corn she might gain by bartering a good transaction. She raised her chin and asked for five more pounds of beans.

The man let out a hard breath and rocked backward, then scrubbed a hand through his hair again. "Here I thought I was bein' noble giving you my best offer up front." His chuckle sounded half amused, half frustrated. "I 'spose, but not a pound more."

She let her breath ease out in a quiet stream, refusing to allow the niggle of guilt that tried to slip into her midsection. "Good. I'll take the supplies now and return in two days for the maps." She hated to hand over the furs without receiving everything owed to her, but they couldn't wait for food. Andy had already become leaner than she liked, even with the steady diet of venison, rabbit, and anything else he could bring down with the rifle. Growing boys took in more food than she'd imagined.

The man eyed her once more over the brim of his invisible spectacles. "Supplies are out back. Don't suppose you have a wagon to load them in?"

"I'll bring my horse around."

As she turned to leave the place, the rush of accomplishment surged through her. Supplies and a map. This arrangement worked better than she'd allowed herself to hope.

When she reached the door, a swell of laughter from the back room stole any joy the happy thoughts might have conjured.

She and Andy would have food for a few weeks and be able to travel on their own, but as long as men allowed themselves to fall under the spell of awful vices like the drinking and gambling taking place on the other side of that wall, she and Andy could never truly be safe.

~

"We'll head out in two days then?" Seth Grant leaned in as he waited for the older man's confirmation. He could practically taste the open wilderness again. A much better sensation in his mouth than the flavors of tobacco and whisky consuming the stale air around this card game.

Elias Benbow nodded. "Daylight morning after next. Meet me back here at the gate behind the trade store, an' make sure your animals are loaded and ready to go."

"Will do." Samuel, Seth's twin brother, extended a hand to the older man.

After taking his turn to shake, Seth stood and turned toward the doorway connecting to the store. He needed fresh air. Not because the scents in this room were luring him back to his former vices. The opposite actually. The stench in here made his stomach want to heave. God had so deeply carved those old desires out of him, he couldn't seem to stand more than ten minutes in a gambling den. And only when the situation required it, like now, to secure their guide on this last leg of the journey northward.

Thank you, Father. He'd take the threat of casting up his accounts any day over the way those habits used to clutch him by the throat.

Samuel's familiar boot steps sounded behind him as they pushed through the hanging buffalo robe that served as a curtain between the gaming room and the brighter chamber where the exchange of goods took place. The fur swished back into place, mostly blocking out the male voices behind them, and a sense of calm settled into his spirit.

The buyer stood behind the counter, sorting through a stack of pelts —mostly deer, from the looks of the fur peeking out of the pile. The man glanced up as Seth stopped before him.

"We need a bit more feed corn or oats for our horses. Do you have any to trade for gold dust here, or do I need to go to the livery up by the river?" Being as this store mostly did business with the Indians, they likely didn't appreciate white men using up all their supplies. Even in exchange for gold dust.

The man's gaze slid over them as he raised one of the furs. "You boys from Helena?"

Seth shook his head. Not that it was any of this man's concern, but he didn't mind being friendly. "California."

His brows rose. "They run out o' gold there so you had to come hunt it in these parts?" The twitch of his cheek was enough to show he meant nothing unfriendly with the question. Yet the curiosity was clear in his eyes. Why would they leave the gold fields of California to come to the much colder panning in the Montana Territory?

"Nope. But I think we're done mining for now."

"Hmm." The sound didn't say much, but the knowing glint in his eyes spoke the rest. Clearly, he felt they'd finally come to their senses. This fellow must have spent a month or two himself digging for yellow rocks. Seen what kind of laborious work the pursuit was for the pittance the average mine returned.

Seth couldn't agree more.

"I have a couple sacks of oats I could sell ya." The man peered up as though looking over spectacles. "Will that do?"

He nodded. "We're headed up to the Canadas through the mountain country, so I guess that'll get us at least part way. Hopefully we'll find a place to restock along the trail."

The man's chin jerked up. "You know the going's a sight easier if you head northeast over the prairies." He spoke as though the trail they took actually mattered to him. Which it shouldn't.

Seth kept his tone friendly. "I'm sure you're right, but the fellow traveling with us lives in the mountains above the Marias River. After we drop him off, we'll head farther north."

The trader ran a hand over his hair, slicking the greasy strands flat. "You're the second person today to say they're taking the mountain trail north. Makes for some hard goin', even in the summer."

His interest honed. "You mean Elias Benbow?"

The man shook his head. "No, a woman come in here while ye was in the back. Asked me to draw her a map o' the landmarks. Sure don't like the thought of any kind of female travelin' that way alone."

"How do you know she was alone?" Samuel stepped into the conversation, surely as concerned at the news as he was.

"'Cause she was in here tradin' fer supplies and askin' directions on her own. If she had a man, he'd be doin' that. 'Specially as jumpy as she was. Looked like she was afraid one o' you men was gonna charge from the back room an' take her by force." The opening in the man's beard where his mouth should be pressed to a thin line.

Seth glanced at his brother to see if he was thinking the same thoughts that were spinning through Seth's own mind. The return look and nod made his unspoken answer clear.

He turned back to the trader. "Do you know where this woman is staying? Maybe she'd like to join our group. It'll just be the three of us, but she'll surely be safer with us than on her own."

The man appeared a little relieved. "The hotel's been full from the passel o' steamboats that's hit the levee. She may be in the camp east o' the fort."

Seth nodded. "We'll look for her." He'd not stop 'til he found her.

The transaction didn't take long to finish, then he and Samuel each hoisted a sack of horse oats on their shoulders. The moment they stepped out into the bright sunshine, Seth turned to his brother. "You wanna store these with our provisions while I go look for her?"

"Nope." Samuel didn't pause to talk, just kept a steady march toward the livery where they were keeping their supplies. "We'll go together."

A stab of frustration jabbed Seth's chest as he trudged forward in his brother's footsteps. Samuel was right, of course. But curiosity blazed inside him about this woman.

What would make her strike out on her own? And why the mountain trail? He and Samuel had good reason—they needed Elias to guide them northward, and Elias was headed to his home in the mountains.

But what would drive her on such a treacherous journey? Something told him this woman wouldn't be like anyone he'd met before.

CHAPTER 2

I've been given so much. I can't help but aid others as I find need.
~ Seth

Seth couldn't help the defeated feeling in his gut as he pushed through the tree cover later that day. No one in the cluster of tents knew of a woman headed north alone. No one even knew of a woman camping alone. One fellow who looked to be half-Indian said he'd seen another tiny campsite set away from town. Tidy and well-hidden.

May have been just what they were looking for.

If they could have found the place. They'd traipsed pretty far from town, checking behind every tree and over each ridge. But still hadn't found any sign of her.

"Wait. Did you hear that?" Samuel's low voice caught Seth's steps short.

He stilled his breathing as he strained to hear. A voice, higher than a man's but...something about it didn't ring like a woman's tone.

The talking sounded just ahead through a patch of cedar and

heavy underbrush. He stepped forward, slower than before, keeping his tread light.

Except… maybe he should allow her to hear them coming. The last thing he wanted to do was surprise an unsuspecting woman. If she knew how to shoot a gun, he'd hate to meet the business end of her rifle. To survive this far, she surely knew how to shoot one. Of course, it'd be even worse if she didn't know how to handle the weapon.

If only he knew her name, he'd call out to announce himself. Maybe best to call a greeting anyway.

"Hello. Anyone out here?" It'd be nice if she would answer. Sound a friendly response.

But of course she didn't. Was she running from the law? Afraid of men? Did she have a violent husband chasing her?

A cluster of bushy spruce sat a dozen strides ahead, so he moved that direction. "Is anyone here?" Surely she'd heard his first call, but he still didn't want to give her the idea they were sneaking up.

A horse's snort sounded on the other side of the trees. Definitely someone there.

Samuel's breath warmed the back of Seth's neck as he reached to push the branches aside, giving them both a glimpse of what lay beyond.

His view made him recoil.

"What do you want?" The woman on the other side of the rifle spoke with a tone edged in steel.

"We mean no harm, ma'am." He eased his hands up. "Just came to ask a question."

"Step out here where I can see you, then ask it." She edged backward, giving them room to comply.

He and Samuel both obliged her, keeping their hands out and well away from their own pistols. Seth wasn't particularly concerned, as they didn't plan to do anything that would encourage her to pull the trigger. Even so, when a man is staring down the barrel of a Henry rifle at close range, it was better to take precautions.

He wrangled away the urge to step back into the trees.

"What's your question?" Now that his view of the woman wasn't blocked by branches, he realized she was much younger than he'd expected. Maybe somewhere in her mid-twenties, a couple years younger than he and Samuel. And she'd be pretty too, if she didn't wear such a look of...well, *hatred* was the word that sprang to mind.

She had absolutely no reason to dislike them that much, and for some reason, he had a sudden urge to prove himself worthy. Once she got to know him, he'd make sure she fully changed her mind about him.

He cleared his throat to get his dry mouth to work. "Ma'am." He nodded in greeting. "My name's Seth Grant, and this is my brother, Samuel. We were in the trade store today, and the fellow there said you might be headed north through the mountains. We're going that way too, so we came to invite you to join our group."

Her hard eyes widened, but the gun never wavered.

He hurried on. "We've one other man riding with us. Elias Benbow. He's lived in this land for a lot of years. A good sort. He's gonna show us the route, then he'll drop out when we reach his cabin right below the line into Canada. We plan to go on to our brother's place a week or so into that country."

He stopped to catch his breath and give her a chance to speak.

Silence filled the space between them. Was there something else he should add? More details she'd need to know to see the wisdom in joining forces?

"Is that everything you came to ask?" Her words held no sign of emotion. No sign of whether she was leaning toward a *yes*. Although the lack of sentiment probably meant she wasn't convinced.

"Yes, ma'am. We thought it made sense to travel together. You know the old saying, 'many hands make light work.' They also make for better protection."

"I appreciate your offer, boys, but no thank you." She spoke with a flat tone.

And she called them *boys*.

"Why wouldn't you want the protection?" He couldn't help the bite of irritation in his tone. She must be touched in the head to deny their offer. She didn't look half-witted, but perhaps that was truly the case. Unless...

was she afraid of them? He glanced down at his shirt and trousers. Clean enough. Maybe he should've shaved and washed better, but he'd have been dirty again by now with all the searching they'd done to find her.

Whatever her reservations, he needed to convince her to drop the crazy notion of traveling alone through this wilderness. He forced his voice to calm. "We mean you no harm, ma'am. We've been in California for the past half-dozen years, but before that we hailed from Yorkville, a little town in South Carolina. From good folks, a family of nine children." He scanned his memory for something else that might help, then looked to Samuel for assistance.

His brother straightened. "Our folks are farmers. They raise corn and cotton mostly. We didn't even have slaves before the war. We worked the farm ourselves."

Her face remained stoic. Unimpressed. Stone. If she was afraid, she had the best poker face he'd ever seen. And he'd seen more than he cared to remember.

Maybe she was touched in the head. Or on the run from the law.

As Samuel's words faded into silence, the woman raised her chin a notch. "I pity your poor mother for having to raise such a brood. Now, I think we're done here. You asked your question, I answered. You can be on your way." Her vivid green eyes held such resolve, there seemed to be nothing left but to turn and leave.

"If that's what you want, ma'am. We'll be leaving Fort Benton morning after next. If you change your mind, meet us at the small gate behind the trade store at sunrise."

"I already gave you my answer." The gun raised a hair, giving the impression they'd best leave.

Seth stepped back. "The offer still stands." Then he made himself turn away. Forced himself to put his back to the gun. To prove he wasn't afraid of her.

Because he had an inkling fear was, indeed, the motivation behind her bluster. The comment about his mother made him think she'd experienced her own hard life and could sympathize with another woman whose path wasn't easy.

A woman as young as she was couldn't know what hardships his mother faced, but she must have her own story. Didn't everyone?

As he and Samuel trekked back toward town, the possibilities of what an innocent young woman might've endured flashed through his mind. Stomach-churning possibilities. Enough to make him want to turn around and force her to travel with them.

He couldn't compel her to make the safe choice, though. The only thing he could do now was put her in God's hands.

Lord, protect her. Do what I can't.

~

Rachel stared at the descent before her, trying to still the roiling in her middle. *God, help me do this.*

"You want me to lead, ma?" Andy reined his horse forward to move up beside her.

She swallowed. "No, I can do it. I just didn't expect the mountains to be so steep yet."

"I think this is only a hill. At least, compared to those over there." He pointed straight ahead, and she squinted to make out the massive forms shrouded in fog.

As her eyes adjusted, the peaks took shape with startling clarity. Yes, peaks. Rising at least twice as high as the terrain they rode now, capped with white and looming tall enough that a fall from them would kill a person without question.

Could she lead them safely through such heights? She had to. There was no other choice if they were to have the new life she'd promised. She and Andy had to fade into the obscurity of these mountains until they reached Fort Hamilton. Once they found Henry, he would help them.

Until then, they had to undertake this journey alone.

Squaring her shoulders, she nudged her gray gelding forward. "Come on, Winter. We can make it."

The horse didn't seem concerned about the descent, tucking his hind legs under him as he shifted steadily downward. Andy's mare, Summer, did just as well.

Still, Rachel had a white-knuckled grip on the saddle by the time they reached the bottom.

"That wasn't so bad, was it?" Andy's tone held a lightness she couldn't help but envy.

She shot a look at him. "One down, twenty more to go?"

He wrinkled his nose. "More like two hundred." His gaze slipped sideways. "Hey, is that the men who came to the camp?"

She followed his focus. Skirting the base of a hill ahead, three men rode in single file, their horses loaded with enough supplies to last for weeks. The two men in the rear had similar builds—at least, similar ways of sitting atop their horses.

Those broad shoulders, squared as if charging into adventure, did look an awful lot like those of the men who'd come stomping into their camp two days before. Seth and Samuel Grant. They shared similarities that made no doubt of their claim to be brothers. Seth must be the older, from the way he'd naturally taken the lead.

A bit of impulsiveness in that one. Probably a tendency that had snared him into more than one unhappy ending. She knew the type too well. Had been married to one with that same propensity to do whatever notion swept into his mind at the moment.

She set her jaw against the painful memories and guided Winter closer to a stand of cedars. The men rode far enough ahead they probably wouldn't look back and notice her and Andy, but they'd do best to stay out of sight anyway.

Although maybe…if their guide was as good in these mountains as they claimed, perhaps she and Andy should follow their trail. Shadowing the men could be the wisest way to ensure she didn't get herself and Andy lost in this wilderness.

Because from the looks of things, the Montana Territory was vast and treacherous enough to swallow them whole.

~

"What are their names again?"

Rachel motioned for Andy to quiet his whisper even more, then moved close to his ear. "The younger man by the fire is Seth Grant. The older is Elias Benbow. The other brother by the horses is Samuel Grant." Though she'd been terrified when they'd come to ask their question, she'd made a mental note of every detail.

Andy nodded, his gaze never leaving the men setting up camp in the little clearing.

Maybe she shouldn't have brought her son along, creeping close to the men's camp to see what they were about. But she'd not been able to suppress her curiosity about how they behaved themselves. After all, if she'd answered differently, she and Andy might be sitting by that fire, even now.

Seth had something simmering in the pot—beans, from the smell of it—and was spooning cornmeal batter into a sizzling pan. Somehow, she hadn't expected him to be the one cooking, tending to women's work. But then, they didn't have a woman among them to attend those duties. Had that been the reason they'd offered to have her along? Maybe now the men planned to take turns at the job.

Within minutes, Seth was handing out tin plates of food, first to Mr. Benbow, then to his brother, who came to sit by the fire. They filled cups from a metal carafe, the kind used to brew coffee. She heard Seth mention water but hadn't caught the full sentence.

Were they truly only drinking water with the evening meal? This close to the fort, they should still have whiskey they'd surely packed for the journey. The wretched stuff had been much more readily available than clean water around the fort.

She couldn't pull her gaze from the scene as the men ate, speaking a bit here and there. Mostly, they seemed to enjoy the food and companionship. An easy camaraderie slipped around them, and they didn't pass a whiskey flask once.

Finally, Mr. Benbow set down his plate and spoke an appreciative comment, then rose with a groan loud enough for all to hear. "Reckon'

I'll stretch my legs a spell. Don't forget to pack all the foodstuffs so we can hang it up away from the bears."

Andy tugged her sleeve. "Let's go."

The boy was right. They'd spent more time watching these men than they should have. She still had to force herself to turn away from her curiosity, to creep behind her son as they retraced their steps up the rocky incline. She stumbled on a loose stone in the darkness but caught herself. She flinched as the noise of the skittering pebble seemed to echo in the darkness.

It wasn't like her to be so careless. She and Andy had become masters at moving soundlessly in the night, even sneaking up on a few Indian camps on their journey along the Missouri.

The ability to remain unseen was a skill that had served her well for many years. Until now. She could only pray the men hadn't heard.

~

"Ma, wake up."

Rachel jerked at her son's sharp tone, springing upright as she blinked away the haze of sleep. A low rumble seemed to fill the air around her, and she struggled to focus on where it might be coming from.

"I think it's a bear." Andy clutched his rifle tight against his shoulder.

She spun to face the direction he stared. Something stirred in the darkness, and the rumble took on more definition.

The crashing of heavy feet echoed through the woods. A surge of unhappy growling sent skitters down her back and arms.

Pushing the blankets aside, she leaped to her feet and reached for her own rifle. They'd paid dearly for these two guns, using the tiny profit from selling the homestead to buy these and the horses. But she'd been thankful every day since then.

"I've got the first shot." Andy's legs were braced in his shooting stance so the force of the Henry's recoil wouldn't knock him to the ground.

The gun was almost as long as he was, and the sight of him there, her twelve-year-old son playing the part of a grown man, made the burn of tears surge up her throat. She shouldn't rely on him so much.

The hungry grunts and growls grew louder. Closer. The shadow moved, then took shape, padding toward them on all fours.

A scream built in her throat, but she held it in as she pumped the lever on her own rifle and raised it to her shoulder.

Andy's gun exploded, ripping through the night.

The bear roared, surging up on its hind legs to a height that froze the blood in her veins.

CHAPTER 3

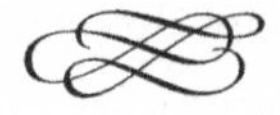

God, let me be enough. Please.
~ Rachel

"Shoot!" Andy's high command pierced Rachel's panic.

She sighted down the barrel, aiming for the bear's exposed chest. But her finger refused to squeeze, her heart booming in her chest. Images flashed before her vision. Blood spraying across a wood floor, staining the yellow skirt a bright crimson. The same life-blood running through her mother's hands.

"Ma!"

She jerked herself back from the memory. Found the bear's chest again as it advanced closer with each racing heartbeat. Closed her eyes tight and squeezed the trigger.

The explosion knocked her backward. The bear roared again.

A second shot rent the air, stilling the roar like a door slammed on the sound.

She forced her eyes open, found the place where the beast had stood. Dropped her gaze to the ground. A massive pile of brown fur lay in a heap.

Andy blew out a long breath, and she turned to him. He looked so young standing there with his hair poking on end, a smoking rifle still clutched in both hands. How could he be the stronger of them?

She wrapped an arm around his shoulders, and they both stared at the beast that would have mutilated them if not for Andy's bravery. "I'm not sure what I did to deserve you, son." She swallowed against the knot in her throat. "I'm proud of you."

He put a clumsy hand around her waist and patted. "It's all right, Ma. I'd best get him bled out." The voice of experience.

They worked together on the job, leaving what they could to finish in the morning. Finally, they washed up and laid weary bodies into their bedrolls. She should have sent Andy to bed earlier. At least he could sleep a bit longer in the morning. They'd need to finish preparing the meat and the hide for travel before they could start back on the trail.

The Grant brothers would get a head start on them. Maybe even make enough distance that she and Andy wouldn't find them again.

But then another thought made her eyes pop open. Had they heard the gunshots? Surely they had, since they were just over the ridge and down the slope. Would they come see what happened? Had they already? The men would be foolish to attempt the path in the darkness, although surely they would investigate come daylight.

The thought gnawed at her sleep. Her hand rested on the stock of her loaded rifle for most of the remaining hours before dawn.

~

By the time Rachel and her son had the meat and the hide prepared and tied on their horses with the other supplies, half the morning had passed. Which meant they'd have to push the horses faster than she liked to catch the Grant party. They hadn't come to investigate as she'd imagined. Was late night gunfire so common in this wilderness it provoked no curiosity? A frightening thought.

And the thought of what lay ahead only tightened the fear coiling in her chest. More ferocious animal attacks, more dangerous precipices—more men, likely more dangerous than Seth Grant and his brother.

Guilt and fear weighed heavy on her. She had no choice.

For Andy's sake, maybe they did need the safety of numbers. The safety that joining the Grant brothers would provide. Her son had been forced to grow up far too fast already due to his father's addictions. She had to stop expecting him to take the place of a full-grown man.

She'd failed him the night before. And she couldn't let her own shortcomings put him in danger like that again.

They took turns riding, then walking while the horses cooled, then riding again. After a short break mid-afternoon, they remounted and nudged the horses into a jog as they charted the base of a mountain. She'd seen signs the men had traveled this way. At least, evidence someone had ridden this way recently.

As the sun sank to the mountains on their left and turned the sky crimson and orange, the sound of male voices ahead made her signal a stop.

"I hear 'em." Andy's low murmur behind her drowned out the noise she strained to hear.

She scanned the rocks and shrubs ahead. The men might be planning to set-up camp among the underbrush.

She motioned Andy forward and guided them off to the side. The last thing she wanted was to barge into their camp without knowing the way of things.

As they reached the fringe of trees, she pulled up and positioned herself and Andy in the shadows. She slid down from her horse, and Andy did the same. "I'm gonna see if they're making camp." She spoke low enough the men wouldn't hear.

"Wait. I see someone." Andy moved forward to peer through the branches.

She padded up behind him. "You're right. Why are they turning back?" Two horses emerged around a rock, following the path they'd been on minutes before.

Realization slipped in, bringing a hint of fear along with it. Those weren't the horses they'd been following for three days now. The slumped shoulders of the men atop them looked nothing like those of the Grant brothers nor Mr. Benbow.

Her chest tightened. More strangers. This was exactly the reason she'd chosen to take this harder route through the mountains, so she could avoid men like these.

"I guess they're going to the fort?" Andy looked up at her, his questioning gaze begging for the answers. If only she had them.

"I suppose so." She rested a hand on his shoulder. "We'll wait until they're out of sight before we move on. Stay with the horses. I'm going to scout through this underbrush." In case the Grant party had indeed decided to camp here. But she suspected she would have heard them speaking with these strangers if they were close.

Which meant she and Andy still hadn't caught up. They'd have to keep riding in the darkness until they found the men they were looking for. Which meant they were likely in for another long night with little sleep.

~

Their fire burned warm as the mountain night wrapped its chilly arms around him, pulling Seth toward droopy-eyed oblivion. Across the blaze, his brother seemed much the same, and Elias had already snuggled into his bedroll. He should lie down, too, and let sleep claim him, but his mind couldn't seem to settle.

Where was *she* camping tonight? The feisty woman with eyes the color of green moss and a loaded Henry rifle just wouldn't leave his thoughts. Had she already left Fort Benton? Was she camping, even now, just over that ridge?

Had she heard the shots the night before? He'd almost gone out to check where the noise had come from, but Elias had warned him against doing so. Said he'd likely be the target of the next bullet, creeping around in the dark like that. By morning, everything seemed calm again, with the birds returning to busy chirping.

Elias bolted upright and reached for his rifle in a fluid movement that seemed unlikely for an older man. "Something's comin' our way." He kept his voice low as he pushed to standing.

Seth reached for his own gun as he stood, turning the direction Elias faced. He'd heard nothing in the darkness save the crackling fire. Years of living in this wilderness had the older man's ears attuned to any sound that didn't belong, even at his age.

A branch cracked somewhere through the covering of pines. Seth raised his rifle. No bear would be so quiet. And a smaller animal wouldn't approach so boldly.

"Hold your fire." A voice slipped through the darkness. "Please." The high tone of a woman. A familiar tone.

"Step into the light." Elias didn't lower his rifle, but his voice was gentle.

A branch shifted. Then she appeared, forming from the shadows. He remembered her hair as a light brown, but the strands looked the color of golden honey in the firelight. Her dress was a dark brown that faded into the shadows, illuminating her face.

His breathing stilled. She was even prettier than he remembered, with those flashing eyes and strong chin.

"Who be you?" Elias asked.

The words pulled Seth from his trance, at least enough to realize the man still held a gun on her.

Seth stepped forward. "She's a friend. Put away the gun."

Friend might be a stretch. The one and only time he'd seen this woman, she had a rifle trained on him and Samuel. But something inside him said she was trustworthy. His instincts were usually right. He'd spent years honing them around the card tables in California.

The woman's gaze hung on Elias for a lingering moment. When the older man lowered his rifle, her piercing eyes turned to him. "Mr. Grant."

"What are you doing here?" The moment the words slipped out, he wanted to slap himself. "I mean, have you come to join us?"

Her gaze turned uncertain. "I...yes. If your offer still stands. Except..." She slipped a glance behind. "It would be me and my son." Her chin raised and the defiant look returned in full. "We'll use our own supplies. We'd only be traveling with you."

A son? "Of course. You're welcome to join us." He couldn't help but wonder where the child was. And where had he been when they'd first met her? The boy must be quite a youngster still. She was so young herself.

She nodded. "I'll go back and get our things." Then she turned and looked as if she might fade into the night.

"I'll come help." He stepped forward, the urge to keep her from disappearing driving him.

"No." She paused, glancing back at him. Something like uncertainty touched her face. "Thank you. I'll return soon."

He needed to respect her wishes, no matter how much it ate at him. So he nodded.

Then she was gone.

He eased out a breath as he turned back toward the campfire, scrubbing a hand through his hair. Samuel met his gaze, raising meaningful brows.

A rough chuckle slipped from Seth. "Yeah." He was just as surprised she'd come. What changed her mind so quickly? The mountain heights? The gunshots the night before? Or something worse? Because she'd been surely determined only three days back.

Samuel dropped to his knees by the food pack they hadn't yet hung in the trees for the night. "I'll fill a couple plates for them."

"Good thinking." Seth should do something to get them settled, too.

Within minutes, the heavy tromping of horses sounded through the trees. One of their animals nickered, and a response came from a gray mount as it stepped into the light of the fire, the woman at its head.

He didn't even know her name. The thought slugged him, spurring his feet into motion.

She pulled her horse aside to allow another golden-colored animal to enter. Leading it was a boy, much older than Seth had expected. Maybe eleven or twelve. Lanky, but starting to spread out—a youth growing into a man. This was her child?

"I'll take yer horses and settle 'em on the tie line." Elias stepped forward. He'd shed his rifle and now spoke in his usual affable tone.

The woman pulled back. "We'll tend them." Her words came out in a bark, just as tense as when they'd first met her.

He had to do something to set her at ease. To let her know they only wanted to help. Now that she'd joined them, she didn't have to carry the weight of her worries alone.

"Ma'am." He motioned toward the older man. "This is Elias Benbow. He's a good fellow and has a way with horses." Then he pointed back to Samuel. "My brother has food ready for you both. If there's anything you need in your packs for the night, go ahead and grab it. Then we'd like to help you get settled in."

She studied him for a long moment. The shadows had settled in her eyes, so he couldn't read her thoughts.

He did his best to keep his expression open. If only he could make her believe they were trustworthy.

He hadn't always been such, but he was now.

She must have seen something that eased her worry, because she turned away and stepped to her pack. "Get what you need, son." Her murmur was so low, he barely picked out the words.

After pulling a few bundles from their packs, she turned to Elias. "Where are your animals tied?"

He reached for the reins, but she pulled back. "We'll tend them. Just show us where."

Seth had to fight the urge to follow and help. He'd never seen a woman so stubborn about accepting assistance. Surely someone had broken her trust in the world.

He kept himself busy with moving the bedrolls around to clear a space for them by the fire. Then he set out two more thick logs for seats. He would have moved the woman's and boy's things in closer, but he had the feeling she'd strike like a venomous snake if he touched them without approval.

At last they returned, Elias first, then the woman marching behind him, her mouth in a determined line. She scooped up as many bundles as she could carry, and her son took the others.

Seth was on his feet. "I don't think I caught your names."

She placed the bundles just outside of their circle and bent to unfasten the leather ties of a satchel. "I'm Mrs. Gray. My son, Andy."

Missus? Was she widowed, then? There were plenty of widows from the War Between the States. Honestly, she didn't look old enough to have a son that big. She must have married young.

Maybe her husband was alive, and they were traveling north to reach him. A small part of him hoped that wasn't the case, which wasn't a Christian way to think at all. He'd need to do a bit more praying than usual on this trip.

"It's a pleasure to meet you, ma'am." Seth motioned toward the empty place they'd created by the fire. "Settle in and let us know what you need."

Her shoulders stiffened. "We need nothing."

He almost let out a sigh but held it back at the last minute. She wasn't taking any favors, that was for certain.

This might be a long journey north.

CHAPTER 4

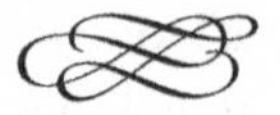

This need intrigues me.
~ Seth

The snoring was the worst part of Rachel's night.

Not the snoring exactly, but the awful memories of lying in the dark, listening to the steady snorts of a man. Her husband, Richard, had only snored when he drank. And he only drank when he played cards. For at least the last year, he snored almost every night. The nights he came home anyway.

She despised snoring.

With her eyes closed, she forced in slow, steady breaths. In *two-three-four,* hold *two,* out *two-three-four.* She occupied her mind with the counting. If she continued long enough, surely she'd eventually fall asleep.

It seemed only a moment later, but when she opened her eyes, daylight filtered in around her. A shadowy form moved to her left.

She jerked upright, reaching for her rifle.

"G'mornin'."

She had the gun pointed before the voice registered.

The attractive man sitting across the fire tipped one side of his mouth up in an easy smile. "Never had a gun pointed at me so often until I met you," Seth said. "And I lived in California six years."

She lowered the rifle to her lap and sat up straighter, then reached to brush stray tendrils of hair back in line. The other men had already risen and must be off preparing for the day. Andy still slept beside her, his face so serene she wanted to press a kiss to his forehead. She could never tire of watching her boy sleep.

But the gaze of the man across the fire seemed to pierce through her, impossible to ignore. Silence stretched between them, and she scrambled to fill it with something. "Where in California?"

"Near Sacramento." He let out a long breath she could hear even across the fire. "The heart of mining country." His words dripped with enough regret to make her look up at him.

"Did you strike it rich?" She should do a better job of keeping the disdain from her tone. Mining seemed like its own kind of gambling. That same lust for riches. The same drive to win. That craving became a sickness before the man realized it. A deadly sickness that affected everyone around him.

"Made enough to live on, but it didn't take long to tell the gold was mostly panned out." He reached for a cup. "Coffee?"

Was he offering the drink to her? The thought startled her more than it probably should. She'd not had a cup of coffee in...well, almost a year. Her mouth salivated, tasting the brew just from the scent lingering in the air. She had to force words out. A statement that brought an almost physical pain. "None for me."

He'd already reached for the carafe, but stopped and looked at her. "You sure? There's plenty to go around. The only other thing to drink is water."

She swallowed. "I can get my own water." Pushing back her blanket, she stood. "Can you point me toward the creek?"

"Here's water for you." He scooped the cup into a pot and raised the dripping tin up to her. "Samuel brought it a few minutes ago."

She had to get control of her situation or she'd be too tempted to accept the things these men tried to give her. Water was a small offering, but this would lead to something more substantial, then another favor even larger. Gifts that would put her in their debt. Under their control.

A situation that could easily place her and Andy in danger.

Standing tall, she squared her shoulders. "Mr. Grant, we'll be providing for our own needs. We'll make our own camp. You've no need to draw water for us or cook for us or tend our horses. The *only* reason we've joined with your party is for the protection a group provides."

He studied her, his brown gaze drilling deep as though seeing through the glare she aimed at him and finding the vulnerable part of her. She fought the urge to look away. To wrap her arms around herself, to conceal the reasons she warned him off.

At last, he nodded. "Very well."

Andy stirred from his bed pallet, probably awakened by her diatribe. She reached for the satchel of items she'd need to mix up a quick corn mush, then softened her voice. "Come, son. Let's walk to find water."

When they returned to camp a quarter hour later, the men were going about their business, mostly leaving them alone. That evening, she planned to have her own cookfire, just so the men didn't feel they needed to do things for her and Andy. They wouldn't be beholden to their travel companions for any reason.

The men were efficient, so it didn't take long for them to start out on the trail. Mr. Benbow led the way with her behind him, then Andy, and the Grant brothers bringing up the rear. Those two looked so much alike, it made her wonder if their other seven siblings looked as similar.

They wound up the side of the mountain, the trail zig-zagging twice as they ascended the steep incline. The higher they climbed, the more her stomach balled into a knot. She'd never been one to prefer heights, but she hadn't expected these mountains to trouble her so much.

At last they reached the peak, and Mr. Benbow called for a stop.

"We'll let the animals rest a minute." He dismounted, and Rachel did the same.

She patted Winter's damp neck. "Good boy." If she kept her focus on the horse, she wouldn't have to look out over the edge of the mountain. She stole a glance at Andy, who'd also slipped off his horse.

"Here, Ma. Hold my horse while I climb up that rock."

"Wait, no." But he'd already thrust the palomino mare's reins into her hand and was clambering onto a boulder as tall as he was. Her heart hammered in her throat and she clutched her neck.

Andy so rarely asked to do playful things, she hated to deny him. And the rock was solid enough, it should be safe. But just being this high up—seeing him even higher—churned bile in her gut.

He stood on the boulder and stepped toward the edge.

Panic clawed inside her like a wild animal. "No!" She jerked toward him, throwing out a hand, dragging the horses with her. "Get back!"

Andy paused and stared at her as though she'd grown a second head. "I'm fine, Ma."

She struggled to regain control of herself. "Please. Get back from the edge." Her voice quivered more than it should, but she couldn't seem to stop it. If Andy slipped on the rock and fell, he'd careen down the jagged mountainside. There was no way he could survive a fall like that.

The disappointment on her son's face was impossible to deny as he shuffled back from the edge, dropped to a sitting position, then slid down from the boulder to land on the ground. She'd not meant he had to climb down, and she hated the fact she'd not been able to allow him at least a few moments of pleasure. But the relief that swept through her was strong enough to drown out the other emotions.

As Andy trudged back to take his mare's reins, she stole a glance at the men they traveled with. Mr. Benbow gave her a sad look that reminded her of her grandfather on Pa's side. She'd not met her father's parents—at least not that she could remember—until a few months before Pa died. It didn't take long to love Grandfather. He seemed to embody everything she loved about her father—and none of the things that scared her.

She'd often seen him looking at her father the way Mr. Benbow now looked at her. She fought the urge to duck away from those eyes. This man knew nothing of her and Andy. He had no right to judge her parenting based on less than a day's acquaintance.

A glance at the Grant brothers showed Samuel staring out over the landscape at the mountains around them, perhaps to give her privacy. Perhaps because she was of such little consequence. Seth had turned to his horse and seemed to be working on his saddle. Did he think her ridiculous, too?

She didn't want to know. The way she raised her son was none of their affair.

Soon they mounted again and, instead of going straight down the mountain, they followed a trail that wound along the side of several peaks connected in a range.

Samuel Grant took the lead this time, and Mr. Benbow dropped back to ride beside her as the trail widened. Thankfully, he rode on the outside edge. Winter seemed comfortable with the man's mule, and they settled into an easy stride.

For some reason, this man didn't churn fear in her like most strangers did, even though he'd first greeted her with his rifle barrel the night before. Something about his demeanor inspired trust, although she knew better than to let down her guard.

"I understand you live in this territory, Mr. Benbow." She might regret starting a conversation, but she should glean as much knowledge of the land as she could from this man.

"Call me Elias. Please. Can't stand that mister word." The wrinkled lines on his face formed a grimace, but they quickly faded as he spoke again. "Yes'm. 'Bout fifteen years now. Used to have farmland in the Kansas Territory. When my family died, I sold it off an' came out here. Some folks are made for farming, ya know? Not me. I just did it 'cause that was what I had to do." He rubbed a hand over his heavily-graying beard.

She knew exactly what he meant. Richard hadn't been meant for farming either. He'd not felt compelled to carry on with it either. At least, not after gambling sank its barbed claws in him. She and Andy had done the work that kept them fed and clothed.

She forced the memories back. "What do you do for a living now?"

He slid her a sideways glance, a touch of humor in his gaze. "Trap an' trade mostly. Pick up a little somethin' here, trade it for somethin' I need there. Hunt for a lot o' my food, an' I have a little garden plot in the summer." He eased out a satisfied breath. "It's a good life. Relaxing."

Relaxing. Did he have no worries? She couldn't imagine a life like that, not in her wildest dreams.

"Look there." Elias pointed down the slope, turning in his saddle to make sure he'd caught Andy's attention, too.

She followed his finger and caught movement halfway down the incline. "Are those…sheep?"

"Mountain goats. You'll see 'em scattered all over these hills. Decent eating if you get hungry, but I mostly leave 'em be." They'd all reined in to watch the creatures grazing. "They can scale most any cliff or rock. The creatures are a wonder."

Elias' words brought back the memory of Andy standing atop the boulder. He had no fear. Not like her. In almost every way, her son was stronger than she was. A thought that filled her with thankfulness.

And utter terror.

~

Even Seth's bones were weary by the time they stopped to make camp for the evening. Samuel looked to be feeling the day's grueling ride as much as he did, although someone who didn't know him well might not see the signs. Hopefully Seth didn't look as worn out as he felt either.

Mrs. Gray and her son seemed to be faring pretty well. They were clearly accustomed to long days in the saddle, although he didn't miss the way she clutched the leather when she peered down from the higher elevations.

It was Samuel's night to settle the animals, Seth's turn to set-up camp and start the fire, and Elias's turn to handle cooking. Likely, Mrs. Gray would want to be in charge of something, but they could accommodate whatever she chose.

After they unloaded the packs, he set about gathering firewood. Andy, too, was walking through the stubby cedar and pine trees, picking up dry sticks and logs. Working together, he and the boy would soon have enough for the night.

"You can set 'em down right here." Elias motioned to the ground near where he worked as Andy approached with arms full.

Seth strode toward the spot to empty his own load, but the boy hesitated before stepping closer. Seth motioned for him to go first.

The lad looked at him, then darted a glance at the place where his mother had laid their packs a few feet away. "I…um. Ma said to put the wood for our fire over here."

It took a moment for the words to take form in his mind. "Your fire? We only need one. We'll just take turns cooking if your ma wants to make her own food."

Andy looked toward his mother, who was tending their horses in a grassy area barely within sight. The boy looked uncertain.

The last thing Seth wanted was to cause trouble between them. "Never mind, son. Do what your ma said. I'll talk with her about it."

The boy looked relieved, but as he turned and dumped his load near their supplies, his brow still wore a troubled crease. He was more serious than any lad Seth had known. Much more than he or his brothers had been, even Serious Sam, as he'd sometimes called his twin.

After Seth eased his own wood into a stack, he grabbed a log that had rolled free of Andy's load and handed it back to the boy. "How old are you, Andy?" He kept his tone as conversational as he could so he didn't scare him off.

"Twelve, sir."

He let a grin slide onto his face. "That's a good age. I remember when Samuel and I were twelve. We'd spend summers helping our pa in the fields during the mornings, then head to the pond to eat our lunch. There was nothing better than swimming in cold water on a sizzling hot day. After we swam for an hour or two, we'd throw out fishing lines and let the sun dry us.

"If we caught something, we'd go home and take it to Mama. If we didn't, we had to go help Pa finish up for the day." He sent a knowing look toward the boy. "I didn't have the knack for catching them that Samuel did, but he always made sure I had at least one fish to take home so I didn't have to go back to the fields."

The boy watched him with so much hunger in his expression, Seth wondered if he'd ever been fishing. Or ever had an easy afternoon swimming. How much hardship had Andy endured in his young life?

"I'd best get back to work." Seth gave the boy a light clap on the shoulder.

Andy flinched as though he'd been struck, then turned away. "I need to start our fire." The lad mumbled the words as though trying to cover up his reaction.

Seth's mind spun as he gathered more wood. He wanted more than anything to march over to the boy and tell him he had nothing to fear from any of them. Andy and his mother were safe here.

But he had the feeling he'd need to do more than speak words. Consistent action was the only thing that would prove their safety. Being steady and dependable would show that he was trustworthy.

But that was something he'd never been good at. As much as he wanted to be solid and capable like Samuel, he always let his impulses lead the way. That certainly kept his life from being dull, but he'd made enough mistakes over the past six years that he'd gladly trade them all for boring and trustworthy any day.

In fact, that's why they'd left California. A fresh start. Another chance.

And this time, with God's help, he'd get it right.

CHAPTER 5

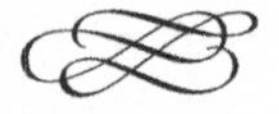

My heart says to never trust again. Yet my heart has been so thoroughly beaten down, I don't know whether to believe it or not.
~ Rachel

"I thought I made it clear to you, Mr. Grant. My son and I are only traveling with you. We'll be cooking our own meals, caring for our own animals, and staying fully out of your way." Rachel kept her hands propped on her hips so she didn't do something with them she regretted.

He didn't seem disturbed by her words at all, just kept that frustratingly calm—almost curious—expression. "I understand. I'm only saying there's no need for you and Andy to have a separate fire. It'd be a sight easier to have one for us all, then take turns cooking."

Easier yes, but she'd do whatever it took to keep her and Andy safe. And that required a bit of space from these men. She worked to level her voice. "We didn't join on to make ourselves a bother. This way, you men can have your space, and we can still have a bit of privacy." Surely he wouldn't argue against that.

His mouth formed a thin line under the edges of his barely-grown beard. He seemed to study her for a moment. "If privacy is what you need, it'd be best to build a partition of sorts that would separate your bedroll from ours, but still give you access to the fire's heat. I bet we could make something easily with a few logs and a blanket." He was already looking around, maybe for branches to construct the idea forming in his mind.

"Wait." She raised a hand.

He stalled, turning back to her. "It's not safe for you to be separated over here." He looked from her pile of logs to the camp where Samuel and Elias were making camp and pretending not to watch the drama unfold. A good ten strides separated them. "A mountain lion or some other animal could strike, and we'd not know 'til we heard you scream." His gaze seemed to drill into her, searing the truth of his words until they pressed into her chest.

Maybe she should just agree. After all, sharing the same fire wouldn't change anything. She and Andy could still keep to themselves. They'd still be protected from another bear attack. It might be the best possible compromise.

She kept her back straight, but nodded. "All right. We'll let our fire burn out and move our bedrolls over."

The corners of his mouth twitched, but at least he had the decency to hold in his triumphant grin. "I'll get started on that partition."

It was almost humorous to watch the Grant brothers as they worked together to build the divider in the darkness. Elias was putting away the food from their evening meal while the younger men worked, and he seemed just as amused.

"It won't hold without a crossbeam there." Samuel Grant's voice maintained a steady resolve, and she tried not to look their way.

"I have a crossbeam. Here." Seth's tone had been slowly building with frustration over the last few minutes.

"It needs another. Right there."

"Fine. Here's another." He tossed a long branch his way. "You want a third, too?"

"This will do."

They sounded as if they might come to blows, and she shot a glance at Andy. Should she take him to check on the horses so he didn't see the argument turn violent?

But a chuckle drew her focus back to the men. Seth stepped away from their work, dusting his hands as he turned to her. "Mrs. G, you now have a partition sturdier than most house walls. Samuel made sure of it."

She studied his face in the dancing firelight. How had his anger evaporated so quickly? Was he just holding it in?

He didn't wait for an answer from her, but turned toward the dwindling campfire in the far camp. "Andy, let's get these things moved over."

~

The next morning on the trail, Seth found himself bringing up the rear of the group. One of the men he used to gamble with had been a cowpuncher in Texas, and called this particular position *riding drag*. That man had hated the rear because of the thick dust a herd of cattle kicked up, but there was no such trouble with this group.

He had the perfect view of Mrs. Gray just ahead, her back tall in the saddle, yet so relaxed with the movement of the animal. She'd clearly spent a great deal of time on the back of her horse. The path was wide enough for them to ride double in most places, and Elias's mule plugged along beside her white-gray gelding. She seemed a little more amiable toward Elias than toward him or Samuel. At least she hadn't bitten Seth's head off yet this morning.

"I noticed you and the boy was eatin' bear meat this mornin'." Elias's tone rumbled easily, conversational. "D'you buy it back at the fort?"

"We shot the beast when he entered our camp a few nights ago." Tension hung in her tone, but there was no visible change in the outline of her shoulders. He wished he could see her face.

Then her words registered in his mind. A few nights ago…was that the shots that had jerked them from sleep around midnight? The ones Elias had stopped him from investigating?

He could imagine the fear of waking to find a bear in their camp. Elias made them hang all foodstuffs and cooking supplies in a tree far from the fire each night, but maybe Mrs. Gray hadn't known to do that.

If they'd had food in their camp, no wonder the bear had come hunting. And three shots had been fired. Did that mean the bear hadn't died with the first bullet? An angry grizzly could be terrifying...and deadly.

The very next night, she and Andy had shown up in their camp, asking for the security of the larger group. Now he understood why.

And he was even more thankful he'd pushed for them to join the rest of them around a single campfire. He didn't like the idea of the woman and boy separated from them, even by a small distance.

Elias had kept her talking with a story about his own run-in with a grizzly, and Seth refocused on their conversation.

"He was an old feller, but his meat filled our bellies for a week at least. Maybe more."

"It's nice to have enough food to last a while."

"Did you make sure you—" Elias cut his words as he threw a hand out to stop them. "Ho up there, Samuel. I see a passel o' deer down the hill."

Seth's gelding saw the animals at the same time Elias did. The horse tensed, ears straining toward the new creatures, every muscle in his body quivering.

About fifty strides down the mountain, a group of six whitetail deer stood frozen. Watching them. Three appeared to be weanlings, just barely old enough to lose their spots. The other three were full-grown, one with a small pair of antlers.

"We need a bit more meat to carry us. I'm gonna take down the young buck." Elias spoke low as he raised his rifle. A moment later, a blast split the air.

A scream sounded within the same breath, and from the corner of his eye, he saw Mrs. Gray clap hands against her ears.

One of the deer dropped to the ground, but the others bolted, leaping down the slope toward a cluster of trees.

"You all can rest yer horses while I take care o' this feller." Elias turned his mule from the trail, working his way down toward the brown heap.

Seth turned his focus back to the woman. Her shoulders had lost their easy line as she now clutched the saddle. Was it seeing an animal die that bothered her? Or did the gunshot remind her of the bear's appearance the other night? Probably the latter.

He eased his horse alongside hers. Her face had paled three shades, but the sight of him seemed to reinvigorate her. At least, the way her shoulders squared and her jaw set in her typical determined look, he assumed that was the case.

He wanted desperately to say something to help her. Something that would ease her fears or maybe clear away the memories that seemed to frighten her. "I had a pet deer once. Or rather Samuel and I both did."

She jerked her gaze to him, her eyes widening in a way that seemed to scrutinize whether he was telling the truth.

"We were just old enough to play in the fields by ourselves, and we discovered a young fawn." He searched the recesses of his mind for any memories of the animal. "I think it must have been a week or two old, and we carried it back to the house. Our sister Noelle set us up with a pap feeder, and we nursed the fawn until it was old enough to wean. It lived in our yard for a few weeks after that. Then one day, it just disappeared."

Samuel had been devastated by the animal's leaving, but Seth had told his brother its family had come back for it. He'd really believed the story, too. Although now, he saw how much more likely it was that another animal had taken the baby. His heart panged at the realization.

"The only pet we had was a horse," she said. "My father called him Alfred and pretended he was a prince that an evil fairy had turned into our gelding." Her voice held a soft edge he'd never heard from her before.

He slid a glance at her. She'd loosened her grip on the saddle, and her gaze lingered in the direction of her son, although her focus seemed somewhere far away.

"Did he ever turn back into a prince?" He couldn't help the question.

She looked over at him, the soft expression lingering a final moment before it turned to something sad. "We eventually lost him. Maybe he became some other girl's prince."

Then she reined her horse back and turned off the trail. "I'm going to see if Elias needs help."

As her horse picked his way down the mountain, Samuel looked at Seth, his gaze making it clear he'd heard their exchange. Her final wording seemed to have his brother wondering, too. *We eventually lost him.* That made him think the animal died, but her next sentence sounded as if they'd sold him.

Samuel shrugged, showing he wasn't going to lose sleep over the comment. "I guess we should all help." Then he turned his horse toward the others, and Andy fell in behind him.

Seth brought up the rear to make sure the boy didn't have trouble, but he couldn't shake off his curiosity as easily as his brother had.

In truth, it was more than just curiosity. This woman's life hadn't been an easy ride, he was pretty sure of it. And the effects of her experiences had left her bruised in a way he craved to make better.

If she'd let him in, maybe he could help her shake off the wounds from the past.

But breaking through Mrs. Gray's shell wasn't going to be easy.

~

Seth scooped out the last of the flapjacks the next morning and loaded them onto a plate. Elias and Samuel had already filled up, then headed out to feed the animals and get things ready for the day.

Awareness tingled his skin even before the sound of soft footsteps alerted him to Mrs. Gray's approach. Every part of him seemed to come alive when she was near.

He reached for the plate of cakes and turned to her. "I made more batter than I should have, and the boys are done eating. I'd be obliged if you and Andy would finish these off since we don't really have room to pack them." That was stretching the truth. They'd always make room for food, and he'd actually made these just for her and Andy. The hard part was getting her to accept them.

She slid a glance at the offering, then turned back to her own pot. "We have plenty."

He grabbed his used dishes and stood, leaving the platter of johnnycakes on the rock near the fire. "Just add these in with your other food." He walked away before she could throw them at him. She probably wouldn't waste good food, but he was learning never to underestimate this woman.

They'd camped a short walk away from a thin creek trickling from the rock face, and he did a quick job of scrubbing the tinware in the icy water. Even with summer coming on strong in the lowlands, these higher elevations still maintained cool nights and icy creeks.

One of the horses neighed in the distance as he worked, and Elias's mule brayed an answer. Even the animals were ready to get on the trail. He stacked the last of the plates and moved on to the frying pan.

A gut-wrenching scream pierced the air, followed by the sharp clatter of iron. *Mrs. Gray?* He struggled to his feet, tossed the fryer to the ground beside the other dishes, and sprinted back toward the campfire.

CHAPTER 6

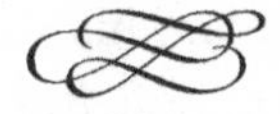

She doesn't make it easy. Yet I'm up for the challenge.
~ Seth

Seth's heart raced faster than his feet as he wove through the underbrush back to camp. Had Mrs. Gray burned herself? Been bitten by a snake?

It wasn't like her to show weakness, which meant her scream had to be caused by more than dropping a log on her foot.

As he neared camp, he could see her form bent over, her son kneeling beside her.

Urgency propelled him faster. His breath came in short gasps as he pulled up beside them. "What happened?"

Andy whirled around, panic in his eyes. "Ma burned herself."

Seth dropped to his knees by her other side, resting a hand on her shoulder as he took in the damage. She clutched her right wrist, the flesh of that hand an angry red.

"My hand slipped on the pot. Poured boiling water on me." Her words ground between clenched teeth.

He'd been burned before—knew well the searing ache that could take a man to his knees—but he'd never experienced anything as bad as this. The flesh of her entire hand was raw.

He turned to Andy. "Go to the creek and get my big pot. Fill it with water. Quick." The icy mountain water would be the best thing for her.

The boy leaped to his feet and tore off.

Seth refocused on the woman, his stomach roiling at the sight of her hand. He took her arm and pulled it toward him. She gave stiffly, releasing her grip on her wrist.

"Is your sleeve wet?" If the cloth held burning water against her skin, the damage could be getting worse. He touched the cloth to see for himself. Not damp. It looked like the searing water had only reached the edge of her palm.

She sniffed, drawing his gaze up to her face. Her eyes were rimmed in red, her nose bright. Yet no tears ran down her cheeks.

A tight knot squeezed in his chest. She shouldn't have to fight to be so strong all the time. How could he let her know she was safe? She could let her guard down when she needed to. Did she ever cry? His mother once said tears were healing for a woman. Maybe if he could help her release her grief, she could start to heal from whatever pain she'd endured in her past.

He leaned forward so he could see her face. "What's your given name, Mrs. Gray?"

Her gaze jerked to his. "Rachel."

He had a feeling she wouldn't have shared that detail if she were thinking straight, but he was thankful she had.

The loud tromping of Andy's boots through the underbrush sounded as he ran toward them, water sloshing from the pot. His appearance interrupted what Seth had planned to say, but that might be for the best. Rachel needed relief from the pain more than anything.

He set the pot down in front of her, and she dipped her hand in the water. She gasped as her skin touched the liquid, but then her mouth closed to a thin line, the muscles in her jaw flexing.

"I'm going to roll up your sleeve to get it out of the way." He reached for her cotton cuff, his fingers large and stubby against her thin arm.

"What's happened?" Samuel's step was almost as heavy as the boy's as he and Elias charged toward them.

Rachel stiffened again, squaring her shoulders. "All is well. Just a burn." Her voice was still strained, but more like her normal, no-nonsense tone.

Seth sent his brother a look that revealed more of the truth, and when Samuel stepped close enough to see her hand glaring at them from under the water, he winced. "Ow."

Even Elias grimaced at the sight. "We're gonna need to wrap that. I've a salve we can put on it to keep it from festering. I'll fetch it."

As he left, Seth glanced at Rachel's face again. "Any better?"

"Some." Her expression didn't look as certain as she made her voice sound.

He scanned for something else they could do to ease the pain. "Maybe you should go to the stream where the water stays cold. That might numb the pain."

She nodded, started to rise without a word, water dripping from her hand.

He took her elbow to help her up, and she didn't jerk away. He made sure he released her as soon as she found her balance. He wouldn't force her to accept his help. He'd just take it a little step at a time.

After she knelt by the stream and eased her hand into the water, she let out a long, slow exhale. Red rimmed her pretty green eyes, but then she lowered her eyelids and sealed them away. She seemed to be forcing deep, steady breaths, which was the best way to deal with pain. How much practice had she been required to endure?

"You feelin' better, Ma?"

She opened her eyes and turned a strained smile to her son. "I am. I'll be fine, honey."

The boy's throat worked, but he didn't look convinced. Smart lad.

Rachel seemed to see it, too, for she leaned over to pat his arm with her good hand. "Go eat the flapjacks Mr. Grant made, then saddle the horses. I'll pack our things, then we'll be ready to leave when the men are."

At least she'd finally consented to eat the food he cooked for them. But they weren't going anywhere until her hand was cared for and some of the pain eased.

Andy didn't move to obey his mother's words, and a glance at him showed his jaw locked. "I'll stay here in case you need me."

A boy trying his best to be the man his mother needed. A lump clogged in Seth's throat. These two shouldn't have to work so hard to survive.

He rested a hand on Andy's shoulder. "She's gonna be fine. But it'll be good to have you nearby."

The boy nodded, his gaze raising to Seth in begrudging thanks.

Elias appeared through the trees, a glass jar and a folded cloth in his hands. He handed the container to Seth. "You might wanna do this, my hands are all bent up from the rheumatis' this mornin'."

Seth's breath hitched. He wanted to help Rachel, but touching her burned flesh would be painful, no matter how gentle he was.

Rachel withdrew her hand from the water as he reached for it, a hard expression taking over her face. She dabbed the water on her skirt to dry it, and he could almost feel the tension emanating from her. Yet she didn't cry out, didn't break her stony look. This woman was stronger than steel.

After opening the jar, he took her cool wrist in his big paw and dabbed dots of the white cream around her hand. With the pad of his finger he spread a thick coat of salve with his lightest touch, doing his best to not even brush her raw skin. He didn't dare look at her face. Pain surely showed there. Looking at this angry flesh was hard enough.

"Now let's wrap it." His voice pitched low and gravely, but at least he got the words out.

Elias handed over the ball of cloth, and Seth shifted it to find the loose end. He placed the edge at Rachel's wrist, where she held it in place with her good hand. Their fingers brushed as she took his place with the fabric. The contact sent a jolt up to his shoulder, even though he was already touching her arm as he supported it.

Maybe his awareness of her was solely because of her injury. He'd better keep it that way. She clearly wouldn't have him, whether he was interested or not.

The bandage was long enough to wrap her hand completely, and within minutes, the limb was fully covered in a white glove. He swathed each finger individually to keep the skin from rubbing. After tying the end in place, he straightened and finally checked her face.

Her eyes were bloodshot, and her nose a bright red, but no tears washed her cheeks. She seemed to be holding them back by sheer force of will, if her locked jaw was any indication.

"I know that hurts, but we should keep it covered a few days in case it blisters." He rubbed his thumb across her wrist, relishing the contact one last time before he released her.

She nodded and sniffed. "I'll be fine." And if determination alone could make her well, she would accomplish it.

He forced his gaze away from her to Elias. "Is there anything else we can do?"

The older man shook his head. "She just needs time to heal. You young fellers wanna stay around these parts today? We can hit the trail again come mornin'."

Seth opened his mouth to agree, but Rachel shook her head violently. "No. We ride on. I won't slow you down."

This woman was too stubborn for her own good. He raised his brows to Elias, silently asking what he thought they should do.

His mouth puckered in a thoughtful frown as he looked at Rachel. "I suppose. But you have to promise to speak up if you get to hurtin' too bad."

They both looked at her, and she met their gazes with a fierce expression. She didn't answer, and it didn't look as if she planned to say anything at all.

So he prompted. "Rachel?" They weren't leaving until she gave her word.

She narrowed flashing eyes at him. "Mrs. Gray."

He almost ducked at the venom in her voice. Apparently, sharing her given name had been an act of weakness during her trauma. "My apologies. *Mrs. Gray*…." He emphasized her name. "Can we have your word you'll tell us if your hand hurts too badly to keep going?"

"You have it." Her words came out measured, as though forced through gritted teeth.

He let out a breath and sat back on his heels. "All right then. I guess let's get on the trail."

But as they packed up and mounted the animals, he couldn't shake the feeling they were making a mistake.

~

Rachel may have given her word to speak up if her hand hurt too badly, but they'd not detailed what *too badly* meant. Her hand had felt like someone peeled the skin off her flesh ever since those first moments when the pain sank over her.

And it wasn't getting any better as the day progressed.

She rode sandwiched between Andy's mare in front of her and Seth Grant's gelding behind, with his brother bringing up the rear. Thankfully, the ground wasn't particularly rough or high up the mountainside, although she probably wouldn't have noticed the scenery with her eyes half shut against the pain. The throbbing had moved into her head, too, and every step Winter took seemed to explode inside her.

But she wouldn't call a halt. Not unless she lost all consciousness. And she wouldn't do that either.

When they stopped for lunch, she kept herself apart from the others. Andy looked worried, and she did her best to reassure him. Seth sent more scrutinizing glances her way than she liked. That man had a way of looking into her that made her feel as though he was seeing her vulnerable places. The things she did her best to hide. Could he see the depth of her pain even now?

If so, he didn't say anything. He did hold Winter's head when she mounted, and she didn't tell him to step away. It was hard enough to climb on the horse without touching anything with her right hand. If the gelding had stepped forward during the process, she might have ended up flat on the ground.

"All set?" Seth looked up at her after she adjusted the reins. Worry lines creased under his eyes. Eyes that seemed to care far too much.

She did her best to give him a confident look. "I am." She'd do this, no matter what it took.

They started off, winding up a rocky trail. The sun beat warmer than it had the past few days, making beads of sweat run down her face. More perspiration seeped down her back beneath the folds of her undergarments. She squeezed her eyes tight as the swaying of Winter's gait pounded through her head with every thrum of her pulse.

One minute at a time. She'd make it through this day.

Without warning, the horse jerked sideways. She squealed, jerked the reins with her left and clutched at the saddle with her right. Fire shot through the limb. Her squeal turned to a scream as her fingers seemed to explode into flame. The horse moved out from underneath her, and she lost her balance.

The world tilted as her foot pulled free from the stirrup. She landed with a blow that slammed through her body.

Another explosion ripped through the air like a gunshot, ricocheting inside her head. She curled tight to get away from it, squeezing her eyes against the pain that stole her breath.

Men shouted around her. Hands gripped her arm, her shoulder. Not rough hands, but she could feel the strength in them.

Yet it was Andy's voice that forced her eyes open.

"Ma!" The desperation in his tone wrapped around her heart with an ache that almost superseded the pain that coursed through the rest of her body.

She searched for him, her gaze swimming as she struggled to right her view of the landscape.

"Are you hurt? Did it bite you?"

She found Andy as he grabbed her good arm. "I'm all right. Not hurt." Except for the fire in her hand and the pounding in her head.

She'd landed on her right side, so she probably hit her injured hand. The appendage felt like it was still drenched in boiling water, so she had no idea if it had sustained more damage.

She pushed her good hand under her and worked to lever herself upright. Strong hands helped lift her, and she knew without looking they belonged to Seth. She could feel his presence anytime he was near.

Sitting upright made her head spin, and she clutched her temple to still the whirling. "Where's my horse? Is he hurt?" It wasn't like Winter to bolt like that.

"Samuel has him. Elias shot the snake before it struck."

She spun to face Seth, but instantly regretted the action as her head throbbed with pain. "Snake?"

His mouth pinched in a grim line as he nodded. "Rattler."

Her throat clutched, not allowing air through. No wonder Winter had spun off the trail. He'd been getting them both out of danger. If her hand hadn't been injured, she could have stayed on when she gripped the saddle.

The spinning in her head finally eased, so she moved to her knees, then to a standing position. Seth tried to help her up, but she shook his hand off her arm. "I'm fine."

She couldn't let them coddle her. Couldn't show weakness that would give them an advantage over her. Letting a man have that power was never a good thing.

Yet with only one good hand, a pounding head, and now an ache in her backside, she was as weak as she could ever remember being. As weak and as vulnerable.

CHAPTER 7

I hate this weakness I can't control.
~ Rachel

As Seth roasted another section of venison for dinner that evening, he couldn't seem to stop his gaze from straying to Rachel. She'd probably string him up from the nearest sturdy pine if she knew he wasn't calling her by her surname in his thoughts.

The thought brought a smile, and he kept his eyes glued to the meat dripping from the spit so she wouldn't know she was the source of the grin. He hated whatever had hurt her before, but he couldn't help loving her spunk.

As he moved the meat to a plate, voices sounded in the distance. Samuel, Elias, and Andy must have been finished settling the animals. The boy's voice pitched higher than the others as he asked a question, then Elias replied in his relaxed drawl.

Seth paused from slicing the roast into individual portions to watch the three approach. Andy still had that gangly look of a boy, yet his stride matched that of the men beside him. A boy growing into a man. Where was his father? How long had he and his mother been on their own?

Although he'd not always appreciated working in the fields alongside his own father, he couldn't imagine trying to maneuver his growing-up years without Pa's guidance. He didn't always follow his father's advice and example, which led to his struggles in California, but they'd helped guide him back to the Heavenly Father when he reached his lowest point.

Hopefully Andy wouldn't fall into the same types of wickedness Seth had, but he still needed a man's example to show him the way to adulthood. Something in Seth's chest ached at the thought of the boy trying to mature without that kind of guidance.

He turned back to the food and speared each chunk of meat onto a separate plate. After scooping out beans to go with the venison, he rose and carried the first two plates to Rachel and her son.

She was attempting to refasten the ties on her pack but jerked her gaze up to his as he set the platter beside her.

He didn't say anything. Didn't comment on how much easier it'd be for her if she ate his food tonight. Just placed the second plate by Andy and walked back to the fire.

Samuel had already scooped up his and Elias's, so Seth reached for his own tin platter and settled onto the ground to eat.

After his first bite, he stole a glance at the woman and boy. Andy had picked up his plate and was looking to his ma, probably for permission.

She nodded to him, but the tight line of her mouth showed she didn't like what she probably considered accepting charity. In his mind, it was more like being a good neighbor, but he knew better than to argue.

Still, he'd eaten half his meal before she finally reached for her plate and forked a bite of venison. With the brilliant reds, purples, and blues of the setting sun behind her and the glow of the firelight on her face, she looked just like an angel. A strong, fierce angel, capable of riding all day with a badly burned hand and likely a few significant bruises from her fall.

The fact she'd come through the snake ordeal with only minor injury proved just how much God cared about this woman. Did she realize it?

Maybe he could find a way to make sure she did.

~

The next morning, it felt like everything Rachel attempted took twice as long as it should have. Maybe because she was working with only one hand. Or perhaps because every part of her right side ached from the fall. If she could cut that half of her body away, she would gladly do it.

But as she finally had their things packed and ready, a glance around showed the men were just as far behind as she. This would be the time to find Andy and see if he needed help with the animals, but her weary body wouldn't seem to obey.

She was still sitting there by the soggy remnants of their campfire a few minutes later when Andy's voice drifted over her shoulder. He was walking toward her, his tone animated as he spoke. "We swam there until the man who owned the pasture moved, and Ma didn't trust the new owner. I was pretty good before we stopped going."

Why would he be talking about their old swimming hole? She held her breath to listen for a response so she could see who he was talking to.

"I'll bet so." Seth's warm timbre answered. "Swimming was my favorite thing to do growing up. In the summer anyway." His voice dipped low where she couldn't hear, and whatever he said must have been funny, for they both chuckled.

Andy's laugh slipped through her, wiping away her pain. How long had it been since he'd laughed? These last few years, he'd grown quieter than when he was young.

Man and boy reached her, and she turned to offer a smile. "Are we ready?"

"Yup." Andy grabbed her satchel and hoisted it onto his shoulder.

Seth met her gaze as the boy turned away. His eyes were warm, but also searching. "You feel up to another day?"

Just once, she wanted to give in to the warmth he offered. Not have to fight her exhaustion and pain—her weakness. She couldn't give in, though.

But she also didn't have the strength to wield her full armor, so she stood—ignoring his proffered hand—and dragged herself toward the horses.

The day seemed to crawl as the sun rose high. Even though these mountains felt closer to the brilliant orb, the air had a nip to it that not even the warm rays could dissolve. They rode through a valley as the afternoon lingered long, and she could only be thankful they weren't navigating steep cliffs. Her weary body didn't have much left, probably not enough to cling to the saddle against a steep descent.

"There's a good camping spot in those trees yonder." Elias's voice called from the front of the line. "We'll stop there."

The relief his words brought infused her muscles with a fresh dose of strength, and she straightened in the saddle. The cluster of pine couldn't be more than half hour's ride. She could endure.

As they neared the woods, dusk settled with its thick, murky coating. Voices sounded from ahead, and her muscles tensed. She peered at the stand where they would be camping. Had someone already settled in for the night? How much longer would Elias make them go now? They couldn't stay close to these strangers, but she may not make it much farther.

Just outside the trees, Elias raised his hand for a halt, then hollered, "Halloo in the camp."

The voices ceased, and footsteps sounded through the trees. A man came into view wearing the same kind of buckskin tunic that had been so common to the men at Fort Benton, as common as the rifle in his hand. "Howdy." His gaze scanned the row of them, catching on her longer than the others.

Elias nodded a greeting. "Name's Elias Benbow. We're travelin' north and planned to stop for the night soon. Just thought I'd let ya know you folks have neighbors."

The man refocused on Elias. "'Preciate it. You folks can join our campfire. We've meat if you need some."

Elias dismounted and pulled his reins over his mule's head. "We have food, but the comp'ny sounds nice." He turned back to her and the men. "All right, folks. Let's get settled."

He wasn't even going to ask if they wanted to stay here? He knew nothing of these men. There was a good chance they weren't decent people, but Elias was willing to bed down around their campfire?

The Grant brothers were dismounting, and Andy started to do the same. She nudged her gelding up beside him. "Wait, Andy. We're not going to stay here." She kept her voice low, but he heard her.

"Will we ride on alone?" Andy kept his voice low, but they still drew Seth's attention, who'd been riding at the back of the line.

He stepped up beside her horse, staring up at her with concern in his warm brown eyes. "What's wrong?"

She locked her jaw. "We're not staying with strangers. Andy and I will ride on. You can catch up with us in the morning." Or maybe they should be on their own again when the sun rose. She wasn't altogether sure she could trust these men anymore either, if they were willing to bed down with perfect strangers.

"Rachel." Seth's voice pulled low.

She jerked upright and sent a sharp glare his way. "Mrs. Gray."

He wrinkled his nose. "If I have to. But how about if I just call you, Mrs. G? Anyway, why don't we meet these people before we decide for sure if we stay or not. If any of us feels it's not safe here, we'll move on to another campsite. Together."

She opened her mouth to protest, but he stepped closer, resting his hand on Winter's shoulder.

His look was so earnest, so…determined, it stilled her. "I won't put you in danger, Rachel. I promise."

She should correct him again. Should refuse to dismount. But a larger part of her wanted to believe him. To trust him. Even if she and Andy climbed down from their horses and met these strangers, Seth was right. They could always remount and ride away.

She let out a breath and nodded. "We'll meet them, but that's all I agree to."

Seth held their horses while she and Andy dismounted, then they walked three-abreast toward the trees. His brother and Elias were already unfastening packs from their animals, but Seth stepped close and spoke in a low voice.

"We need to make sure these men don't mean harm. How about if we go meet the group before unpacking. If any of us don't like the feel of things, we can move on and camp a bit farther down the trail."

Elias shrugged. "Suits me either way. Most o' the folks along this trail are a decent lot, but there can be a bad apple every now an' then."

As they tied the horses to the trees, that old familiar panic surged in Rachel's chest. "Andy, why don't you stay here and watch the animals."

"Ma." His voice dripped with more than a little frustration. "I'm old enough to come with you."

Was he? So much of her wanted to shelter him. This world would attack as soon as he was on his own. But she had to teach him how to deal with it. How to spot an untrustworthy man.

Inhaling a strengthening breath, she nodded. "All right."

They trekked through the trees, the canopy of limbs blocking out most of the remaining daylight. Seth walked just in front of her, holding aside branches and clearing the way. She kept Andy behind her, and Samuel brought up the rear. These two seemed to do that often, as though bracketing her and her son inside their protection. Did all brothers work together so well? She'd never witnessed a connection like this. Never seen grown men who communicated without speaking as these two did.

The light of a campfire shone through the trees, and low voices hummed in the distance.

As they stepped into the light, the bulky forms of three men took shape around the campfire. One stood—the man who'd greeted them before. "Come in and sit yourselves. I'm Rufus Cook. These are Alonzo and Milton."

Each of the men raised a hand as his name was announced, and Rachel's eyes locked on the flask in Alonzo's grip.

Her stomach churned, threatening to send bile up to her throat. She backed a step, reaching for Andy. Her hand found his arm and closed around it.

At the corner of her vision, Elias waved them forward, and the drone of his voice tried to break through her senses. Yet the panic swirling in her chest blocked everything out except that bottle.

The man raised the container to his bearded lips, and she turned away as a wave of vomit rose up to her chest, burning her throat.

She sucked in a hoarse breath, struggling to keep her insides in place. A gentle arm slipped around her shoulders, steering her away from the fire and toward the blessed relief of the darkness.

CHAPTER 8

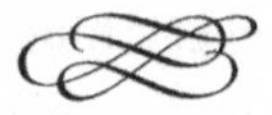

Even I didn't expect this much adventure.
~ Seth

Seth knew Rachel was afraid. Knew she had scars from whatever awful things happened in her past.

Nay, these weren't scars, they were open wounds. Festering and bleeding so she was forced to limp through life in a miserable condition.

He should never have forced her to approach the men when she so clearly dreaded it. Pushing her wasn't the way to heal the injuries from her past. She needed kindness and understanding before anything else. Those and the healing touch of a loving Father.

Be there for her, Lord.

When they reached the horses, he was relieved to see Rachel's son and his brother close behind them.

"Elias stayed to make our apologies and bid them farewell." Samuel spoke in a low voice.

To smooth things over. Good. Seth turned his focus back to the woman bent under his arm. "You're safe, Rachel. We're not staying near those men. You've nothing to worry about."

She raised her face to him, and in the vivid light of an almost-full moon, her eyes glistened with pain. No tears leaked from them, but the anguish was impossible to miss, and it pressed his chest with a powerful ache. She seemed to be struggling to shutter the emotion, and seconds later her back stiffened and her shoulders squared.

"I'm well." She inhaled a deep breath, her chest rising with the effort. He forced his gaze to stay on her face.

"Well enough to ride farther?"

She nodded, then turned toward her horse, reaching for the leather that tied the gelding to the tree. "Let's go."

They rode another quarter hour, then camped beside a narrow creek under the weepy branches of a willow. A much more exposed campsite than the one Rufus Cook and his friends occupied, but this one was quiet. Since it was so late and the weather mild, they opted not to build a cookfire.

Rachel seemed dead on her feet as they made camp and ate a cold meal of roasted venison and corn cake. She tucked into her bedroll before the rest of them finished eating.

He leaned forward to speak to her. "Do you want the screens put up?"

They'd erected some form of partition each night, but that would be harder to do with only the willow tree nearby. Lack of wood was another reason he was thankful they'd not attempted a fire.

"Don't worry about it tonight." The last word trailed into a yawn, and her eyes drifted shut.

Andy looked just as weary, but he appeared determined to sit up with the men. It was time they all bedded down.

He glanced around, scanning the land outside their camp. All seemed quiet. "Think we'll be safe here?" Maybe he was being too cautious, but a bit of Rachel's concern about the men they'd just left had worked its way inside him.

Mountains lined either side of the valley, protecting them like fortresses. Yet it was the length of the valley that gave him pause.

Without tree cover, they could be seen for a long way in either direction. Of course, anyone approaching could also be seen. If they were awake to watch.

He swiveled to face the others. "Should we set a guard?"

Elias rubbed a hand over his beard. "I think we'll be safe enough. As long as we sleep light."

Seth hesitated before nodding. Should he accept that they weren't taking action to assure their safety? The safety of Rachel and Andy.

Elias may well be right. Rufus and the others would likely drink a little, then sleep away their weariness.

His own exhausted body begged to do the same.

But as he stretched out on his blanket, his muscles couldn't quite seem to relax. He was a man of action, not one to turn away when something—or someone—he cared about might be in danger.

He'd sleep light, as Elias said. But still, he felt powerless.

God would have to stand guard tonight. He let the thought sink in fully, bringing with it the shame that was his due. His thoughts should have turned to the Almighty from his first moment of concern.

Sorry, Lord. Would he ever get it right the first time?

~

When Rachel pushed her eyes open the next morning, daylight had already settled over the valley. She'd not slept this late in years.

The faint rustle of movement met her ears, but she took a moment to stretch under her blanket. She should rise. Make up for the time she'd wasted. But she couldn't remember a time she'd felt so relaxed.

"You sick, Ma?"

She turned to Andy and smiled. "No, son. I'm just resting." Pushing the blanket aside, she sat up. "Sorry I slept so long."

"Nothing to be sorry about." Seth's voice sounded behind her, and she turned to see him holding out a steaming cup. She'd never seen such a beautiful sight. The man, with a thin layer of beard shadowing his pleasing features, presenting her with the rich aroma of coffee. She'd not had coffee in a month of Mondays.

She should refuse the offering as she had that first morning and every morning since. But today seemed different. Not only did she feel fully rested, she felt…at peace. Or at least, more peaceful than she could ever remember.

So she took the tin mug he offered, murmured a "thank you," and raised the cup to inhale an aromatic breath. Why had she ever rejected an offer so luxurious? Sure, she believed in making her own way, not accepting gifts or charity, especially from men. But honestly…one should have her priorities straight.

She sipped the brew, letting the strength of it warm her all the way down.

Seth dropped to his haunches beside her. "How's your hand this morning?"

She glanced at her bandage, which was looking rather soiled. The searing pain had slipped to a dull ache, so she'd barely thought about it until he asked. "Better."

"Elias says we should unwrap it and apply more salve. I have clean cloth we can use for a fresh bandage."

The thought of disturbing the wound didn't appeal, but she nodded. "I'll prepare the morning meal, then take care of it."

He nodded toward a pan by a small fire, which hadn't been there the night before. "My brother made corn mush. He's not as good a cook as I am, but it fills the empty places." His eyes held a twinkle that would draw her if she allowed it.

Instead, she took another sip of coffee. "Which of you is older?"

She shouldn't ask questions that would make him think her interested, but this was something she'd been wondering. Was Seth the elder, with his unnerving smile and intense gaze, his tendency toward action when an idea took hold of him? Or Samuel, who was so quiet and reserved, she still didn't know much about him? He always seemed to be there when his brother needed him, yet he never instigated whatever action Seth had them embroiled in.

He squared his shoulders. "I am." Then a grin tugged the corner of his mouth. "By about five minutes."

His words took a moment to register. "You're twins?"

He nodded, a true smile widening his face. The flash of his white teeth only made him more handsome.

She glanced toward Samuel, more to quell the longing in her chest than anything. She didn't need a man. Wouldn't have one, not even a fellow who appeared honorable, like Seth Grant.

She forced her tone to stay light. "You don't look exactly the same."

He shrugged. "Some twins are identical, some aren't. Now I answered your question, I have one for you."

Her gaze jerked to him as wariness crowded inside her. His grin still sat easy on his mouth, no sign of anything diabolical.

"I think I heard you were going to Fort Hamilton, but what's there for you? Family?"

The weight on her chest eased a notch. Speaking of Henry wouldn't bring harm, surely. And no pain. "My brother is there. At least, he was when he wrote last summer."

His head tipped in a curious expression. "Is he your only brother?"

"He is." Even a topic as safe as Henry found a way to surface painful memories.

Maybe Seth saw or felt as much, for he pushed to his feet. "I'll get the salve from Elias, then we can fix up your hand and hit the trail."

~

"We'll probably see Indians today."

Seth turned in his saddle to see if Elias wore a jesting smile.

The man only nodded, his hands propped on the horn of his saddle as he rocked to the rhythm of the mule's gait. "Last time I came through here, there was a band of Apsalooke camping just over that hill yonder." He motioned ahead of them. "They were nice enough, but I just said howdy an' moved on."

Howdy. Interesting word choice for Indians. He and Samuel had seen a band of redskins in the distance on their journey from California, but they'd not spoken with them. "Are most of the Indians friendly in these parts?"

"Well." Elias drew out the word in his relaxed way. "It depends. Usually if you mind your own business and act friendly enough, they'll be pleasant back."

Pleasant? He'd never associated that word with Indians, but best hold his tongue and see.

As they climbed the ridge, Elias took the lead. At the top, a small cluster of teepees appeared in the valley below. A few figures had been moving around outside the lodges but stilled, then moved closer to the tents. Probably because they saw the strangers riding down the hill.

"Wouldn't it have been better to ride around this camp?" Seth kept his voice low, just loud enough for Elias to hear.

The old man glanced to the side. "Wouldn't be an easy ride to scale that mountain range. Besides, if you're gonna spend time in this territory, ya need ta get used to meetin' with Indians."

The man did have a point.

Two men stepped from the camp as they approached, each of them clad in buckskins like Elias. That was the extent of their similarity to the bent older man. These braves were younger, about the age of him and Samuel, and stood straight and proud. Both wore their glossy black hair in braids, but the leaner of the two had hung feathers from the leather tie fastening the plaits.

Elias reined in about ten strides from the men, and Seth pulled up beside him. "Howdy." The older man raised a hand.

The Indian with the feathers raised his own hand in greeting.

"We're just passing through. Don't plan to bother you and your people."

Did the Indians speak English then? Again, the man with the feathers was the one to respond. "You make trade?" The words were clipped but understandable.

Elias shook his head. "Nothing to trade this time."

The Indian nodded, then spoke a string of sounds that had to be in his own language.

Elias nodded and raised a hand in farewell, then reined his mule in front of Seth's gelding and moved on the direction they'd been traveling.

The lead Indian also raised a hand in farewell, and Seth did the same as he turned his horse to follow the mule. That was it then?

He couldn't help a glance back at Rachel, just behind him. Her face wore no expression, not even the grim determination that usually marked her features. How did she so clearly wipe away every trace of her thoughts?

That was a talent he'd never mastered, not even in his gambling days. Since he couldn't eliminate expression from his features, he'd perfected a teasing smirk. A look that hadn't endeared him to the men at his table. But at least they weren't able to read his hand.

When he and his fellow travelers crested a low hill and descended out of sight from the Indians, Elias halted and turned in his saddle, propping a hand on the cantle. "You folks made it through all right?"

Seth reined his horse over so Rachel could ride up beside him, giving him a better view of her and her son, who rode behind her. The boy's face was a little paler than normal, but they were safe. He met Samuel's gaze at the rear of the line. A guardian angel for the group.

He almost chuckled at the thought. His brother, tall, broad-shouldered, and every bit a ruddy man. Not the way he pictured an angel. Yet Samuel was always there, ready to lend aid when needed, guarding Seth's back without being asked.

Seth brought his gaze back to Andy. "Are those the first Indians you've seen?"

"No, sir." The boy's eyes darted to his mother.

Seth turned his gaze that same direction, raising his brows. He made sure to let his face show nothing more than a curious smile. Nothing that would raise her guard.

Rachel's chin lifted. "We saw several bands as we traveled west."

"From the steamboat?"

A confused light touched her eyes, then faded an instant later. "On land."

"You rode horseback from…" He searched his mind for where she said they'd come from. Had she said? No, in fact.

He gave her an expectant look, waiting for her to fill in the location. And to answer the question he'd started to ask. Would he be so lucky as to get her to answer both questions?

She dipped her head in a single nod. "Yes, we rode alongside the Missouri River and saw several Indian camps, as Andy said."

One out of two questions was better than nothing. "Did you ever have trouble from them?"

"None."

As they started out again, her few words wandered through his mind, creating images that stoked more questions. How long had they traveled and from where? How was it possible that a woman and boy journeyed without trouble, both from Indians and the rough sort of white man who traded whiskey to the natives?

Maybe they *had* run into trouble. Did he want to know what they'd experienced? His blood ran hot just thinking about it.

Well, now she was riding with him and Samuel, and they'd make sure she and her son never had to worry about that kind of trouble again.

CHAPTER 9

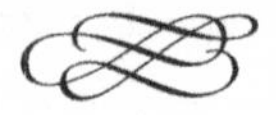

If this is freedom, why am I still broken?
~ Rachel

Rachel should be used to long days in the saddle. After more than four months of this wearying journey, her muscles no longer screamed each morning from the previous day's tortures. But the closer they drew to the Canadian border, the more she itched to be done with this final phase of her old life.

It was past time she and Andy started fresh.

She'd been riding second in line behind Elias since they stopped for the noon meal two or three hours before. Her gelding breathed hard as they ascended the rocky incline of a low rise between two peaks. She couldn't help a sigh of relief as she glanced up at the mountain on their right. Its snowcapped crown rose high enough to steal her breath, and she was more than thankful they wouldn't be scaling its top like the mountain goats did.

"In a few minutes, you folks'll lay eyes on a sight ya won't soon forget." Elias's voice drifted down to them.

"What is it?" Andy seemed to be growing a little bolder each day he spent among these men. Not dangerously bold, just more comfortable in his own skin. Exactly what she wanted for him.

Elias glanced back with a grin. "You like to swim, boy?"

Andy jerked back. "Swim? I..." He glanced at her as though for permission. At the same moment, her horse surged forward to climb a steep section, occupying her focus so she couldn't give her son the encouragement she would have liked to.

"I do." His voice took on strength as he responded to the man in the lead. Perhaps he didn't need her support after all.

Elias reined in at the crest of the hill, pulling off to the side so all the animals could stand and catch their breath from the climb. Even though the altitude was much lower than the peaks on either side of them, she still had to ease herself into looking down toward the valley below.

Her stomach swooped as she gradually lowered her gaze. But then the glimmer of crystal captured her focus. Sparkling green stretching out in the most beautiful lake she'd ever seen.

"Is that water?" Andy's voice sounded as awed as she felt.

"Sure is."

"Let's get down there," Seth said. "It's been far too long since I've given Samuel the dunking he deserves."

She looked over just in time to see Seth shoot a grin at his brother.

Amazingly enough, Samuel Grant—the one who rarely spoke—returned the same look. "I think you'll find that just as impossible as you did fifteen years ago. But if you can best me in a race from one side to the other, I'll give you a chance at a dunking."

"Oh, ho." Seth turned to Andy with a wink. "He talks much, but can he stand behind his boasting?"

Andy's eyes had widened with the interchange, almost as though he expected them to come to blows. Her heart panged at the thought. He'd seen too much of the evil side of men.

When the horses had rested sufficiently, they started down the incline, and even the animals seemed eager to reach the water.

Two trees of the same variety stood along near the water's edge, their white bark and heart-shaped leaves similar to the grove of aspens behind their house in Missouri.

Elias halted beneath the shade of their branches and dismounted. "This is as good a place as any to stop for the night. That way you boys can play fer a while."

Once the animals had been hobbled in the grass around the edge of the lake, there was still another hour or so before dusk fell in earnest.

"You want me to look for firewood, Ma?"

She glanced up from the painful task of unfastening the pouch that contained their cooking utensils. Everything was still so much harder, even though her burn was healing well.

But just before the *yes* slipped out in answer to her son's question, she caught the shift of his gaze toward the clear green of the water. She'd gladly gather wood one-handed to allow him a moment of pleasure, but did she dare let him swim without someone out there to help? It had been three or four years, at least, since the land containing the swimming hole was sold. And even before they lost the right to use the spot, he'd not been adept at much more than making a good splash.

But he needed time to be a youth. She had to allow him the chance.

"Enjoy the water before it gets dark. Just stay in the shallows, please."

He spun back to her, eyes wide and eager, perhaps checking to see if she were playing a cruel joke with the offer. She gave him a warm smile but couldn't help adding, "Be careful. Don't take risks."

"Yes, ma'am." He was already pulling his shirt tail from his trousers as he slipped out of his boots.

"I say we all take a swim." Seth's voice tore her gaze from her son, and she swiveled to face him.

He met her look with raised brows. "What say you, Rachel? Elias?" He turned to the older man before she could call him to task for using her given name.

He did it only to tease her, she was fairly certain of that now. And for that reason, she should ignore the prod. Yet she still didn't like how the intimacy of her name on his lips lowered the barriers she was so careful to keep around her.

"I think that water's a mite cold fer these ol' bones." Elias reached a hand to his back with a boyish twist to his mouth that said his excuse may not quite be true. "Mrs. Gray should try out the water, though."

Seth turned and stepped toward her, a devilish smile on his face. For half a breath, it looked like he might hoist her up and toss her in the lake.

Her body tensed, remembering the last time she'd been manhandled. She scrambled to her feet and backed away, her heart pulsing like a hummingbird's wings. "No." She took another step back, wrapping her arms around herself. Hating the fear that closed off her throat. "No."

He froze, his smile slipping away as he took in her reaction. "Rachel, I didn't mean..."

She took another step back, half-turned away. Just enough to draw a clear breath of air. To regain control over her reactions.

"I'm sorry. I would never have forced you." Seth's voice came low and earnest, truth marking each of his words.

She breathed in another cleansing breath, letting it steal out of her and take the terror with it. Another inhale, another exhale. Finally, her breath didn't quaver with the leaving.

Squaring her shoulders, she turned back to him. "I'd rather not swim, but I'll not stand in your way."

His dark eyes held such a well of sadness, they were almost her undoing. "I understand."

Did he? The way he seemed to see inside her, all the way to her core, maybe he did. She wrapped her hands around her, trying to conceal his gaze from seeing too much.

Yet covering herself didn't seem to make a difference. She turned away again, back to the pack she'd been unfastening. "I'll make a stew while you swim. Something warm for when you all come out with your teeth chattering."

"Thank you." His voice kept that earnestness.

She hunched against his words and his gaze, which was still drilling into her.

Long moments passed before his footsteps finally faded behind her. More moments before his deep tenor joined in with his brother's and Andy's higher tones.

Not until then did she finally take in another breath.

~

Seth forced himself to push Rachel's reaction out of his mind so he could focus on Andy in the lake. The boy hadn't been exaggerating when he said he'd had only a little experience swimming. In truth, his movements in the water were choppy and held more than a hint of uncertainty.

Drawing up beside the lad, he sank down in the water until it reached his chest, where his undershirt clung like a second skin. "When I taught Samuel to swim, we used a side stroke that made it easy to learn the feel of the water. Shall I show you?"

Before Andy could answer, Samuel interrupted. "When you taught me to swim, you pushed me under the water and climbed on my shoulders. 'Tis I who taught you the side stroke."

Seth winked at the boy. "He doesn't remember well when his brain is water-logged. Shall I show you the stroke?"

A hint of pleasure lit Andy's green eyes as he nodded.

Working together, he and Samuel demonstrated the method, then coached the lad through the process until he was making good progress through the water.

The first time the three of them reached the far end of the narrow lake, he stood with a wide grin. "I did it. I made it across without stopping once."

That pride glimmering in his eyes—those eyes so like Rachel's—pressed on Seth's chest so much, it felt like he might burst from pleasure. "That's something Samuel can't even claim."

His brother took on a look of mock indignation. "I only touched down once. And that was to see why you were lagging so far behind, brother."

Seth took the teasing with a grin. "You ready to head back?" He posed the question to them both but watched Andy for signs he was pushing the boy too hard.

He nodded firmly. "Beat ya there."

~

Rachel tugged the wooden spoon through the stew but couldn't stop her focus from drifting toward the water.

She'd never seen grown men play like boys, not with the gusto and laughter that now drifted from the lake. Andy's higher pitch sounded among the deeper male tones, and the happy voice swelled her heart.

This was what he needed.

Splashing mingled with a burst of laughter and shouts, and she sharpened her gaze to make sure Andy wasn't in danger. They appeared to be having some kind of splash fight. Seth was deep in the midst of the battle, instigating, most likely.

He lived life so fully, so intensely. Whether he was skinning a deer carcass, bandaging her burned hand, or teaching her son to swim, this man dove into whatever he set his mind to. Felt every part of it. Spent himself in the act.

So different than she, who did everything possible not to feel. Not to allow herself to be entrenched by what was happening. She had to keep herself separate. It was the only way to survive through the pain of life.

A flash of movement drew her gaze upward again. As if her thoughts had summoned him, Seth Grant slogged up the bank, emerging from the lake like a sea creature, water dripping from every part of him.

His undershirt and trousers clung to his body, outlining every curve of his muscular chest and arms, his lean middle. She was staring but couldn't seem to look away. He was the most beautiful specimen of a man she could ever remember seeing.

As he drew nearer, her gaze flicked to his face. His eyes met hers, his mouth tipped in a half-smile that seemed to be enjoying her attention.

She dropped her focus back to the stew, heat surging to her face that had nothing to do with the fire.

He moved into the campsite and plopped down on one of the logs Elias had found. "That fire feels good."

She needed to say something that would prove she wasn't tongue-tied by the sight of him. "The water's cold?"

"I think this lake is fed by run-off from snow in the mountains."

She raised her face to the white-capped peak keeping guard above them, then looked to the lake where Andy made small waves in the water as he talked with Samuel. "Perhaps it's time everyone came to get warm."

"I think he's enjoying it." Seth's tone was low. Not chiding, but she could feel his suggestion that the time of leisure might be good for her son. He was right, even though the suggestion that he might know better than she what her boy needed riled. Yet, she knew better than to let emotion overwhelm good sense.

So she turned her focus back to the meal, reaching for a plate. After scooping a goodly portion from the pot, she handed the tin to Seth. "This will warm you."

"Mmm…Just what I need. Thank you."

She shouldn't allow his appreciation to bring so much pleasure, but she couldn't seem to stop herself. She'd worked hard to squelch the desire to be wanted, even needed. Letting that craving arise now would impair her ability to protect herself.

And Andy.

"There we go." Elias's high voice broke the stillness between them. "I think this'll be enough wood to see us 'til morning." He dropped his load and brushed the dirt from his hands. "Come mornin', I imagine we'll all be hankerin' to hit the trail."

Yes, they should push on tomorrow. Every day would bring her closer to her brother. Closer to the day she'd leave these men.

She only had to make sure she didn't leave her heart at the parting.

CHAPTER 10

'Tis a stronger attraction than I want to feel.
~ Seth

As darkness settled over the valley, a thick layer of clouds smothered the light of the moon. Seth kept an eye on the sky as the conversation flowed around the campfire. Maybe it was the hearty meal Rachel cooked, or maybe high spirits from the pleasure of a swim, but everyone seemed a bit more talkative than normal.

And none more so than Elias.

"Have you met any other old trappers like in that story you told?" Andy leaned toward the older man, his gaze hungry.

"Let's see." Elias stroked his beard. "I'll never forget the story ol' Joe Meek tells about when he was a younger man an' assigned to guard duty with another fella one night. He an' this other fella—Reese was his name—both fell asleep. The boss woke up an' called out, 'All's well?' But neither one of 'em was awake to answer.

"The boss man, he was hoppin' mad, and he stomped toward the two that was supposed to be guardin'. He was loud enough, he woke Reese, who realized right quick they'd been caught.

"Reese calls out in a loud whisper, 'Indians! Get down!'" Elias leaned forward, ducking low as his voice took on the same tone of those in his story.

"The boss knew 'xactly what those words meant, so he drops to the ground and says, 'Where?'

"'Right out there,' says Reese.

"'Where's Meek?' asks the boss.

"'Tryin' to shoot the Indians.' Reese is still talkin' low." Elias spoke in a stage whisper as they hung on his every word.

"The night was about as dark as this'n." Elias motioned toward the starless sky. "So Reese crawled over to where Meek was sleepin', then woke him up and told him what was happenin'. The two of 'em crawled back to the boss.

"He asked all kinda questions about the Indians, an' Meek told him there'd been more than he could count. The next mornin', turns out there was a set of Indian moccasins right where Meek an' Reese said they saw the Indians."

"So the Indians really came?" Andy's eyes grew round.

Elias curled his thin lips under as he chuckled. "Meek didn't own up to it, but it wouldn't surprise me if those were his moccasins. He was a wily one. And never lost a chance for a good joke, even though sometimes the joke came back on him." He leaned back an' slapped his hands on his knees. "I sup—"

A bolt of lightning lit the sky just as a crack of thunder boomed loud as a gunshot.

Seth startled at the sound, and beside him, a half-scream broke from Rachel. He jerked his gaze to her.

She'd clapped a hand over her mouth and clutched Andy's arm, as though to protect him. When the sound died away, he felt, more than heard, her tremulous exhale.

"Whew. I thought we'd get some rain, but I didn't expect all that with it." Elias shook his head. "We'd best get these supplies covered up. If we're lucky, we'll have a few extra furs to huddle under."

Seth rose with the others and pulled out the pelts Elias used for his bedding. "All Samuel and I have are wool blankets. Don't suppose they'll keep anything dry."

"We have a few small hides. Rabbit and such." Rachel turned to her packs, then stilled, looking back at Elias. "There's a bear hide, still salted, but not yet dried." Her voice hung with question. Seth wasn't familiar enough with animal skins and the tanning process to know what she was asking.

One fact he was fairly certain of, the bear hide she possessed was likely the one she and Andy had killed the night before joining them. The episode that must surely have terrified them both.

Elias seemed to weigh his answer. "The salt might help keep the fur safe, but it's likely the rain will ruin any trading value. The hide will do plenty well to keep you dry, though."

Her lower lip slipped under her teeth as uncertainty tugged her features. A look he wasn't sure he'd ever seen on her face. "All right."

After turning back to the pack, she extracted a large bundle of oilcloth, which was wrapped around the dark fur peeking from inside. She began unfolding the pack as white crystals fell from inside. "This is likely large enough for two or three of us to sit under. We can use the oilcloth for shelter, too."

While they set to work piling the goods that should be kept dry, Seth let his mind spin through the next few hours. It was nigh time to bed down for the night, but that wouldn't be fruitful if this was a heavy downpour. How long would the storm last?

Heavy drops began pelting, and lightning lit the air twice more, followed closely by thunder. The second blast was almost as loud as when they'd been sitting around the fire.

While Seth unrolled a fur, he moved toward Elias. "You think the horses are all right?"

The man glanced toward where they'd left them, but the darkness was too thick to see. "They're hobbled, so they can drift toward the trees on the other side of the lake. There's not anything else we can do to help them."

The rain drove harder, and Seth slipped back into motion. "This pelt is big enough to shelter one person."

"And I have a wolf hide that'll work for another." Elias raised a mottled fur. "You want it Mrs. Gray?"

"Andy and I will use the oilcloth." She motioned for her son to join her as she sank down against one of the trees.

"That's all we have then. Best we sit close an' maybe we can all get covered." Elias moved toward them and settled on the other side of Andy.

Seth wasn't sure they'd all be able to snuggle under the three scant coverings, but he and Samuel had both donned their coats before the drops came. Water ran down his face, and his collar was already soaked, but this certainly wouldn't be the first time they'd gotten wet in a rainstorm.

He scanned the camp to see if there was anything left needing attention. The supplies and wood were covered, and the fire had sizzled to a thin stream of smoke.

"Come sit." Rachel's voice broke through the din of raindrops. She held the oilcloth over her head with one hand, and patted the ground beside her with the other. There was enough space there for him and Samuel to sit under the shelter of branches.

He strode toward them and took the spot beside Rachel—no way was he leaving that place to Samuel.

Especially when she inched closer to her son and bid Seth move nearer. "I think if we all scoot in, the oilcloth will cover you both."

It had been a lifetime since he'd sat so close to a woman, and her warmth seeped all the way down his arm, his hip, his thigh. She didn't seem to mind the closeness, which was the biggest wonder of all. Or maybe she cared enough that he and Samuel not sit in the rain. Either way, he would relish these few minutes.

The rain fell in sheets, drenching everything in sight, including the ground. Water soaked into the seat of his trousers, but he could live with the discomfort. The pounding drops were too loud to allow for talking, and the steady noise combined with another long day in the saddle soon had him yawning.

A few minutes later, Rachel touched his knee to get his attention. She pointed to Andy on her other side, his head resting on her shoulder. His thin frame rose and fell with deep breaths.

The sleep of the weary. And rightly so. If the ride hadn't exhausted the boy, the hour of swimming should have finished the job.

Rachel looked back at Seth with a smile, and he lost himself in the thick emerald of her eyes in the darkness. She was so beautiful, this woman. So strong, yet so achingly fragile. As much as she fought to take on a man's role, she was woman, every part of her.

His hand longed to reach up and touch her face. To lean closer and kiss her lips. He wouldn't do it, of course. But that didn't stop the ache.

He looked away before she could see the turn of his thoughts, bringing his gaze back to Andy. After a nod and a smile, he settled back against the trunk of the tree. As much as he loved sitting so near her, she made his body come to life more fully than when he'd jumped into the icy lake.

In fact, he may just need another dunking in the water when this was over. Clearly, there would be no sleep for him tonight.

~

Rachel woke to an ache stabbing her neck. She attempted to raise her head, but the pain pierced harder. So she took a moment to make out her surroundings in the dim light of early dawn.

She was sitting upright, Andy pressed against her shoulder. And her cheek rested on…

Awareness crept in with a heavy weight. Her first response was to jerk away from the man she was leaning against. But if she did, he'd awaken and know she'd spent the night pressed against him. And her pride just couldn't stomach the thought of giving him that satisfaction.

Except this was Seth.

He didn't act like the other men she'd known. Not like Richard. If she could trust her instincts, she was fairly certain Seth wouldn't gloat or try to press his advantage if she gave him quarter.

Still, she eased her head off his shoulder, biting down against the pain spearing her neck. She couldn't stand without waking Andy, but the ache in her middle told her she'd need to do so soon. Her morning ministrations called, and she should check on the horses after the night's storm.

As if he felt the loss of her touch, the man to her left shifted, his body stiffening in a stretch as he extended his legs in front of him.

She dared a glance at his face, and he met her look with a sleepy smile. "I guess we made it through the storm." His voice came out in a low murmur, its sleep-roughened timbre sending an unwanted tingle down her arms.

"We did." She kept her voice soft, but it must have been loud enough to wake her son, for he raised his head.

He looked around, his hair pressed up where he'd leaned against her shoulder. "Is it morning already?" The words summoned a yawn.

"It is." She leaned forward and pushed herself away from the tree. "I'm going to check the horses."

After finding tree cover to attend to morning needs, she headed toward the grassy area where they'd left the animals. "Winter. Here, boy." The morning seemed so still, she almost hated to break the quiet with her voice.

The horses and mule weren't where they'd left them, but she heard a snort through the fog that had settled in this end of the valley.

As she moved forward, Elias's mule appeared through the mist. He ripped up a bite of grass, then raised his head to eye her as he munched.

"Hey, boy. You look like you weathered the storm just fine." She rubbed his shoulder, scanning the rest of his body for injuries. All seemed well.

Moving on to the two burly geldings the Grant brothers rode, she accepted an affectionate snuffle from one as she took his jaw in both hands. "It's good to see you, too." Animals were so much easier to be around than people. You never had to worry about artifice or ulterior motives.

She patted his shoulder, then stepped forward and did the same to the other gelding. These two were a matched pair, perfect for twin brothers. Were the animals brothers, too?

After stepping past the second chestnut gelding, she scanned the fog for her and Andy's horses. "Winter. Summer. Where are you?"

Andy had named the animals for their colors, and she still loved the titles. Winter's white-gray coat reminding her of snow, and Summer's golden body just like the warm sun of a summer day.

She made her way farther, extending a hand through the dense white crystals that blocked her view beyond the reach of her arm. The lake's edge appeared suddenly, only a step away.

Altering her course, she followed alongside it. "Winter. Come, boy." The horse didn't answer, and she strained to make out the sounds of grazing or something else that would alert their presence.

She wasn't quite sure where she was around the edge of the lake, but she must be somewhere along the short end. A tree suddenly loomed in front of her. A dark trunk with spiny needles above her. A pine.

"Winter, Summer. Come eat." She must have walked past the animals without seeing them.

Turning, she retraced her steps, keeping the lake on her right side. Hopefully, she'd see them on her way back to camp. If not, she'd have to wait until the fog faded. Either way, this would give them a chance to graze.

The animals needed plenty of fodder to ready themselves for another long ride.

CHAPTER 11

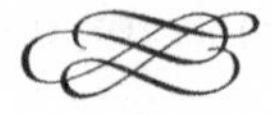

I should have braced myself better for this blow.
~ Rachel

When the fog lifted, their horses were nowhere to be found.

Rachel fought the fear surging in her chest as she called out across the valley for the animals. Elias and Samuel were gathering in the mule and the two chestnut geldings, removing hobbles so they could bring them to the camp for their morning ration of oats.

Where had the other two gone?

"I'll go find them, Ma." Andy reached for a rope and slung it over his shoulder.

"I'll look, too." There was no way she was staying here to clean dishes while their prize possessions wandered away through the woods at the edges of the valley. "You hike along the tree line that butts against the mountain. I'll go through the center of the woods at the far edge."

"*I'll* look through the center of the woods." Seth's strong voice made her spin to face him. “My legs are longer. I can cover more ground. You can search to the right of us.”

He was right about his ability to move faster than her shorter legs —especially since she was wearing skirts—but it irked the way he took over and reassigned her role. These weren’t his horses, they were hers.

“This is the way I can help best.” His voice dropped in volume, the words spoken only to her. His eyes begged for her to allow him.

She stilled. There was wisdom in his suggestion, but the path was quite likely the place they'd find the horses, as it contained the most space where they could be hidden. Could she give over control of the hunt to him?

She inhaled a deep breath, then exhaled. “All right. But call out if you find them.”

A half hour later, she’d hiked to the mountain cliff they descended the day before, with no sight of the missing animals. She halted at the incline, scanning the slope for any sign of the horses.

The animals would be hard-pressed to mount that grade wearing hobbles. And it only made sense they would seek shelter in the trees.

Turning toward where Seth had gone, she strained to hear any sound that he’d found them. Should she head that way and see if he needed help?

He said he would call out.

She should turn the other way and search through the thin copse of trees on the left side of the lake. It wasn’t likely the horses had traversed that far—they’d have had to walk by the camp to reach it. But she should cover every possibility.

Searching that area proved fruitless, and soon she trudged back toward camp to see if Andy or Seth had found the horses. Where could the animals have gone? And what in the world would she do if she couldn’t find them?

The possible reality of that last thought slugged her like a rifle bullet. Her shoulders sank under the weight, and she forced down a burn in her throat. She would not cry, no matter how bad things grew.

As she reached the campsite, it was easy to see the forms of three animals and two men working amongst them.

But no others.

Samuel Grant met her with a grim set to his mouth. "Where all have you searched?"

She motioned toward the areas. "I'm going to see if Seth or Andy found them. They must have. There's no other place the horses could have gone without climbing a mountain."

He scrubbed a hand through his hair, the same motion Seth did when he was frustrated. He scanned the camp. "I'll come with you." Then to Elias, "Do you need anything else before I join the search?"

"No, son. I'll hold down the fort 'til you bring 'em back."

When they reached the edge of the woods where Seth searched, Samuel cupped his hands around his mouth and called for his brother in a booming voice.

"Here." Seth's voice wasn't far away, maybe fifty strides or so into the trees. "Andy and I are coming back."

Rachel's pulse jolted. "Do you have the horses?" They must have found them.

"No."

The single word crashed through her hope, shattering jagged pieces inside her. She could do nothing but wait as the sound of their heavy steps drifted through the woods. Where could the animals have gone? Maybe Seth saw signs of them and was only coming back to get help for a more thorough search.

As they appeared through the trunks, she tried to study their faces in the dim light of the woods. Both seemed grim, but neither Seth's large frame nor Andy's smaller profile looked despondent. Maybe they had an idea where the horses had gone.

For to be left without mounts in this massive wilderness would surely be enough to make her son's shoulders slump.

Seth met her gaze as he neared, stopping before her. He propped his hands on his hips. "I walked as far as the rear edge of the trees. The mountains form a sort of canyon in that area, like a river once ran through it. I picked out a few hoof marks in the mud left from last night's rain."

The fragments of hope tried to form in her chest again. "Then we should follow them." She started forward, moving around him to hike the path he'd just trod.

"Wait." He grabbed her arm.

She froze, her heart pounding in her throat. Every instinct told her to jerk away. His grip wasn't tight, but it seemed to be clutching harder with each passing second, pressing on her chest so she couldn't breathe.

He released her, and she forced herself to take in a breath.

"Wait." His voice was softer this time, almost gentle. Did he realize how she struggled against so much fear? Irrational fear in this case, yet she couldn't seem to stop herself. So many times, Richard had grabbed her arm when the drink took hold. And never was it a harmless gesture.

She forced herself to focus again on the horses. What had Seth been trying to tell her? "Why should I wait?" She didn't dare look at his face, for he would see too easily the turmoil in her gaze.

He let out a breath, and the sound almost drew her focus. But she stopped herself.

"Elias said we'll be traveling that way when we leave, so I thought it best we pack up our camp and head out. I found this."

She jerked her gaze to what he held up. A strip of leather—one of those used for hobbles—dirty and ragged at the torn edges.

She sucked in a breath and looked to his face. "Do you know whose it is?"

He shook his head. "I suspect the other horse broke loose from his, too. That means they're free to move as far as they want. We'll stand a better chance of reaching them on horseback."

She looked back toward the camp, her mind swimming. "How can we all go on just three animals?"

"We can double up. You and Andy are both light. Our geldings are of good size to add another small person. We've used up a lot of the foodstuffs, so Elias's mule can carry most of your things. If we don't carry dry firewood for tonight, we should be fine."

He was probably right, although the thought of riding so near one of these men made her throat clutch again.

But she could do it. She had to.

~

Seth tried to act as though nothing moved him about the woman sitting in front of him in the saddle, but it was impossible.

In truth, everything about this woman moved him. From her indomitable strength to the vulnerability he glimpsed every so often when she struggled to overcome her fears. He'd seen enough to have a few suspicions about what had occurred in her past, and just the thought of someone taking a hand to her was enough to make his blood boil in his veins.

He couldn't focus on that now, though. She needed him to be calm. To be strong for her in the face of this possible loss.

She began the journey with her back so rigid she rarely touched him. He kept one arm loose around her so he could hold the reins. All three saddles had gear stacked high behind them, so it was necessary for her to ride in front. Hopefully, this doubling up would only last a few hours so the extra weight wouldn't be too hard on the horses.

Maneuvering through the woods with the animals so loaded wasn't easy, and he fought to keep the branches from striking Rachel's face and arms.

She did an admirable job catching limbs and holding them aside as they passed, but the frequent movement kept her brushing against his arms, his chest, his shoulders. Every touch made him achingly aware of her.

Maybe by the time this ended, he'd be fully numb to her. The effects of overexposure.

He could only hope.

They finally emerged through the woods, where the mountain

ranges on either side drew together to form the ravine. Rachel had relaxed through the twisting and bending the forest required, and she now sat easy in the saddle, as though she were born on a horse.

That ability to make riding a horse look easy could only come from much time spent in the saddle. Was it only the journey west that gave her this ability? Maybe he could ask in a roundabout way.

"How long have you had these two horses?"

She seemed to startle at his words. Maybe he'd spoken too loudly.

But she didn't hesitate long before answering. "We bought them back in Missouri with what was left from selling the house. That was last autumn, so they've been with us a little less than a year. They're good horses. I'm not sure what spooked them so badly in the storm. We've surely been through worse before."

He wanted to tuck her in his arms, to soothe away the worry lacing her voice. But he'd have to do it with words, for he'd learned his lesson about touching her when he'd not been invited to do so.

After sitting with her pressed against his shoulder much of the night, he'd not thought twice about reaching for her arm to halt her earlier. But the way she recoiled made it clear a sudden touch wasn't welcome. The panic in her eyes would be seared in his mind for a long time to come.

He struggled for something to say that would ease her worry. "I don't know why they ran. Maybe the lightning struck too near them. I'm sure we'll find them soon, though."

They were entering the canyon now, and he pointed up to the rock wall that rose in stair steps on either side of them. "Look at the way the rock changes color with each layer."

She followed his motion and was silent for a moment as she took in the red and white lines in the stone. "I like the view much better from down here."

He bit back a chuckle. "Not much for heights, huh?"

"Am I that obvious?" Her voice seemed to hold the hint of a smile.

"Not really." He shouldn't say how much he was drawn to watch her.

As they rode on, he did his best to keep her occupied with little tidbits and casual questions. Anything to keep her thoughts from worry. She relaxed into him a little more every few minutes, especially as the uneven path meant the horses had to shift and strain to maneuver, which jostled them both.

"These tracks seem like they're gettin' fresher." Elias pointed to a muddy print the shape of a horseshoe. "If I remember right, there's a little grassy spot on the other side of that hill. Might be that's where we find 'em."

"I hope so." She echoed the words in Seth's own mind.

The sides of the canyon leveled off as they ascended what Elias called a *hill*. It looked more like a cliff, and the animals strained to climb. There wasn't a place to stop and let them rest partway up, but thankfully, this wasn't as high as the true mountains they'd maneuvered.

As they crested the top, Seth reined his horse in beside Elias. "Oh." The scene stretching below them was breathtaking, a narrow valley spanning from the base of their hill and extending three times as far as he could throw a stone. Beyond that, three mountains rose in magnificent splendor, each of their peaks capped with snow.

"Does the snow ever melt here?" Andy's voice sounded beside him where Samuel had also reined in.

"Some o' these peaks keep it all year 'round," Elias said.

The gelding underneath them shifted forward, and Rachel grabbed his arm that held the reins. It was only then he realized how tense she was from the height they stared down from.

He brought his other hand around to help grip the leathers, then eased his arms back to hold her a little more securely. "Easy." He spoke to the horse but meant it for her as well.

She moved her other hand to grip his arm, too, and he closed her in a little tighter, careful not to touch her with his hands. "You're safe." He spoke only loud enough for her ears, and he ached to wrap his arms around her fully instead of this loose hold that offered a sense of protection without pressure that would scare her. If she would only let him through her defenses, she would see his intent was to care for her. Never in a thousand summers would he let her be hurt like before.

Her only response was rough breathing, as though she struggled to get the air in, then out again.

He scrambled for something to say to distract her, but before his mind could form a line of conversation, Elias motioned them forward.

"Down we go. Seems like I might see somethin' that could be yer horse."

Seth held his gelding back from following the mule and leaned close to Rachel's ear. "Do you want to wait a minute longer?"

She shook her head. "Go."

All right then. She planned to face this fear head-on like she'd faced everything else. This woman's strength continued to amaze him.

He nudged the gelding forward, and the animal picked his way through the rocky terrain. At a steeper step, he gathered his haunches under him and dropped down with his front legs.

Rachel let out a squeak and pulled Seth's arm tight against her. He tucked his hand around her side, holding the reins with his left hand. "I've got you." She didn't fight his grip. If anything, she held him closer.

CHAPTER 12

All my life I've wanted to be a better man. Something about this woman makes me think I may actually achieve that goal.
~ Seth

As much as Seth would have loved to relish Rachel's trust in him, it took all his focus to guide the horse down the descent. The gelding was usually sure-footed, but this cliff would be a test even for a mountain goat.

The clatter of rocks behind them signaled Samuel was making his way, too. *Keep them safe, Lord. Let us all get down without incident.*

Halfway through, his gelding stumbled. Seth jerked up on the reins to keep the animal's head up. The horse scrambled but finally gathered his hooves underneath him.

Rachel gripped Seth's arm with a hold tight enough to hinder the blood flow, but it was nothing compared to the strength with which he held her.

The slope was too steep for the horse to stop and rest, but Seth kept a tight hold on the reins to help the gelding take things slow. One measured step at a time.

When they finally reached the bottom where the grade leveled, he both felt and heard Rachel's long exhale.

"Good, boy." Seth leaned around her to rub the animal's shoulder, which brought his face almost beside hers.

She rested her head back against his shoulder and turned a weary smile to him. "I wasn't sure we would make it."

The ride down, or maybe the fear she fought with each step, had more than exhausted her. Had stripped away her protective shell.

Their faces were mere handbreadths apart, and he could feel the warmth of her spent air on his cheeks. But he wouldn't take advantage of her vulnerability. A kiss would spoil this moment, this warm celebration in his chest. And too, her son was looking on. *Later*. He could only pray for another opportunity later.

Samuel reined his mount in beside Seth's. "I'm gonna walk a while. This boy scraped his knee on a rock."

Rachel lifted her head from his shoulder as she turned to the pair. Yet she didn't stiffen her back. Stayed soft in his arms.

Which meant he had to pull on every bit of self-control he possessed to say, "I should walk, too. This boy needs a break after all that work."

Elias let out a laugh—really more like a cackle—as he gave his mule an affectionate slap on the neck. "That's why you fellers need a mule. Can take you anywhere you wanna go and won't wear out doin' it."

He forced himself to release his grip around Rachel's waist, and his arm missed the warmth of her body. She leaned forward as though she would dismount, but he rested a hand on her shoulder. "You can stay put. I won't kick you as I climb down."

"I'll walk, too." She shifted her leg over the gelding's neck and slid out of his hold.

By the time he'd dismounted, she was stroking the horse's muzzle, murmuring soft words to him. That would make the horse feel better, no doubt. Having her whisper sweet words would heal any man's aches.

As Seth gathered the reins, she turned her focus to her son, slipping her arm around his shoulders. Then she looked to Elias. "Which direction did you see the horses?"

The older man raised a hand to shield his gaze from the sun and scanned to their left, along the base of the mountain. "There's some heavy brush out there, but I think I saw the yellow mare mixed in with it."

"Let's go see." Rachel released her son and started that direction.

~

The horses greeted Rachel with welcome nickers, as though they'd been casually waiting for her to come. She and Andy easily caught the animals, but saddling them and refastening their packs required dismantling all the careful organizing Elias had done on the mule and the two chestnut geldings.

Finally, they were back on the trail, and it seemed like the sun should be much farther along its arc than just past the noon mark.

"Hard to believe it's been less than a full day since we were swimming in the lake, huh?" Seth rode on her right, his gelding's nose even with her stirrup.

"That was a lot of fun. Can we swim the next time we come to water?" Andy seemed like a new boy since they're play time the day before. Lighter, as though he'd washed off some of the seriousness that marked his bearing these past years. It had come on so gradually, she'd not even realized how different he'd become.

Growing up with a father like Richard did that to a boy.

She pushed the thought away. Despite the fear from losing the horses, it felt as though she'd shed a layer of worry, too. Or maybe she and Andy had already stepped into the new life this trip would bring them.

"I reckon' we can do that." Elias called back from the lead. "It'll be a few days before we hit another."

The rest of that afternoon passed easily and with blue skies, for which she couldn't help but be relieved. She'd never again complain about a long day in the saddle, because it meant she had a horse to ride.

And she was mostly able to keep that promise over the next few days. They rode through one rain shower, but with no thunder or lightning, the horses did little more than duck against the wet.

In the wee hours of the third day after that awful storm, Elias took the last swig of his morning coffee, then set the cup down and rubbed his hands together. "We reach Two Rivers later this mornin'."

"What's that?" Rachel laid strips of bear meat on the pan to sizzle over the fire. She'd become adept at using her left hand for work that would soil the bandage still on her right.

"Two Rivers be the little town about a half day's ride below my cabin. I need to stop in an' deliver a couple things I promised folks. There's a lake above the place that's the source o' the rivers flowing on either side o' the town. Figured we could maybe spend the afternoon there, then push on to my place tomorrow."

That old familiar tightening squeezed her chest. "A town?" The question slipped out before she could stop it, the words laced too heavily with her angst. That was a testament to how familiar she'd become with these people.

Yet she wouldn't allow them to force her through the town. Under no condition.

"How big is this place? What businesses are there?" Seth's voice still held a trace of sleepy gravel, yet its strength worked its usual magic to calm her.

"Just a few buildings. A trade store, a smithy, a leatherworker who can also build a wagon if ya ask him to."

And at least one of those places sold whiskey and served as gambling den, she had no doubt.

She raised her chin to Elias so he had no doubt of the seriousness of her intent. "Andy and I will ride on and meet you at the lake." They could follow one of the rivers to the source, surely.

He cocked his head to study her. "There's no need to worry 'bout these folks. I know 'em all well. An' I won't do more than say howdy and unload what I brought, if'n yer worried about the time."

"I've an idea." Seth leaned forward, his cup cradled in both hands. "You see your friends, Elias. The rest of us can follow the river up to the lake and get started on that swim. You join us whenever you're finished."

Yes.

Seth must have heard her relieved exhale, for a corner of his mouth curved as he slid her a glance, then returned his focus to Elias.

"I reckon' that'll work fine."

"Maybe you'll have enough time to finally best me." Samuel reached up to tousle Andy's hair. The ruffle didn't muss it any more than his sleep had already done, and Rachel couldn't help the surge of love that warmed her chest at Andy's answering grin.

Seth and Samuel Grant were men unlike any she'd ever known. In fact, she'd long given up believing such existed among ranks of the male population. How close Andy had come to never knowing their good influence.

It would have been a loss for him. But as much as she appreciated their attentions to her son, she couldn't allow herself to be affected. It was one thing to be thankful for their encouragement to her child during this journey. Quite another to let her own heart be cracked open.

Yet as Seth leaned near to refill his tin with coffee, her senses came alive in the way that always unsettled her. She'd let him in too far already. In a few weeks they would reach Canada and go their separate ways.

Carving him from her heart would be torture. But she'd have to do it.

~

As they settled into their usual rhythm on the trail, Seth couldn't help wondering exactly why Rachel was so skittish of people.

He'd assumed she didn't trust strangers, and he was pretty sure her wariness was mostly directed toward men. He'd supposed someone in her past had planted the fear deep within her over a span of much time. Probably her husband, if he'd read her reactions correctly.

But her distrust seemed so extreme, was there something more? Was she fleeing from a crime she committed?

And the bigger question...did that change how he felt about her?

His chest ached every time he thought of what she must have suffered. At the same time, fury sluiced through his veins. No woman should be mistreated, especially not such a tender heart as Rachel.

If the abuse had turned her to violence, well... Should he talk to her about it? God knew exactly how much wrong he'd done, even though none of his misdeeds had been technically against the law. Still, so many people had been hurt, some even ending in death.

And yet the Lord had forgiven those sins. Cleansed him completely when Seth had finally turned in desperation. Maybe Rachel needed to know of that same grace. *Show me your way, Father. Help me get this right.*

A few hours into the morning, they reached a wide creek flowing with trees on either side.

"I reckon' this is where we part ways fer a bit." Elias paused at the river's edge. "You just follow this upstream 'til you see the lake. I'll catch up in an hour or two."

"Take your time." Seth raised a hand in farewell, then turned his gelding the direction Elias had pointed.

In a half hour they reached the lake, which wasn't as large as the first one they swam in. The water wasn't such a clear green either, but it was still a welcome sight with the warm sun running beads of sweat down his back.

"Those trees'll make a good campsite." Rachel motioned toward a cluster of a dozen trunks.

"Can I swim after I unsaddle the horses?" Andy was already eyeing the water.

"You may." She couldn't deny that longing in his gaze.

The boy hurried through his task and had Winter and Summer

stripped of their saddles and set out to graze before she'd even unfastened the food pack.

Her gaze followed her son as he tugged off his boots and shirt, then stepped into the water. He waded forward with no concern slowing his progress.

She couldn't help but call out to him. "Be careful of rocks."

He shot her a grin. "I will." But he didn't slow a bit. When the water reached the top of his trousers, he ducked low to submerge his chest, then turned toward them. "Come on. It's warmer than the other lake."

Seth and Samuel had already unsaddled their own mounts. Seth gathered wood for a fire, and Samuel organized their packs—their normal process to set up camp.

She motioned toward the water. "Go swim. This can wait." In truth, she would feel better if Andy weren't in the water alone. None of them knew the dangers in this water, and his skill was still so limited.

A look passed between the brothers, so quick she almost missed it. Then Seth turned to her. "Samuel will join your son. I'll get a fire started first."

Her relief spread a warmth through her chest that flowed out to her smile. It was just like Seth to know her concern even when she didn't express it. To watch over Andy without leaving her to bear the brunt of the work.

She had the food pulled out for the midday meal by the time Seth kindled a blaze for the campfire. He sat back on his heels to study the flame, and she couldn't help a glance at his strong profile. From his wide shoulders to the way every part of his face dove into his expression. This man was too appealing.

Forcing her focus away from him, she scrambled for something to distract her attention. "Do you want to eat before you swim?"

He reached for one of the strips of roasted venison. "I'll just have this to hold me over." The grin he sent her started a fluttering in her chest, and she looked away.

A minute later, he pushed to his feet with a little groan. "These long days in the saddle can wear you out."

Oh, how she knew that to be true.

"Anything else that needs doing before I join the others?"

She shook her head, not daring to meet his gaze. "Nothing. I'll have food and warm coffee when you finish swimming."

"Thank you."

Those two simple words, spoken with an earnestness that she could feel to her core, finally broke through her defenses.

She met his look, forced herself to nod. Did her best not to fall into the intensity in his eyes.

Then those eyes softened, crinkling at the edges. One corner of his mouth tipped up. "You're welcome to join us in the water. You might find you like it."

He didn't step forward like he had the last time. Did nothing to stir her fear. And for a moment, part of her craved to go with him. To set aside her worries and free herself in the water.

However, that would also require setting aside her skirts, and that she couldn't do. "Thank you for the offer, but I've things I need to accomplish. Go. Enjoy your swim."

The sparkle in his eyes faded, and she hated that she'd been the one to dim it. But she couldn't let herself grow too fond of this man.

That would only make it harder later.

The sounds of the men and boy playing rang freely as she took the opportunity to do some washing now that she'd finally removed the bandage from her burns. Her spare shirtwaist and undergarments were in dire need, as well as Andy's shirt and stockings. Perhaps she should ask Seth and Samuel if they had things that needed cleaning.

She sat back on her heels and watched Samuel throw a pine cone over his brother's head, right into Andy's hands. Seth dove for the cone, making a mighty splash as he fell short of the prize.

"I got it." Andy's voice held a cheer as he raised the cone high, then sent it back over Seth's head to Samuel's waiting arms.

She had a feeling Seth wasn't putting as much height into his jump for the 'ball' as he could have, but with the grin spreading Andy's face, she wouldn't be calling foul.

CHAPTER 13

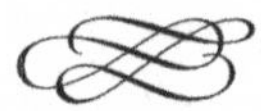

A tiny piece of the normal life I crave.
~ Rachel

"There she is. Home."

Rachel strained to see through the trees as Elias motioned toward a glimmer of sunlight that proclaimed a clearing. He reined his mule off the main trail toward where he'd pointed.

The sun's rays streamed onto a small log cabin, rough-built and not much larger than a single room. Yet as they reined in beside the structure, it was clear the logs were large and sturdy, well-chinked and constructed to last for scores of years.

"There's a lean-to out back with a pen for the animals. Might wanna unload at the cabin door first." The pleasure on Elias's face was hard to deny. How wonderful it must be to finally reach home.

Their little group had developed a lean efficiency, each person unpacking the gear they carried that would be needed for the night. Rachel would normally begin preparations for the evening meal. It'd become clear rather early in the journey that her skill for cooking a decent meal over an open fire was more advanced than that of the others. She didn't mind the work, and the appreciation from the men felt better than she wanted to admit.

When Andy led both their horses toward the back of the cabin following the other men, she stepped into the cabin and paused to glance around the room. A stone hearth covered most of the left wall of the building, with a few pans hanging from the logs on one side.

It was just past the time they'd normally stop for the midday meal, so she should prepare food for the group. Yet this was Elias's home. She didn't want to intrude on his space.

For now, she could put together a cold meal like they normally ate on the trail. As much as she longed for something hearty and nourishing, maybe that would come this evening.

The occasional call of a male voice drifted through the cabin walls as she worked, and just as she finished laying out the food, their tones drifted around the side of the building. A moment later, the door latch lifted, and the parade of men tromped in.

She hadn't been overly conscious of being the only woman in a group of towering men until that moment. It was really only the Grant brothers whose presence seemed to fill the place, and Seth who made her senses spring alive, following his every movement.

She was careful not to make eye contact, just motioned toward the food spread across Elias's small, square table.

"Sorry the place isn't really big enough for all you folks. Me an' the mule don't get much comp'ny up here." Elias hung his hat on a peg and raised his rifle to the hooks mounted above the door.

"I'll just be glad to wake up without dew on my face tomorrow morning." Andy's white teeth flashed in a grin that revealed a hint of the man he would become.

Samuel was the last one in and closed the door behind them. "Good construction, Elias. How long did it take to put this together?"

While the two of them talked methods of notching logs and various chinking materials, Rachel handed out plates. The little table wasn't large enough for them all to sit around it—and only contained two chairs—so most would need to sit on the floor.

Normally they didn't worry with plates for the midday meal, just took slabs of roasted meat and hunks of corncake from the sections she laid out.

But again, this was Elias's home, although the floor was packed dirt and the entire place needed a good cleaning. Just for today, they could attempt to live as civilized people. After this meal, she'd get to work clearing the cobwebs and setting this place to rights. It was the least she could do for the man who'd guided them safely through miles of treacherous trails.

The thought of leaving Elias behind the next morning started an ache in her chest. She forced herself to push the feeling aside. Tomorrow she could face that struggle. Not today.

Through the afternoon, the men kept busy outside, mostly making repairs to the cabin and corral fencing. For about an hour, the steady *thwack* of an ax against wood rang through the clearing.

She'd kept Andy busy hauling water from the creek and carrying off piles of leaves and scraps she'd swept from in the cabin—probably most had blown in during Elias's absence. Andy completed each task she requested, but it wasn't hard to see his longing glances toward the sounds drifting through the open door.

When she finished sweeping as far into the chimney as she could reach from the hearth, she paused to catch her breath and see how much progress the boy had made scrubbing the base of the walls where spatters of dry mud looked to be several seasons old. "Makes you glad we never had a wood floor, doesn't it?"

"Yes, ma'am." His voice held none of the enthusiasm that had filled it these past few days, and his scrubbing was a methodical back-and-forth movement that might very well put her to sleep. Seth's voice sounded from outside, and Andy's attention was pulled to the open door again.

She barely held in her sigh. The place was so small she could finish on her own in the next hour. He should learn how to work alongside a man while he had the chance. His father certainly never gave him the opportunity. Those last few years, Richard had been so besotted with his drink and gambling, he'd had little time for things around the house. What she couldn't teach Andy, the boy'd had to learn on his own.

"Why don't you go see if the others need your help outside?"

"You mean it?" But Andy had already dropped his rag and bolted halfway to the door before he turned back to wait for her answer.

"Go." She made a shooing motion with her hand, and couldn't help a chuckle as her son dashed out into the sunshine.

~

The aroma of something tantalizing tugged at Seth for a full hour before Rachel finally called them in to eat. With the way that woman could cook mouthwatering meals over a campfire, he had high hopes for what she would accomplish with a stone hearth and hanging hooks. Too bad Elias didn't own a real cookstove. They might be in for homemade bread and pies and who knew what else.

"What's got you smiling like a man who's panned a dozen ounces of gold?" Samuel nudged him with an elbow.

Seth shot a glance at Andy to make sure the boy hadn't heard. He wasn't quite ready to answer questions about his intentions toward Andy's mother. "Just lookin' forward to a good meal after a hard day's work."

"Well..." Samuel drawled the word so it held much more meaning than those four letters should possess. "Me, too. But no food has ever made me blush like a schoolgirl."

Again, Seth glanced toward Andy, who was animatedly describing the way a nail he'd been hammering had shot away when he helped fix the fence. There was no way he'd heard Samuel's comment.

Seth turned a glare on his brother. "I'm not blushing. I like good food. There's no shame in that."

Samuel's pressed lips quivered in a way that made Seth want to send a fist through that mouth. Not hard, just enough to wipe the smirk from his smug face.

Instead he settled for a "knock it off" just loud enough for Samuel to hear.

But his brother's words replayed in his mind through the evening, and as Seth lay on his bedroll in the single-room cabin later that night, he couldn't seem to force them away.

He was definitely attracted to Rachel Gray. He ached to fix the wrongs that had been done to her, but this was more than just his overblown desire to protect her. She intrigued him. She drew him like no woman he'd ever known. And yes, she was stunningly beautiful. But that seemed like a small piece of why his mind wouldn't let her stray far.

When they reached the Canadian Territory and found her brother, was he prepared to let her step out of his life? Andy, too? The lad had begun to open up this last week or so, and Seth was becoming fonder of him by the day.

If he wasn't going to take a permanent role in the boy's life, he should probably ease back. Not let either of them become too attached.

The thought formed an ache in his chest strong enough to steal his breath. Andy needed a strong man in his life. Seth could be that man. With God's help, he'd left his vices in the past. He still wasn't the kind of man he wanted to be, but if he could just point Andy to the Heavenly Father instead of any earthly man, he'd do the job well.

And what of Rachel? He'd not known her long enough to say for sure what he felt was love. In truth, there was still so much he didn't know about her. But he could imagine them making a life together. Could imagine loving everything about her.

If only she would open up to him.

Show me the way, Lord. Guide me in Your path for us both. Rather, for all three of us.

~

Saying goodbye to Elias was so much harder than Rachel expected.

He shook Andy's hand first, looking him in the eye as he would a grown man. "I'm proud to know ya, Andy Gray. You take care o' your mama, and don't ever miss a chance to take a swim." He paused, and his hand that gripped Andy's shook as though with emotion. "If you're ever 'round these parts, you come back an' see ol' Elias."

Andy nodded. "I will." His voice cracked at the end, squeezing Rachel's heart. He shouldn't have to say goodbye to so much at such a young age.

Elias pulled the boy close for a one-arm hug, still gripping his hand with the other. When they stepped apart, Andy turned away quickly, but not before she saw the red rimming his eyes.

Next, Elias turned to her, moisture brimming in his gaze. He wrapped a hand around each of her upper arms. "I surely am glad you two joined up with us."

She had to swallow down the lump in her throat before her voice would come through. "I am, too." Her own voice was in danger of cracking, and she shored up her defenses. And she put a little space between them. "Thank you for everything."

The creases at his eyes deepened, and she saw understanding in his gaze. He didn't let her go. "I meant what I told your son. If you're ever in these parts, I expect a visit."

She nodded. "Yes, sir."

He released her then and moved on to Seth, leaving her to pull herself back together. She'd been through much worse than this without crying.

When the goodbyes were said and everyone mounted, they started toward the trail, Samuel in the lead.

Rachel allowed herself a final glance back just before they turned to walk among the trees that would hide them from the clearing. Elias stood in front of his cabin, hands propped at his waist.

When he saw her look back, a grin split his beard, and he waved.

She swallowed down the emotion that threatened again. Forced herself to raise a final farewell. Elias hadn't been perfect, but he'd been good to them. And that couldn't be said for many people in her life. He'd always hold a special place in her heart.

Now it was time to turn her gaze forward. There was much distance left to travel before they finally reached their new home.

Home. The word stirred the same hope it usually did, except... finding Henry would mean they had to part from Seth and his brother.

And with every day that passed, the thought of losing Seth Grant made her heart ache far more than it should.

CHAPTER 14

In moments like this, I come to life.
~ Seth

"You want me to take the lead?" Seth called up to his brother as they neared the rocky base of another looming mountain.

This second day out from Elias's place had brought them through rough terrain, maybe the hardest going yet. And the mountain ahead bore more rock than vegetation.

Lord, help us get up and over without event. He hated subjecting Rachel and Andy to the dangers of traveling through this country. They were both doing admirably so far, but they hadn't reached the peak yet.

"Nah. I'll take this one," Samuel called over his shoulder as he leaned forward to give his horse freedom to climb the ascent.

Rachel held her horse back to put space between her and Samuel's mount, then let the gelding move on. Andy did the same, and Seth held his breath as he watched the boy ascend. An excellent horseman already.

He nudged his gelding forward to follow them, keeping his eyes more on the animals ahead than his own path. Partway up the mountain, the hard-packed ground turned to loose stone, as though remnants of a rockslide covered their path.

Andy's horse stumbled and fell hard on his knee.

"Pull his head up," Seth yelled, his heart climbing into his throat.

Andy was already doing it, but the horse still struggled to get his feet on solid ground. Seth couldn't see if the horse was down on both front knees or just one, but the boy had raised his reins high to hold the animal's head up, pulling some of the weight off his front end so he could get his footing.

At last, the horse heaved upright, planting both front hooves on rocks underneath him. Uneven footing, but secure for the moment. The horse heaved, and Seth found himself doing the same.

"Are you all right, Andy?"

"Yeah." The boy's response was unsteady.

Seth's own heart still surged in his chest. "I think we'd better walk the rest of the way up."

Andy was off the horse before Seth could lean forward to dismount. As the boy landed, the loose rocks slid underneath him. He leaned forward and clutched the saddle, tugging the horse off balance.

"Whoa, there." Seth hit the ground and scrambled toward the pair, leaving his horse where it stood.

Andy's mare had regained her footing, and the two of them stood on tenuous ground. Seth slowed his movements as he neared them, but he couldn't seem to ease his breathing, nor the speed of his racing heart.

"I got her." The boy was breathing hard, too.

"I'll lead her the rest of the way up. Hold my horse steady and I'll come back for him." Seth reached for the reins.

"I can do it." Andy's tone wasn't obstinate, but determination locked his chin. He gazed up the rest of the slope. "I can do it." This time he seemed to be confirming within himself.

Seth eyed the same incline, all the way up to the two horses and riders at the top.

"Are you hurt?" Rachel's voice sounded from far above, echoing off the stone that spanned between them.

He cupped his hands around his mouth to call up to her. "No. All are well." At least, he hoped the horse was.

Leaning forward to check the animal's knees, he saw a gash on the right leg from the stones. Not a bad cut from the looks of it, but they could make sure once they were all on level ground.

Seth straightened and turned his gaze back to Andy. "You'll go slow and stay well away from the mare's hooves?"

"Yes, sir." His face held more seriousness than Seth would have expected from a lad his age. He was accustomed to matters of danger. Hadn't Rachel said the boy did most of the hunting? It seemed impossible for one so young, yet looking at the earnestness in his face now, not as unbelievable as before.

Seth blew out a breath and nodded. "Be careful. I'll be right behind if you need anything."

Boy and horse picked their way up the mountain, one laborious step at a time. But Seth didn't mind the slowness. As long as they were safe. The lad took such care with his responsibility, Seth could see why Rachel entrusted him out alone with the rifle.

They finally arrived at the top, and Rachel reached for her son, wrapping an arm around him. "What happened?"

"Summer slipped in the rocks, so I had to lead her up. She's all right now." He let his mother embrace him, but it was easy to see the struggle inside him to be a man in his own right.

Rachel's gaze lifted to Seth, and he met her searching eyes with a nod. "They're both fine."

The worried line of her shoulders eased, and she gave her son a final hug, then stepped back. "Well then." She inhaled a breath that raised her chest. "I suppose now we have to go down the other side."

Seth turned his focus to his brother. "Easier I hope?"

The line across Samuel's brow didn't bode well as he turned to look over his shoulder.

Seth pulled his gelding up to the top of the ridge to view what his brother saw. When he reached Samuel's side and looked down, the sight almost made him swoon.

Not quite straight down, but they'd have to travel back and forth in switchbacks to keep from tumbling head over heels. Riding the horses wouldn't be possible. They'd all be walking. "Are you sure this is the way down?"

Samuel raised the paper that held Elias's sketch of the remainder of their journey, more detailed than the one Rachel had brought with her. "The line he said to travel seems to go down from here."

Seth scanned the incline to the right, which turned into a steep drop. Then to the left, which looked much the same before meeting another mountainside rising upward.

This was the best of the available options, but so very treacherous. He let out a breath. "We lead the horses in zigzags?"

Samuel nodded. "Probably best for you and me to handle the animals, one at a time. Go down, then come back up for the other two."

"I can lead my mare." Andy's voice sounded beside Seth, and he turned to find that same determined seriousness.

"That's a pretty steep grade." Samuel's tone sounded clearly unconvinced.

"Andy, no." Rachel's voice was as desperate as Samuel's was uncertain.

Seth studied the boy, who was taking the measure of the descent. Then Andy raised his gaze to meet Seth's. "I can do it. I'll stay right behind you, do everything you say." Those eyes begged a chance. Begged trust.

Did he dare allow the opportunity? Andy might have as good a chance at getting down as he and Samuel did. "I tell you what. If your mother agrees, we'll let Samuel go first, then you and I hike down with our horses, you staying right behind me."

A smile bloomed across Andy's face, and Seth raised a staying hand. "If"—he paused for effect—"your mother agrees."

Andy turned that beseeching gaze on Rachel, who stood behind them with her horse—a safe distance away from this steeper side of the mountain.

"I don't know." She rolled her lips together, uncertainty tightening the lines of her face.

"I can do it, Ma." Andy's voice held a quiet conviction that reinforced Seth's faith in his offer.

Rachel shifted her gaze to Seth. "Is it safe?"

He met her gaze. He had to be completely honest, even if she didn't like what he said. "Nothing's completely safe, but I think he's capable if any of us can."

She nodded, then turned her focus back to her son. "Make sure you do exactly what Seth and Samuel tell you."

Andy gave a grave nod. "I will."

"All right, then. We'll see how Samuel manages the descent." Seth looked to his brother.

Samuel returned a grimace. "I suppose that makes me the test."

"I can go first if you prefer." In truth, it shouldn't be his younger brother who risked his life to see if it could be done. "I'll go. Just keep Andy close."

Samuel gave a firm shake of his head. "No. Let me go first. Once I'm down, you and Andy start."

There was simply no good way to keep everyone safe. He'd have to trust his brother—and most of all, trust the One who *could* keep them from harm.

As Samuel and his gelding started down the incline at an angle, breathing came a little harder for Seth. *Don't let them be injured, Lord. Please.*

A motion beside him barely registered until he realized it was Rachel, stepping forward to the place where Samuel had stood.

Her gasp was just loud enough to snag his focus. Her face had paled, and she seemed to sway.

He reached for her, but instead of grasping her arm, slipped his hand around her back. She eased closer, surely more for the stability he offered than any tenderness. But she stirred everything inside him—his need to protect her, his desire to love her.

With his arm tucked around her, they watched his brother descend. Twice the rocks slid from under Samuel's feet, bouncing down the mountain until they reached the base far below. He could have fallen with them, but both times he was able to grasp a bit of the stone face to hold him. God's hand alone kept the horse from slipping down to its death.

"He's almost there." Andy's voice clogged with tension.

The words jarred Seth, making him realize just how hard he was gripping Rachel. Or maybe she was doing the clutching, because one of her hands covered his at her waist, squeezing hard enough to whiten her fingers.

Samuel was nearing the bottom, and soon he jumped the last stride, then turned to coax the gelding to leap down from the short ledge where he perched. At last, his brother turned his face upward and waved.

Seth breathed deeply to clear the knot in his gut. "I suppose it's our turn." He didn't fear for himself, but that descent would be hard on Andy. And even harder on Rachel.

He turned his gaze to her honey-colored hair. The shimmer of the sun made the strands look so soft. His fingers itched to stroke it, but he didn't dare.

She must have felt his gaze, for she looked up, meeting him with eyes so green his breath caught. He had to swallow to summon moisture to his mouth.

"Should I come down behind Andy?" The fear—the vulnerability—in her eyes speared him.

"No." The word came out breathy, as though he'd already descended the mountain and climbed back up it. "I'll return for you. Wait for me."

She held his gaze another minute, possessing more than just his focus.

Then she looked away. Not down, but far out over the valley. Maybe even farther. "I'll wait."

The words seemed to cover more than simply this moment. This situation. He'd have to unpack them later.

For now, he had to get a boy and two horses down the mountain without injury. Then he'd come back to the woman waiting for him.

~

Going down the mountain took everything she had. And she may not have ever stepped off the edge of the cliff without having Seth's hand to cling to. The trust she placed in this man should scare her more than the mountain, but she couldn't bring herself to regret it. Seth had proved himself a good man. Maybe better than a good man.

As she slid her way down the final stretch, his grip stayed firm. And when her feet landed on flat ground, his hold was the only thing that kept her knees from buckling.

"You made it, Ma." Andy's grin seemed wider than his face. "That was fun, wasn't it?"

A jerky laugh slipped out before she could stop it. The sarcastic kind, and probably more a release of nerves than anything. "I'd use a different word for the experience."

When Seth gave her hand a gentle squeeze, she realized she was still holding his. Heat flamed to her face, and she slipped her grasp away and brushed tendrils of hair from her face.

"Anyone wanna eat a bite before we head on?" Samuel was searching through his pack, where they stowed most of the food.

"I do." Andy was always ready to eat.

Her own stomach roiled at the thought of food, but the others needed sustenance. "I suppose it's time."

"I think I saw a little spring over there. The horses need water." Samuel motioned to their left. It seemed he'd taken over the job of trail guide.

Walking the thirty or so strides on solid ground helped rid her body of the rest of its nerves, and she worked quickly to lay out food while the others watered the horses and themselves.

Summer in these mountains was so much cooler than it had been back in Missouri, but still the sun shone hot as it hovered over them.

Finally, the others finished their meal and returned supplies to their packs.

As Rachel fastened the ties on her own, she heard Seth say to his brother, "I'm gonna step behind that rock, then I'll be ready."

She should probably do the same once he finished. The hours ahead would be long enough without an aching bladder.

A moment later, Seth shouted. As she turned toward the noise, Samuel grabbed his rifle from its scabbard and sprinted the direction his brother had gone.

Rachel's pulse raced as she started toward them. What could have happened to him within seconds of disappearing behind the boulder?

"What is it?" Andy darted past her.

"Wait. Andy." What if there was danger? A wild animal?

A gunshot ripped through the air, the boom echoing off cliff walls, reverberating through her head.

She gripped her temples as crimson flashed through her vision. Blood dripping from a hand. She squeezed her eyes shut, pushing the image back. Then she forced them open, focusing on the commotion around her.

Seth was coming out from behind the rock, one arm draped around his brother's neck. Andy walked on his other side. Seth wasn't putting weight on his left leg.

Raising her skirts, she ran toward them. "What happened?" Had the shot injured him or something else?

Samuel raised a grim look as she neared. "Bit by a rattlesnake."

CHAPTER 15

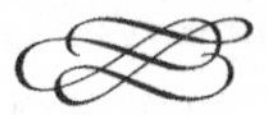

God, don't let me show my fear. Please.
~ Rachel

Rachel's heart seized. She inhaled a breath, forcing herself under control.

She knew exactly what had to be done. "Lay him down right there." She motioned to the place they stood. "He shouldn't move. We have to keep his blood from spreading the poison."

Samuel obeyed and lowered Seth to sit on the ground. She dropped to her knees beside his left leg. "Where's the bite?"

He pulled up the hem of his trouser to reveal the pale skin of his calf. Twin red marks marred the top where a bump was already swelling. At least the bite wasn't in the thick part of the muscle. Although the man's leg seemed to be all muscle. Defined and solid.

She forced her attention back to the fang marks. "Did you see the snake? Are you sure it was a rattler?"

"Saw and heard it." Seth spoke through his teeth.

"It's lying in pieces if you wanna look at it." Samuel's tone held more tension than she'd ever heard from him. "Do you know what to do?"

She nodded. "I've treated two rattlesnake bites before. Do you have a handkerchief?"

His brows rose. "No. You need a bandage?"

They didn't have time to search for things. Raising her skirt hem, she ripped the seam, then tore off a strip long enough to tie around Seth's leg. "Get me some gunpowder and salt, equal parts. We don't have egg so mix enough water to make a paste. Quick."

Samuel sprinted toward the horses.

After wrapping the cloth around Seth's leg a handbreadth above the wound, she tied the knot tight. "Andy, go get him a cup of clean water to drink."

"Yes, ma'am." He darted away too, leaving her alone with Seth.

She glanced at his face. Pale, but that could be from fear of the snake. Even a man as strong as Seth Grant had the right to lose color when he stared death in the face. Beads of sweat slid down his temples, dampening his hair.

She returned her focus to his leg, straining to recall everything the doctor had said when Richard was bitten, which was the only time she'd been lucid enough to remember. The wound had been in his hand, and the doctor had dosed him with more whiskey than anything, but he'd also used the gunpowder poultice. Was there something else?

The skin was beginning to darken over the wound, and the swelling had definitely worsened. No doubt about it, the snake had been poisonous.

She forced her body to remain calm, her heart not to race. Where was Samuel with that poultice?

A glance back showed he was adding water to the mixture, then he used his finger to stir as he jogged toward her. She needed something to hold the concoction in place over the bite, so she grabbed her skirt and tore another swath.

She dabbed the thick mixture on the bite, then tied the cloth to hold it in place. After brushing the rest from her hands, she leaned back to survey him. "Are you having trouble breathing?"

Seth leaned back, his hands on the ground, his weight propped against them. Moisture wicked his brow. He took a few breaths. "I don't think so."

"Tell me if you struggle for breath or if your chest hurts."

He nodded, all sign of his easy nature stripped away. "Is it bad?"

She looked back at the leg, though there was nothing left to see except the swelling skin that showed around the bandage. She inhaled a steadying breath, then released it. Better to be honest with him. "I've seen worse. But there is poison in there."

"It's not bad, though? He'll live?" Samuel dropped to his haunches beside her, his voice ringing with hope.

Did she dare encourage that optimism? *Be honest.* She could only speak the truth as she knew it. Nothing more, nothing less. "Based on the two rattlesnake bites I've seen before, I'd say he stands a decent chance of surviving. If there's no infection." She turned her focus to Seth. "You need rest, and you should drink plenty of water. That's all we can do right now."

Samuel rose to his knees, his presence looming beside her. "There has to be more we can do. Don't you know anything?" The demand in his tone struck like accusation.

She met the fire in his eyes with a level gaze. "I'm telling you the truth as far as I know it. My experience is limited to two occasions, so I may be wrong."

The flame in his look blazed. "Don't you care whether he lives or dies?" He spit the words through clenched teeth.

They hit their mark, spraying sparks that singed her calm façade. She tightened her own jaw lest her emotions broke through her control. "I do care. I'm doing everything I know to help him recover."

"Sam." Seth's tone was soft yet held a hint of warning.

His brother huffed out a grunt, then scrubbed a hand through his thick hair. He seemed to be fighting a battle within himself. She'd seen that look before. Richard sometimes wore that tortured look just before his vices dragged him to town for drink and gambling.

Finally, he eased out a long breath. "Rest. All right." He turned to scan the area around them. "There's not a good place to camp here. No trees for shelter. Is it all right if we ride a little farther if we take it slow?"

She shook her head before he finished the question. "No. He needs to stay as still as possible for a few more hours so the poison doesn't spread through his body."

Seth eased himself down so he was lying flat on the ground. "I'm fine right here. You don't need to worry about me. Just see to the animals."

"Here's the water, Ma." Andy's voice was a welcome distraction.

She turned to take the cup from her son and tried to summon a smile to ease the worry marking his face. "The bite isn't as bad as it could be. Mr. Grant needs to rest for a while."

He nodded, sliding a long look to Seth.

Seth managed a better smile than she had. "I'll be fine. I'm gonna need you and Samuel to unsaddle the horses, though. Your mama won't let me up yet."

"Yes, sir." Andy looked to Samuel.

The man heaved out another breath and pushed to his feet. "Let's go set up camp."

A thought struck Rachel, and she turned to his retreating back. "You should check the rocks to make sure there aren't any other snakes."

He waved an acknowledging hand but didn't turn to her. "I'll do it."

She had to stop herself from nibbling her lower lip as she returned her focus to Seth. "He's angry with me."

"That's just his way of worrying. He's thankful you're here."

A half-laugh, half-snort slipped out. "I can feel his regard."

One corner of Seth's mouth tipped up. "He'll show it better once he simmers down."

She raised the cup, more than ready to take the focus off herself. "Can you sit up to drink this?"

He used his elbow to prop himself up, then took the tin and held it to his mouth. As he swallowed gulp after gulp, his eyes found hers.

She should look away, but that intense brown gaze had a way of pulling her in, holding her until he chose to release her.

He finished with a long exhale and lay back as he handed over the empty cup. "I, for one, am also quite thankful you're here. And not just to cure me from snakebite." His lips pulled in something of a roguish grin, although the pain around his eyes showed through.

She sent him a look meant to silence his teasing. "Does your leg hurt as much?" Peeling up the edge of the bandage, she checked to see if the blackening of the skin had spread.

"It's better. The band you tied around me smarts more than the bite."

"Good." She lay the fabric back in place, adjusting it so the poultice better covered the injured area.

"Tell me."

She shot a glance to his face. "Tell what?"

His eyes had softened. "About the other times you treated rattlesnake bites. Your mother? Brother?" A short pause. "Husband?"

That last word on his tongue nearly made her flinch, but she forced herself to hold firm. Now that he'd spoken it, her former marriage no longer hung like a secret between them.

Of course he would assume she'd been married. She had a son. But her life with Richard felt like something to hide from this man who was so very different from the man whose name she still carried.

Now, Seth was giving her the chance to speak of it.

She inhaled a silent, fortifying breath and kept her eyes focused on the wound as she spoke. "It was my husband, Richard. Andy was less than a week old when Richard came stumbling into the house clutching his hand. I ran for the doctor, and he came right away. He had Richard drink a great deal of whiskey while he made a poultice like this one, except he added egg to the mixture instead of water." She glanced to Seth's face. "I used everything we have here. I hope it will be enough."

He nodded. "I'm mixing in a large dose of prayer, so that will more than cover what we're missing." He slid a glance at her. A look that should have warned her about his next words. "Your husband is...?"

The breath caught in her throat. She could say it, just spit out the words. "Died. Earlier this year." They came out a bit garbled, but at least she'd said them.

He nodded, his eyes softening. "How about the second snakebite you mentioned?"

She turned back to his wound so she didn't reveal too much by her face and worked to keep the memories distant. Only facts. "The second time I was bitten as I worked in our garden. Andy was nearby and mixed the poultice for me. The viper struck through the leather of my boot, so the bite wasn't a bad one."

"What of the snake?" The surprise in his voice was clear.

"I killed it with the spade."

"After it bit you?"

"Yes."

"What of needing to be still so the poison didn't travel through your body? Did you know that at the time?"

She raised a casual shoulder. "I didn't want the snake to strike Andy. It was best to kill it immediately." Why did he press so about details that didn't pertain to the bite itself?

"Where was your husband?" His tone was gentle, yet relentless.

"Not home." She steeled her jaw. If he pushed farther, she'd not answer his questions.

"Did your wound look similar to mine?" He shifted, trying to see down his leg.

"Somewhat. Yours is swelling more than mine did. The blackening of the skin is similar." She pressed his shoulder. "Lie still."

He was silent finally. Yet the quiet made her want to fill it. What did he think about what she'd shared? He was hearing more about their life beneath the words than she'd spoken, she was almost certain. Especially from the questions he asked.

Did he judge her? Judge Richard? He didn't know the details, so his thoughts could only be speculation. And he *wouldn't* know the details. More than this she wasn't ready to share. Wouldn't share.

She needed to create some distance between them, both physical and emotional. Reaching for the cup, she started to push up to her feet.

"Rachel." He touched her arm, stilling her.

She couldn't draw in a breath, but it had to be from his nearness, for no memories sprang through her. Nothing that made her want to quiver in fear.

"Yes?" She forced out the word. Then pulled in air through her tight lungs.

"I'm sorry for all you suffered."

She shouldn't look at him, but her wayward eyes refused to obey. Her gaze searched his face, finding a depth of feeling that seemed to sear through the middle of her. Flaying her wide.

He could have meant he was sorry for the bite from the venomous snake. But he meant more. It was all there in his eyes.

She wanted to believe him. Wanted to crawl into the safety he offered. But she couldn't let herself be so vulnerable. Not with anyone, especially not with a man.

Dropping her gaze from his face made it easier to stand. To turn.

To walk away.

CHAPTER 16

I can handle everything. This shouldn't be too much.
~ Rachel

The snakebite was a frustration all the way around, except for the peek Seth was given into Rachel's life. But after those few minutes of openness, she'd closed up again like a turtle retreating into its shell.

And if she was anything like a turtle, she wouldn't be pried back out. He'd have to wait until she was ready to come of her own accord.

Samuel was the one who worried him most in the group. He spent most of the afternoon pacing with his rifle beside the cliff wall like a sentry, then checking the horses and asking Rachel whether there was anything else they should be doing for Seth's leg.

She answered with a surprising amount of patience each time. In truth, Seth had never seen his brother so worked up. At least, not as a grown man.

When darkness came and Samuel still wandered around, not even stopping to eat a bite with Rachel and Andy, Seth motioned him over.

Samuel's stride turned purposeful as he moved toward him. "What is it? What do you need?" So much tension radiated through his voice, but Samuel hid it with such a gruff tone, some might be afraid of him.

Seth patted the ground beside him, the place where Rachel had knelt when she'd told him about her husband. "Sit and keep me company."

The shadows didn't hide his brother's reluctance, but he sat. Seth could hear Rachel murmuring to her son, something about checking the horses. Giving him a private moment with his brother, no doubt. *She's perfect for me, Lord.*

But just now, he needed to keep himself focused. He and Samuel had never minced words between them, so Seth didn't bother to do it now. "You think I'm dying?"

Silence hung thick in the air for a long moment before Samuel answered. "Are you?"

"No. The leg doesn't hurt half as much now as it did earlier. I'd say that means I'm over the worst of it. Between God's healing and Rachel's care, I'm a blessed man. We'll have to check with my nurse, but I imagine I'll be ready to ride again come morning."

He felt Samuel's exhale more than he heard it. The tension lacing the air eased away, and Seth couldn't help the affectionate tug in his chest for his brother. If anything like this happened to Samuel, he'd be a bundle of distraught nerves, too. Much worse, in fact.

"I'll talk to Rachel about whether we wait another day or not." Samuel sounded much more like himself.

"Fine, but I doubt I can make myself lie here past tomorrow morning. If we're not riding, I'll at least be up and moving around."

"You give that lady trouble, and you'll answer to me." Samuel's voice was teasing, but the words rubbed the raw edges of the annoying pain Seth had fought all afternoon.

"I won't give her trouble, you louse."

His brother chuckled as he stood. "You sure won't."

~

Rachel worried about Seth spending the next day in the saddle, but he seemed so much recovered, she couldn't justify waiting an extra day to continue their journey. However, if they came upon any mountains like the one yesterday morning, she'd put a firm halt to their travel until he was stronger.

Samuel seemed to have a new regard for her, or maybe that was her imagination. He'd always been respectful—more so than most men. But he appeared to listen more closely now when she made an observation or offered her opinion. The same way he did with his brother.

They camped early that night, mostly because she and Samuel were both worried about Seth. For his part, Seth didn't mention his leg unless asked. The blackened skin around the wound must have been painful, and by the time she inspected the area after they made camp, the swelling had increased much from when she'd checked it that morning.

"I'll be good as new by the morning." Seth adjusted his trouser leg after she applied a new poultice.

"I hope so, but for now, sit with your leg flat so this mixture can take effect." She poured water from the cup over her hands to rinse them, then stood and brushed out her skirt. "I'll work on our meal now."

"Bring the pack over here and I'll take care of it." He motioned toward the satchel containing the food and pan she usually used.

She hesitated. He really needed to rest to bring the swelling down. She'd learned with Richard that when she wanted him to do something, she'd get the best response if she made herself as genial as she could be. She forced an expression that should pass for a smile. "I won't have anything to do if I don't cook." In truth, she had washing and mending to do, and Andy's hair begged for a trimming.

"Sit with me. I may even let you help." He patted the ground beside him, and the tug at the corners of his mouth started a longing deep in her chest.

Maybe if she worked with him, she could assign easy tasks that would keep him still. "Only if you'll make certain you don't move your leg."

"I'll be the best patient you've ever had." His mouth pulled into a cheeky grin, which pulled a matching smile from her. She turned away before he could see the effect he had on her.

When she'd positioned the supplies and herself beside him, she reached to untie the leather strap. "I was thinking we'd finish the last of the bear meat, maybe in a stew with the beans I soaked last night."

"An excellent idea." He covered her hand with his to still her movement, then worked the satchel free. "I'd very much like to do the part I can, although I'll need your help to fill the pot with water for the beans."

He accompanied the words with a wink, and the gesture raised such a flurry in her midsection, she didn't have the nerve to do more than take the dish he offered her.

After filling it with water from the creek, she positioned it near enough the flames so the liquid could come to a boil.

"Wanna check for stones in the beans while I cut the meat?" The sharp blade of his knife glimmered with light reflecting off the flickering flames.

She didn't look at Seth as she settled beside him again and took up the bag he handed her. He hummed a light tune while he worked, and the sound eased her nerves as she scooped a handful of beans and sorted them in her skirts, picking out two stones from the bunch.

"So, your home in Missouri," he said, "was it in town? On a farm? You mentioned a garden, but I suppose that could be either." His tone was so casual, he might have been asking if she preferred rain or sunshine.

There was nothing dangerous in his question. Nothing that should concern her. Nothing save the memories those days resurrected. But she had to stop letting those memories hold power over her. The life she'd lived with Richard was in the past. She'd endured, and she was stronger now for coming through them.

She squared her shoulders and forced her tone to sound as casual as his. "Our farm was about an hour's ride from a little town near the river."

"A farm, eh. What did you grow?" He cut chunks off the slab of meat she'd roasted the morning after the bear roared into their camp. If only she'd known then how much would change when they chose to join with these men.

She forced her mind back to those days. "We raised produce to sell at market. The riverboats would dock outside town and buy our vegetables."

He nodded. "Sounds like a good living. We raised corn and cotton down on my pa's farm. I think sometimes that's why they had so many young'uns, to always have help in the fields." He chuckled.

She listened for a hint of bitterness in the laugh but couldn't find any. "I'd forgotten there were so many of you. Nine, you said? Where do you and Samuel fall in the order?"

"Second from last." The word came out on a weighty sigh.

She dared a glance at his face, and the way his nose wrinkled caught her unawares. She tried to stop the smile that pulled at her cheeks, but it wouldn't be denied.

"That funny, is it?" He gave her a sideways look that only made the grin harder to hold in.

"I can't imagine it's as awful as you make it sound."

His eyes narrowed. "You must surely be the firstborn."

She raised her chin. "I am. Four years older than my brother, Henry. The one we're traveling to find."

His gaze searched her face. "That does explain a lot."

She turned her gaze back to the beans. "Like what?"

"Like why you're so driven. You don't let anything stop you from what you set out to do."

"That has nothing to do with my childhood." She'd become this way out of necessity, when Richard chose cards and drink over their family. When he'd slowly gambled away their lives, piece by piece.

"Maybe your growing up years aren't the only reason." He reached toward her and brushed a strand of hair from her cheek, tucking it behind her ear.

She froze, her lungs unable to breathe with the fire of his touch.

"But I think that played a part. I'm sure much has happened to develop the strong woman I'm privileged to know."

His words sank over her like warm water over frozen hands. Their balm was a blessed relief, yet as her insides awakened, the ache was almost too much to bear. So much had happened. Things he'd never know, things she somehow wanted to tell him. Wanted to drown in the safety of his touch, his tenderness. The way he seemed to know her, even without her revealing herself.

And the most wondrous part of all—he didn't shun her for the way her past had changed her. He didn't shun the person she'd been forced to become.

The sting of tears struck before she realized they were coming. She forced air in and out, turned her head away so he wouldn't see the redness. She wrinkled her nose. Anything to stop them.

She didn't cry. Couldn't. Through everything, she'd not cried.

Now, before this man, she would not break down. Locking her jaw, she returned her focus to the beans. A rock sat among the bunch in her hand, and she grabbed it up and threw it in the fire, imagining the weakness and tears burning with it among the flames.

"Rachel." Seth's voice hummed low, calling to her. Drawing her back from the fierceness of her determination.

"Yes?" Her throat was both dry and clogged with emotion. Just one example of the way this man tied her in knots.

"Tell me about your father. What was he like?"

The words plunged a knife into her chest, slicing through her with a sweet agony that brought another surge of tears to burn her eyes.

She didn't have to answer his question. Didn't owe Seth any more details of her past.

But that didn't stop the words from spilling out. "He was wonderful. He taught me games and played make-believe. When he came home from trips for business, he always brought me a trinket or sweet. One time it was a doll he said had once been a little girl like me. Her greatest wish was to have a special friend, so her fairy godmother turned her into my Molly and sent her to live with me."

She swallowed to push down the lump in her throat. "After Molly came, Papa's trips took him away more and more. For longer each time. My mother never liked Molly, and I thought it was just because she believed Papa giving me the doll proved he loved me best. I hated how it always felt like we were vying for his love."

The emotion clogging her throat seemed to grow, closing off her breathing. She inhaled a long draught of air, willing her body to relax. Was she really going to tell the next part? There was no reason she should. Except a part of her wanted him to know. Wanted to share the weight of this burden that still threatened to smother at times.

With her gaze locked in the flames, she let her mind call back the memories. "One time he left for weeks. I don't remember how long exactly. I only know this horrible feeling took over our home. Mother didn't get out of bed some days. I had Henry to take care of, and I made sure he ate and got to school on time. I remember keeping Molly with me wherever I went in the house, even though I was too old to play with dolls by then. Molly was my one reminder of happiness."

Her mouth ceased moving of its own accord, trying to save her from the pain that would come next. She'd journeyed this far, though. She had to finish.

Yet as she tried to recall the start of that awful day, the memory wouldn't come. Seemed her mind had blocked it. That couldn't be true, for she saw those awful moments in vivid detail, heard the gunshot every time a loud noise reverberated near her. Why couldn't she find the beginning?

Seth's warm hand slipped over hers, prying open her clenched fist, weaving his fingers between hers as though they belonged there. His thumb stroked the back of her hand, and the warm caress eased the tension clawing through her.

An image of that awful day slid into her mind. From a distance, like she was seeing her younger self through a window. "I accidentally left Molly in Mother's room one morning when I brought her food. I'd already sent Henry to school, and maybe I left the doll there because I wanted a chance to see Mother again. To know that she was eating. That she'd get better. But I had to go back for Molly, too. I would never leave her alone with Mother. I think part of me worried Mother would hurt my doll."

The picture in her mind dimmed a little, like soot smudged the window she peered through. "When I opened Mother's door, she was out of bed. The first thing I thought was how wonderful it was that she'd changed from her dressing gown into her yellow calico day dress." She forced in air to slow the rapid thud in her chest. "I never saw the gun. Only heard the blast. Saw the smoke cloud around her hand. Then the blood.

"At first I couldn't move. My mind wouldn't register what had happened. I must have screamed, but I don't remember. I don't remember any sound after that gunshot. I ran for her. There was so much blood, I didn't know what to do. She'd shot herself in the shoulder. I guess aiming for her heart, but she must have shifted. I remember seeing my mother's face, her mouth wide like she was screaming, but I couldn't hear her.

"Her eyes..." She pressed her own lids shut against the image, but the gaze only seared deeper. "Looking into them was like drowning in a sea of desperation. I'd never imagined such sadness could exist. And in that moment, I realized I might lose her. I realized she *wanted* to leave me."

A flash of understanding slipped through Rachel, the kind that could only come with distance from the situation. She turned to meet Seth's eyes. "Maybe she didn't actually mean to leave *me*. She was desperate to escape the suffering in her life. But I took it personally. I truly believed I was the misery she wanted to flee."

He met her gaze, and the warmth there slid over her. Filled her with strength to continue. She turned back to the fire to gather her thoughts. "Anyway. I saw how weak she was. And even as I pressed a wad of cloth to the blood spurting from her shoulder, I promised myself I'd be strong."

The memory of that vow slipped through her, infusing her determination. She would never be like her mother. Never let herself be brought so low by the actions of another person.

"Did she make it?" Seth's gentle voice pulled her from the swirl of her thoughts.

She inhaled a stabilizing breath. "A neighbor came and sent for the doctor. Mother lived."

Those months after were only a haze in her memories. People came and went in such a blur. She only remembered working so hard to separate herself from the chaos. To suppress the pain of losing her mother—not physically, but every tiny thread of connection had been severed that day.

"What of your father?" Again Seth's voice pulled her back, kept her from being sucked into the mire of her memories.

"He came home sometime during the days after. I don't know if he was already sick or if it started to come on him then. As Mother started to get up from the bed, Father spent more time there. It wasn't until I saw his handkerchiefs stained with blood that I realized something was wrong." She swallowed down the lump in her throat, forced back the burn in her eyes. "He was gone before Christmas."

Silence settled between them, broken only by the crackle of the fire. Seth stroked his thumb across her hand. His touch eased the tension in her limbs, pulling her back to the present little by little.

Voices sounded in the distance, and it wasn't hard to pick out Andy's higher tone laced with Samuel's tenor. She blinked as she scanned the dusky landscape for them. "I'd better finish these beans or we'll never get to eat." Extracting her hand from Seth's, she went back to work picking out rocks.

"No worries as long as we have this meat to snack on. We can be a patient bunch when we need to be." As he maneuvered his knife through the thick meat again, something about Seth's tone made her think he was talking about more than just the meal tonight.

CHAPTER 17

'Tis more than I deserve. And may well be my undoing.
~ Seth

Darkness settled as they finished the meal, both the cooking and the eating. Seth hated that he was forced to stay seated by the fire instead of helping the others. Rachel's story had his mind churning, and he'd do better if he could get away for a walk to gather his wayward thoughts.

But time away couldn't be had, so he forced himself to focus on the others. The four of them sat around the fire, empty plates still showing remnants of beans and bear meat—the best beans and meat he could ever remember. With Rachel on one side of him, Samuel on the other, and Andy just across the flame, eyes bright as he told of the deer he and Samuel saw when they watered the horses, a feeling settled in Seth's chest he couldn't remember experiencing in years. If he had to name it, he'd call this...contentment.

As the lad's tale came to a close, Rachel reached for his plate. "As soon as I wash these, I'll cut your hair. It's in dire need of a trim."

Seth ran his gaze over the boy's head. A little shaggy, perhaps, with some loose curls drooping over his ears, but nothing compared to his own mop of straight brown hair.

His fingers reached for the strands at his neck, testing the length. Just over his collar. Certainly not the longest he'd ever kept it. He'd had a cut and a shave when they left California, and hadn't worried about it since then. Maybe when they reached Simeon's place in the Canadian territories, their sister-in-law would have the tools necessary for another cut.

Andy didn't grumble when his mother sat him down with his back to the fire so she could see. She unwrapped a pair of scissors from their protective cloth and set to work. On a journey that required they bring only the most needed supplies, he found it interesting that she'd considered scissors necessary.

Her adept fingers wove in and out of the boy's hair, which was a darker brown than her light honey tint. Andy must have inherited his hair color from his father, although he certainly had his mother's intriguing green eyes.

She seemed absorbed by her work but must have felt his gaze on her, for she turned to send raised brows his way. "How's the swelling?"

A smile tugged his mouth as she returned her focus to the boy's hair and snipped another piece. Always the practical one. He'd come to realize busyness was one of the tactics she used to guard herself from getting too close.

Now that he understood it, and now that she was allowing him glimpses into her past, her attempts to keep him at a distance only made him smile.

And love her all the more.

Maybe this wasn't full-fledged love yet, but he was pretty sure he wouldn't be letting this woman go once they reached her brother.

Seth raised his trouser leg. "The swelling looks better than it did when we made camp." Or rather, when the others set-up camp. He'd been assigned the job of watching. Holding the ground in place.

Not a role he wanted to make permanent.

Within a quarter hour, she'd worked a difference in Andy's appearance, although not nearly as much as if she'd let the hair grow more before she'd gone after it. She sat back on her heels to examine the result, reaching up to stroke a few strands in place. "Very nice. Much improved."

Andy turned a longsuffering look on her, dramatic enough that the shadows cast by the firelight couldn't hide the expression. "I don't know why my hair has to be so short all the time. Seth and Samuel get to have long hair."

"I'm not their mother." Her voice held an arch in it, like a cat's back responding to insult. "But I *am* yours, and you'll keep yourself well-groomed."

It was hard to know what made him speak, whether the desire for her to think him better than a slovenly boor or simply to encourage Andy into obedience, he couldn't say. The words simply tumbled out. "Hope my turn's next."

All three faces spun to him. Andy's curious head tipped, and Rachel's eyes widened in the shadows of the dancing flame. Samuel, of course, had the corners of his mouth pulled in a wide grin. His hands wrapped around his knees, and he looked quite content to watch his brother make a fool of himself for a woman.

Just to squash that look, Seth turned back to Rachel. "Samuel will have his hair cut as soon as I'm done."

"Actually, I think the horses need a final drink tonight. Will you help me, Andy? We should move their tether rope to fresh grass while we're at it."

"Yes, sir." Andy was all arms and legs as he scrambled to his feet and darted toward the animals.

As Samuel pushed to standing, Seth gave his voice just enough volume for Samuel alone when he said, "Coward."

His brother's only response was a chuckle as he ambled away.

Re-gathering his wits, Seth turned to Rachel. She seemed to be wrapping the scissors in the cloth again. "What of my hair?"

She jerked her head up. "You're not serious?"

"Completely." Apparently it had *not* been only a desire to encourage the boy that prompted his statement, because the thought of having Rachel's fingers run through his hair the same way they had her son's stirred his blood.

"I'm not sure it would be proper." Was it just his imagination, or did her words seem breathy?

"I'll behave, you have my word. Or if you prefer, we can call my coward of a brother back to act as chaperone."

The laugh she gave seemed to stutter with nervousness, and he pulled the joking from his tone. "In truth, Rachel, you have nothing to fear from me."

"I know." Her words were soft, vulnerable in a way that made his chest ache.

She stood and edged toward him with an air of nervousness she so rarely revealed. In fact, he'd only seen this look in her eyes when she was forced to peer over the edge of a cliff.

He had to keep himself perfectly still to set her at ease. Let her see she had nothing to fear from him.

When she dropped to her knees behind him, his muscles tensed for the feeling of her fingers in his hair. Instead, her voice sounded. "Can you turn a bit so I can have the light from the fire? How short do you want it?"

He shifted as she'd asked. "The way you cut Andy's is perfect. Or different, if you think it's best. You have my permission to cut as much of my hair as you'd like." He wanted what she wanted. And not just in the style of his hair. He couldn't think of anything he'd refuse to do if it made her happy.

"All right." Her inhale was just loud enough for him to hear, and the next moment, air brushed his scalp as she lifted a section of hair.

He wasn't sure she breathed again as she worked. He knew the feeling, for he had to consciously think to draw in air, then release the spent breath. Her fingers brushed his ear, his neck, the ear again, and he forced himself not to react to each touch, nor shiver at the tingles that slipped down his back and arms.

After finishing the back, then his right side, she shifted around to his left. Occasionally the warmth of her breath grazed his skin. So she was breathing now. She must be feeling more confident with him. *Thank you, Lord.*

He kept his head as still as possible, only letting his eyes slip to the side for a glimpse of her profile. After a few more minutes, she let out a breath. "All right. Let me make sure I have it even."

She moved around to the front, as she had with Andy, kneeling beside his injured leg and turning his face so she could look on him fully. Her gaze scanned the top of his head, then from one side to the other, never touching his eyes.

For his part, Seth couldn't stop looking at her mossy green orbs, except for the one time his focus slipped to her lips, but he pulled it quickly back upward. She was so beautiful—he'd known it, of course, but seeing her so close constricted his lungs so much he could no longer draw breath.

"I think that's good." She reached up to brush the hair across his forehead, and the burn of her touch slid all the way through him. As much as he tried, he couldn't stop the tremble of pleasure.

Her gaze jerked to his eyes, concern raising her brow. She must see the feelings he was doing his best to hold in check, desire not the least of them.

She made a little sound, like breath rushing through her lips, and she looked as though she would draw back.

But then she didn't. Simply held his gaze, her eyes a fathomless depth. He sank deep, the longing in him almost outweighing his good sense. His body longed to look to her mouth, to savor her kiss. He could already taste it, already feel the warmth of her lips. But he *would not* let his gaze be drawn there.

And then her focus slipped.

Her eyes lingered on *his* mouth. She seemed to lean toward him, and that movement broke the last of his resolve.

He met her partway, pausing for a moment as the wonder of her nearness washed over him. Their breaths mingled, and her warm air soothed his skin.

Then he closed the distance.

Her lips were softer than he'd expected. Vulnerable. This was not the Rachel she worked so hard to be. He let his mouth caress her, relishing in the taste and feel of her. This woman had burrowed so far inside him, he'd be hard-pressed to extract her.

And he didn't plan to.

~

Rachel couldn't believe she was kissing him.

Yet she couldn't bring herself to regret it, nor to stop. He was breath to her lungs. Air that infused her with steadying power. A sturdy beating in her chest.

This wasn't Richard, and every touch of his mouth proclaimed it. Seth was gentle, his kiss caressing. His hands at her elbows secure, not wandering where he might long to go.

That last thought slowed her. Even though this was Seth, she still had to be careful. She wasn't ready to give her life to a man again. Would never be ready.

And she shouldn't pretend she was.

She pulled back, breaking the seal of their lips. The separation felt as if she were ripping a piece of herself away, and she embraced the ache. A just punishment for letting herself be carried away.

He was breathing hard, the same rhythm that heaved in her chest, and he didn't move far, just enough so she could see his eyes in clear focus.

His hand moved to cup her cheek. "Rachel."

She'd never heard her name spoken with such reverence, and the way he looked at her made her yearn to move into his arms. Let him cradle her in his protection. Let him care for her as his eyes promised he would.

But she couldn't let herself be that weak.

She inhaled a long breath to gather strength, then pulled back. "I… think that's it for your hair." She dropped her gaze to the scissors, and it took a moment for her mind to register what she should do next. Get herself out of there. And quick.

Pushing to her feet, she flipped the cloth over the metal blades and slipped them in her pack. "I'm going to see what's taking them so long with the horses."

Without looking back, she stepped out of the firelight and into the darkness.

~

Seth had trouble keeping a grin off his face the next morning, even when Samuel gave him a nudge and one of those raised-eyebrow looks as they saddled the horses. His brother might as well get used to this. Seth had a feeling he'd be smiling a lot with Rachel Gray around.

Rachel didn't seem quite as convinced. She wouldn't meet his gaze through the morning hours, except for the one time he made a joke about seeing another snake. Then she slid a narrow-eyed look his way, and he offered a sloppy grin. He might be making a fool of himself, but the smile had the effect he'd been going for.

The corners of her own mouth twitched, and by the way her cheeks appled, her thoughts must be returning to their kiss, just as his were constantly.

She'd need some time to get used to the idea, but he'd wait as long as he needed to.

The next two days fell into a rhythm, especially as the path they took included mostly smaller mountains and long valleys between ranges. The swelling and pain in his leg had lessened a great deal. He was glad of that, but not so glad that he no longer needed Rachel's ministrations. In fact, she seemed to be doing her best to keep her distance from him.

He took every opportunity to prove himself worthy. That he was different from whatever she hated in her past. She'd never actually said her first marriage was a poor one, but something had instilled in her this fierce independence and fear of men. He'd stake money it had been the man who Andy called Pa.

It was only in the dark of night, as he lay staring up at the wide span of stars, that his mind wandered to the places he couldn't seem to forget. Was he really any better than the man in Rachel's past?

Those days in California were a blur, but he remembered enough for the shame to wash over him again. The drink, the games, the women, the power—he'd never meant to fall prey to any of it. But one led to another, and just once became just once more, until he was caught in a cesspool he couldn't drag himself out of.

Thank the Lord for hearing his cry. For pulling him from the jaws of addiction. For sending Samuel to haul him away from that life. He'd never let it gain hold over him again.

God had given him another chance. This time, he had to get it right.

CHAPTER 18

In an instant I'm proved helpless.
~ Rachel

"What's that sound?" Andy's voice jerked Seth from his thoughts as they skirted the base of a mountain. Three days since that kiss with Rachel, and he still couldn't keep his mind focused.

He strained to decipher the noise, something like a distant roar. "Might be a waterfall." Turning in the saddle, he glanced at his brother, who brought up the rear. "What do you think?"

"I see it." Rachel pointed in front of them, and he spun forward to see.

A glimmer like crystal shone on the face of the mountain farther ahead, about fifty strides up. The sparkle grew brighter the closer they rode, almost blinding.

The sound of rushing water intensified, making the horses edgy as they neared the spectacle. The fall cascaded down four tiers, each landing on a rock ledge, then rushing forward to drop off again.

When the water finally reached the bottom, it ran in a narrow river about three horse-lengths wide.

They'd already stopped for lunch, but he reined in anyway. "Anyone wanna go for a swim?" He had to yell to be heard, and he turned to see the responses of the others as they halted beside him.

"Yeah." Andy looked like he'd slide off and dive in right then, but his mother put a staying hand to his arm.

"Is it deep enough to swim?" Her brows lowered as she eyed the water.

"Maybe we'll just water the horses." He dismounted, then led his gelding toward the narrow river.

As all the animals drank, his gaze wandered to the steep rock face, broken in places where stones had fallen. He'd heard of caves behind waterfalls, but this one probably wasn't large enough for that.

Still, when his horse finished, he and the gelding ambled toward the cliff. At the falls, he reached into the spray and splashed a handful on his face and neck, wiping off as much sweat and trail dust as he could reach.

Since Rachel trimmed the hair off the back of his neck, it was much easier to stay cool.

"Think I'm just gonna dunk my head in." Samuel stepped up beside him, and Seth eased back to allow him room. His brother did just that, letting the water pound on his head and run in streams down either side of his face.

When Samuel pulled back, he shook the water from him like a dog, then raised his head with a grin. "Whew, that felt good."

"My turn." Andy left his mare in Rachel's care and slipped between their geldings.

Seth glanced at Rachel to make sure she didn't mind. A soft smile curved her mouth as she watched her son. It broadened even more when the boy hooted as water ran down his face and neck.

When he drew back and shook the same way Samuel had, his voice came out at a higher volume. "Boy, that was fine."

They were making this look like too much fun. "Guess it's my turn."

The icy water jolted him when it first struck his head, running in tiny streams down his face and neck. The sensation definitely woke his nerves.

When he pulled back and scrubbed the water from his face, he couldn't help a grin at the others. "You should try it too, Rachel."

She shook her head firmly. "Not a chance." But then her smile slipped back into place as she met his gaze. Something about her look made his insides come alive, even more than when the water had cascaded over him.

This woman had the power to stir him with only a smile.

~

Rachel was glad Samuel took the lead after they left the waterfall, for she wasn't sure she'd have been able to focus if Seth had been riding just ahead of her.

Not that Samuel wasn't attractive, but something about Seth called to her. And now, with water slicking his shirt against him, every stolen glance at those wide shoulders and broad chest did funny things inside her. Especially when he turned a grin on her.

He may not be a danger to their physical safety, but he was causing a ruckus in her emotions. No matter what, she had to keep him out of her heart. No man had ever found his way there. She'd thought Richard had in the beginning, but when his other loves took precedent, she realized how easily her feelings toward him changed.

Now, with Andy in front of her and Samuel leading the way, at least she could keep her focus on her son. The brown shirt he wore was in dire need of washing. And she should stitch the hole at his shoulder while she was working on it.

"Ho." Samuel's hand flew up to halt them.

Rachel reined in her gelding and strained to see what brought on the command. They were riding on a well-worn game trail with thick brush on their left and a mountain on their right.

"Indian ahead." Samuel's tone was tight and just loud enough for them all to hear.

The two words sent her pulse hammering in her throat. Indians like the ones they'd met with Elias? Had he said they would encounter any other camps? She didn't remember any comment about them.

"Let me by." Seth pushed his gelding up alongside hers, and she steered her horse toward the brush, as did Andy.

It was then she saw the lone rider, not a dozen strides ahead and coming toward them. The man wore long braids as had the members of other tribe they'd met, and a thick bone necklace that fit his neck tightly. He had a slightly different look than the other Indians, though. Face a little more rounded maybe, cheek bones not as sharp. But still, very much Indian.

And the rifle he pointed at them bespoke a far different reception than they'd received before.

"Keep your hands away from your guns." Seth murmured. Then raising his volume, he spoke to the man. "We come in peace."

The man gave no sign he understood the words. His horse halted a couple lengths in front of them, but with both hands on the gun, there seemed to be no way he could have reined in.

Seth raised his hands away from his sides. "We're only passing through. We mean no harm."

The stranger's horse shifted sideways off the trail—once again without an obvious signal from the rider—and he motioned with his rifle along the path. "Follow me."

"I think he wants us to go with him," Seth murmured.

Fear clawed in Rachel's chest. "What do you think he wants with us?" She'd heard of things Indians did to their captives. Tortures, ravishments. That was why she'd been so careful to avoid Indian camps as they'd traveled along the Missouri River.

They'd never come face-to-face with an Indian on the trail, though.

"Maybe he'll accept me alone and let you three go." Seth glanced at his brother, a long look passing between them.

As though she had no say in the matter. As though she would allow Seth to trade his life for theirs. "You're not going by yourself, Seth." They would all come through this alive.

Except... She sent a glance to Andy. She would endure what she had to, but she couldn't let her son be captured.

"Let's just see what he wants for now." Samuel's low tone seemed to still the tension in the air.

The Indian barked a command. He motioned again along the path, accompanying the gesture with a string of sounds.

Seth turned his gaze back to her, his eyes forming the question his mouth didn't need to.

She didn't want to go. But she would. For now, they'd stick together. Once they had a better idea of what this Indian planned, they could form a strategy.

She nodded, and Seth turned back toward the Indian, nudging his gelding forward. Samuel reined in behind him, probably to give as much of a barrier as possible between the Indian and her son. Maybe to protect her, too.

When Seth reached the Indian, the man spun his horse to face the same direction, then motioned for Seth to continue. The brave kept his horse still as all four of them passed, even though the trail was barely wide enough for two horses.

Rachel met the man's gaze with a hard look as she rode by him. Perhaps she shouldn't have, judging from the way his grim mouth took on a hint of amusement. She no longer backed down to men who meant her or Andy harm, yet would that kind of behavior make things harder with Indians?

The Indian's horse fell in behind Andy, a position that didn't make Rachel comfortable at all. She'd just about decided to have the boy move his horse up in front of hers when three more Indians swept in around them—two came alongside, and the other rode in front of Seth, blocking them on three sides with the mountain on the fourth.

These men had appeared as if by magic. One moment they weren't there, the next they rode with backs straight, faces stern, and rifles in hand.

Her anxiety crept up several notches, and with a brave riding at her heel, there was no way she could exchange places with Andy now. Nor would it help buffer him from these men.

She wanted to call up to Samuel or Seth. To ask what was happening. In truth, what she really wanted was Seth beside her. Yet that wasn't possible, and it was better for them all to remain silent. Their captors—for surely that's what they were now—might understand English.

Soon, the mountain on their right curved away from the trail, and trees filled the space on either side of them. With the Indians still flanking them front, left, and rear, did they dare try to escape to the right?

The trees would make for slow progress, and they'd surely be shot down within a moment of trying.

A short way ahead, the lead Indian veered off the path into the woods, and the guards beside them motioned for them to follow. It was hard to tell so far back in the group, but it didn't look as if they were traveling a regular path now. Where were they being taken?

She slipped a glance at the tawny man riding beside her. Would it hurt to ask? It might anger him, but there was always the chance he'd offer a clue. "Where are you taking us?" She hadn't meant for the words to come out like an accusation, so she softened her shoulders and expression.

But the Indian ignored her, just kept his expression impassive as he navigated his horse around a tree.

If talking wouldn't have an effect on their captors, she'd have to wait for a chance to break loose.

~

They'd been riding through these trees forever, and Seth's muscles were balled tight as he gripped the butt of his rifle resting in the scabbard by his leg. One gun against four, already primed and trained on them, were not good odds.

But he'd take the chance if he could find an opportunity for Rachel and Andy to escape. Samuel, too, although he had a feeling his brother wouldn't leave him to fend for himself.

Daylight shone through the trees ahead, and he strained to see the terrain. An open meadow maybe. As they broke through the edge of the trees, he had to squint against the bright sunlight.

They stepped into the narrow end of a valley, something like a bottleneck, with the woods closing off their left and a wider section open to the right. He scanned the area for anyone else, but there was no sign of other Indians, only their captors.

Except…he inhaled a deep draught of air. A faint scent of smoke tickled his senses. Their camp must be nearby.

With other Indians? Most likely. These men weren't painted like he'd heard they sometimes did when planning a battle or traveling in a war party. Yet their behavior indicated they had known strangers were coming.

Maybe they were always prepared to capture travelers who ventured too near their hallowed ground.

The Indian riding in front continued straight ahead, into the opposite tree line. Seth darted a final glance around the clearing before following the man into the dim light of the woods.

As his eyes adjusted, he scanned the trunks and saplings they wove through. No other Indians appeared. A small relief, but he was grateful. The thought made his chest pang. Why hadn't he called on God for help the minute the Indian pointed his gun at them?

Sorry, Lord. Protect us, please. Rachel and Andy especially. And Samuel. Show me what to do to get them away safely.

A glance over his shoulder showed tension lining his brother's face, but at least his horse was still tucked in close to Seth's gelding. Rachel rode just behind him, her face a fierce mask. The sight would have made him chuckle if their circumstances weren't dire. She worked so hard to present herself as one who shouldn't be crossed. And she possessed a strength of will that was daunting, for sure. Yet she was also achingly vulnerable inside. The fact that he'd allowed her and Andy to be part of this danger made anger sluice through him.

He had to protect her better than this. *God, help me get her away from these men.*

A sound from ahead jerked his attention frontward. The Indian leading them reined his horse to the side, then motioned as if he wanted Seth to keep riding forward.

They'd come upon a path again, like the game trail they'd been following before.

He studied the man. Surely he wasn't letting them go. Yet there was nothing ahead except that trail that led deeper into the woods.

The other captors were backing their horses away also. The lead Indian motioned again, this time with a grunt that stung of impatience.

"I think he wants you to ride forward." Samuel's murmur came from just behind him.

"Should I?" He threw the question back as he kept his focus on the Indians.

"Best to do what they say until we find a way out."

Seth inhaled a breath to clear his thinking. Nothing about this made sense.

The man who seemed to be in charge grunted louder than before as he jabbed toward the trail ahead. Seth obliged, nudging his gelding forward.

The Indians stayed where they were, letting them ride away. Every nerve in Seth's body stood at alert, waiting for the sound of horses moving through the forest. Any signal that would give notice of what the Indians planned.

When about fifteen strides separated them, Seth spoke to his brother. "Take the lead while I slip behind Andy." He didn't like the boy being exposed should one of the men decide to take a shot.

Reining to the side, he kept his focus on the Indians as Samuel rode by him, then Rachel, then the boy. He wanted desperately to say something to ease Rachel's fears, but he didn't dare take his gaze from their former captors. Maybe the Indians had changed their minds about keeping them as prisoners. Maybe something else was happening here.

But he didn't dare lose track of the most obvious threats.

They rode on, and after a few minutes, the trail crested a slight hill, dropping the Indians from sight.

Andy huffed out a loud breath. "Do you think they're gone?"

"I'm not sure, but I'd like to get a bit farther before we stop or talk too loudly." Seth kept his voice low. As easily as the Indians had appeared around them before, they could be watching even now, preparing to surround them again.

The boy rode up beside his mother, and Seth longed to do the same. But he kept his mount right behind them. Thankfully, the horses had spent enough time together they didn't mind riding nose to tail.

It felt like an hour but might have only been a quarter hour when they came out from the woods to bright daylight again, this time with a mountain range in front of them.

Samuel pulled his map from a pocket and glanced at it. "We're still moving the right direction. We go over that lower section there." He pointed to the dip between two peaks.

Seth rode alongside his brother. It was easier to see that no Indians surrounded them now. "Did Elias say anything about an Indian camp around here?"

Samuel met his gaze, eyes narrowing. "Not a thing."

He wanted to growl in frustration. "Why do you think they did that? What did they want?"

"I wonder if they were trying to keep us away from something." Rachel's voice broke through for the first time since they'd come upon the brave.

He turned to study her, mulling over her words. "What would they be hiding?"

She raised a shoulder. "Their camp maybe. Perhaps a sick chief. I don't know."

Possible. Unless they'd simply changed their mind, he couldn't think of a better reason.

Letting out a long breath, he rubbed at the tight muscles in his neck. "Does anyone need a break before we ride for the mountains?"

Rachel looked to her son before shaking her head. "Let's put distance between us and them."

His thoughts exactly.

CHAPTER 19

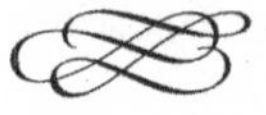

Understanding comes more each day. If only I didn't have to wait.
~ Seth

The last few hours of daylight passed before they reached the base of the mountain they would need to cross. Seth scanned the area as his brother called a halt for the group.

"You think we should stay the night here?" There wasn't much cover, only a small patch of cedar shrubs that would barely serve as a windbreak.

"It's getting too dark to scale the ridge tonight." Samuel looked up to the dip in the mountain top they would need to cross.

Seth sighed. "I guess you're right." They'd need to stand guard tonight. He couldn't allow the Indians to sneak in and take Rachel or Andy. The earlier events still made no sense, but now that he knew danger was near, he'd not let the threat gain ground again.

They made camp quickly, sharing as few words as possible. Tension hung as thick in the air as it did through his shoulders. His body ached from the strain of the day, especially the leg still healing from snake bite, but he pushed the pain aside. He had to be at his best tonight.

As they finished a simple meal, Seth kept part of his attention focused on the darkness beyond the flickering light of their tiny campfire. There was little wood to be had, but it would be best to let the fire die anyway. Of course, the Indians could easily find them without aid of a campfire, but without the fire, Seth and Samuel could see into the dark better.

Seth finished his last bite, then set the plate in front of him and looked to his brother. "Can you take the first watch? I'll spell you in a few hours."

"I can take the first watch." Rachel's tone was strong. "Or the second."

He sucked in a breath. Couldn't she just allow them to protect her and Andy? Why did she always have to pretend to be so tough?

Even as his frustration mounted, he knew why. Rachel still had so much to overcome from her past. She wouldn't trust him fully until she let her hurts and fears go.

Still, he could try to ease her angst for tonight.

Turning to her, he leaned in and let his passion bleed into his voice. "I know you're capable of standing guard, Rachel, but Samuel and I want to do this. Will you let us? Please."

She seemed hesitant to meet his gaze, but at last she did. That fierceness was there in her look, but he could see the vulnerability, too. He wouldn't have recognized it as such if he hadn't come to know her so well. His hands ached to reach out and take hers, to cradle them. But he didn't, not with the others watching.

At last she nodded, then looked away. "Fine. If it's so important to you."

Now it took even greater strength not to pull her into his arms. He sat back and turned toward his brother, more an effort to push the impulse away than anything else. "All right. I'll spell you in the middle of the night. Wake me if I don't get up on my own."

~

Rachel lay still in the darkness as the whispered exchange of the brothers drifted across the camp. She couldn't make out what they were saying, but it must be the changing of the guard. Seth should have let her take her turn at the post, for she surely hadn't slept much these past hours.

Had his night been much better? She'd heard steady breathing at one point, but not for very long.

After a few minutes, stillness settled back over the camp, except steady breathing from Andy, and maybe Samuel. Even the night animals had settled in for a deeper sleep.

Yet her nerves would have none of it. If anything, she was more awake now than when she laid down hours before. And her body was tired of lying still.

Pushing her blanket aside, she eased herself up to sitting. Her bedroll was beside Andy's, who was sandwiched next to whichever Grant brother was taking his turn to sleep—currently Samuel. It was good she'd stopped asking the men to build a partition for her. That had been a silly requirement from the beginning, especially out here where cover was sometimes so scarce, they had to do almost everything in plain sight of each other. *Almost* everything.

Seth had turned to her at her first movement, which meant he was staying alert. Maybe his brother had shared news when they'd exchanged whispers.

She stood and padded toward him, then sank down to sit on the ground beside him. He had a small piece of firewood behind him for a backrest, and he reached for a second to position behind her.

"Thanks," she whispered. The log didn't provide much support, but the thought was nice.

He nodded with a half-smile before he turned back to scan the darkness around him.

She leaned close and kept her voice in a low whisper. "Did your brother see anything?"

He ducked his head toward hers and responded in the same whisper, but kept his gaze forward. Ever vigilant. "Saw some shadows a ways out, but before he could alert us he realized they were deer. The animals stuck around for a while, which they wouldn't do if people were moving. Other than that, nothing."

Their shoulders were touching, and as he spoke, his warm breath brushed her cheek. The musk of his scent washed through her. A scent she'd come to recognize as his alone—man and hard work and something rich, something that made her feel protected.

Even though he'd stopped speaking, she didn't pull back. Kept leaning in, relishing that protection while she had the chance.

For long moments, they sat there in quiet. Him scanning the darkness, his chin roving in every direction around them. She pretended to be watching and listening for a potential enemy, but in truth, she was savoring his nearness.

That would only cause her pain later, when they had to part, but she would accept that as her due when the time came. For now, she would simply absorb Seth Grant's strength.

"You keep watch as though you've done it before." She wasn't sure why she said that. Why she felt the need to break the silence. Maybe just to hear the deep timbre of his voice, even in a whisper.

He slid a glance at her before looking back into the darkness. "Once or twice. I'm ashamed to say I didn't take it as seriously then as I should have. But I'll not let you and Andy be captured again. I think I would have done most anything earlier to get you free. That's not a feeling I want to repeat."

She couldn't seem to stop those words from sinking through her like a warm drink on a cold night. This man wore his role as protector like a second skin. She'd never experienced that before. She was almost afraid to allow it. When he slipped up, the disappointment would be all the worse.

He'd done so much, it seemed as if she should offer something in return. She had nothing, though. Nothing except herself and her son and a past she wanted to leave far behind.

"Samuel and I joined up with a group coming back from California. The boss man had a strong dislike for Indians and always set a watch. It only took a few days before we figured out the Indians probably had a good reason to dislike him back. Seemed like a decent man when he was sober, but when he started drinking, the fellow turned vicious. We figured we were better off making our way alone."

She had to steel herself not to flinch. "A lot of men get mean when they're in their cups."

The burn of his gaze pressed into her, but now it was her turn to stare out at the darkness. "Do you know that from experience?"

His question was personal, yet he'd spoken with a gentleness that didn't make it feel like prodding. Even still, she had to fight the urge to pull away from him. Had to fight to keep her hackles lowered.

This was Seth. He seemed to truly care. And hadn't she been thinking minutes before she wished she could give him something in return for his help and protection? The least she could do was answer his questions.

"I do." Her voice came out weaker than she liked, even in a whisper. She forced strength into it. "My husband drank some."

"Did he hurt you?"

She'd known that question was coming. Still, anger flashed through her. Only for a second, yet he must have sensed it.

"I'm sorry, I shouldn't have asked that." He inhaled a long, audible breath. "You said he passed away. What happened to him?"

She'd started down this road, she may as well finish. And part of her wanted to tell. Wanted someone else to know what life with Richard had been like. She'd not had anyone to talk to at the time. Now Seth...he was her safe place.

She took in a steadying breath. Where to start? Probably from the beginning. If she was going to do this, she may as well tell all in one fell swoop. "Richard didn't always gamble. When we married, I thought I loved him." Bitterness slipped into her words before she could stop it. "I was so young, I didn't know any better." But she'd had nowhere else to go. Not after Papa died. Mama had remarried, and Rachel wasn't about to move in with her new stepfather. In truth her mother was only a shell of a woman by then, probably hoping the man would finally push her into the grave.

She blinked, driving away the image that threatened. This was about her life with Richard. "I didn't know how much he drank for a while. His trips to sell our produce began to take longer and longer. Sometimes he'd come home with more money than we'd ever earned before. He would tell a story about the wealthy husband of a sick woman tipping him well for the healing foods we offered. Other times, he'd return with almost nothing."

Anger stirred anew in her belly. "I knew something wasn't right, so one week Andy and I followed him into town. My son was only toddling around then, and I remember how hard it was to carry him all the way, since Richard had the wagon. He sold our produce within a few hours, then I watched him go into the hotel that also housed the only restaurant and bar. He didn't come out for a long time, so I snuck around to the windows. I knew people would recognize me if I went inside."

She gritted her teeth against the rage that still seared her at the memory. "He sat there for hours, playing game after game. Others at the table came and went, but he spent every last coin he had. *We* had." She forced herself to breathe out the anger roiling inside her.

"Finally, when dusk was coming on, the woman whose husband owned the place came and tapped him on the shoulder, then stood there with her hands on her waist until he walked out. She gave him a pouch, which he must have asked her to keep safe for him, because it was the same pouch he brought home and said was all he had earned from selling the vegetables."

She'd thought she lost this anger years ago, yet it curled inside her like smoke filling a cookstove. She had to separate herself from this story or she'd never get through it.

Drawing another deep breath to settle herself, she forced that wall she'd summoned so many times before. "I took over selling the produce after that, but Richard still found ways to slip off and gamble. I'd come in from the gardens, and he'd be gone. I confronted him a few times, but he always denied it. Told some kind of story about helping a neighbor or seeing a young child on the road he had to take to town. Confronting him never helped, so I stopped.

"Then he started drinking to excess, too. He'd come home late at night, so soused he could barely stand upright. Since he didn't have money from the produce to gamble, things started disappearing around our home.

"One morning when I awoke, I realized he'd not brought the horse home when he returned in the middle of the night. I asked when he would be going to retrieve it, and he said the animal wasn't his, not anymore. That was the first time the liquor made him mean."

"It might not have been only the drink." Seth's words came quietly, breaking through the past. "Loss like that can gain power over a man."

She turned to look at him. He was facing her, his face shadowed. Was he defending Richard? Why speak at this point when he'd been silent until now?

Maybe he read her thoughts, for his jaw worked, and a bit of steel crept into his tone. "I'm not defending him, Rachel. Not in the least. Just saying more than the drink was probably feeding his anger."

She nodded, turning away from him again. "I'm sure his rage came from many places, and the whiskey made it worse. I didn't confront him again until my grandmother's brooch disappeared. I'd already hidden my valuables, anything that would be worth money. But Richard found that particular hiding place. And others."

If she didn't bring this to a close, she would be in danger of letting the emotions take control again. "Anyway, by the time Andy turned ten, the drink was wasting his father's body away. There was some kind of fight at the card table. Richard wasn't strong enough to defend himself, or maybe he was too drunk.

"One of the men he gambled with came by the next morning to tell me they'd laid out Richard's body and asked if I wanted to come pick it up for burial. He also took our milk cow that he'd won in the game before the fight began."

"Oh, Rachel." The depth of sorrow in Seth's voice would be enough to break her if she let it. In truth, if he touched her, she wouldn't be strong enough to continue.

She kept herself rigid. "I went to town, arranged for Richard's burial. I sold our home and land to pay off the lien on half the property caused by his gambling. With what was left, I bought these two horses and our guns, then Andy and I headed northwest."

She inhaled a cleansing breath, releasing the past with the spent air. "We'll start a new life when we find Henry. Our own life."

The strength of Seth's gaze finally left her face as he turned to stare out at the night. All was quiet. Blessedly quiet. Only their breathing, the soft snores drifting from behind them, and the gentle snort of one of their horses.

"It's peaceful out here." And why did she feel she needed to break the silence again? Maybe to distract him from her tale. Or perhaps distract herself.

"It is if you're not watching for Indians." But his tone had a light tinge that sounded as if he agreed. Then it grew serious. "Thank you for telling me your story. Now and the other night. I wish more than anything you didn't have to go through all that. Andy, too." His voice seemed to crack, although it could have been the effort to keep his words soft. "Thank you for trusting me with it."

Trusting him. She did trust him. And even more now that he'd not condoned Richard's actions nor railed against him. In truth, Richard had made poor decisions, but those vices swallowed so many men, taking control and ruining lives. Now that she was free, she would never allow herself to be in that situation again.

As the silence settled, her mind wandered back through the events from earlier that day. Amusing how being captured by Indians felt less threatening than her former life.

A yawn forced her jaw open before she could stop it.

"Why don't you get some sleep?" Seth touched her arm. A light brush of his fingers. For once, the touch didn't make her jerk away. Instead, she almost leaned in, like when she'd been whispering earlier.

But instead she nodded. "Wake me if you see anything concerning."

"I will."

Before she could push to her feet, he stood in an easy motion. After brushing his hand on his trouser leg, he extended it to her. Taking that hand felt like more than simply accepting help to rise.

Almost as though placing her hand in his would mean accepting something beyond his friendship.

But that was silly. He was simply being Seth. Caring for her even when she didn't realize she needed—or wanted—his care.

So she slipped her hand in his, feeling the warmth of his contact. Accepting his strength to help her stand.

When they stood, face-to-face, he didn't release her. His gaze searched hers. Just enough moonlight shone to see the glimmer in his eyes. For a moment, it looked as if he might lean forward and kiss her.

Her breath seized. Part of her almost bolted out of his hold. Back to her bedroll. Yet she stood, rooted, because the other part of her, apparently the stronger part, longed for his touch. Longed for his arms around her, pulling her close.

He didn't move though. Didn't come nearer. Did nothing more than brush his thumb across the back of her hand.

Then he released her. Stepped back. "Good night, Rachel. Sleep well." Something in the words felt like a promise.

Of what, she wasn't quite sure. But as she curled onto her pallet and pulled the blanket over her, she couldn't help a longing for what might be to come.

She shouldn't want it. But she did.

CHAPTER 20

Why can't the good moments last?
~ Rachel

The Indians never came. Or if they did, they didn't leave a sign. And they didn't attack.

Seth finally found a moment alone with his brother while they saddled the horses. "You think they'll ambush us today?"

Samuel scanned the open land around them, just as they'd both been doing all morning. "Couldn't say as I know what they'll do. I'm a bit tired of trying to guess it."

He couldn't help a snort. "I know what you mean."

His brother's mouth tipped as he met Seth's look. Then he sobered, his gaze drifting toward the mountain they'd be climbing soon. "I think we have enough to worry about getting over that. We'll watch for the Indians, but we can't lose our concentration up there."

Samuel was right. Getting Rachel and Andy over this peak safely had to be his main focus today. "All right. Onward and upward."

His brother nodded as he pulled the cinch tight on his saddle, then gave his gelding a pat. "Let's get to it then."

Rachel and her son had already saddled their horses and were finished packing their gear by the time Seth led his gelding to the camp. Within minutes they'd tied the last of the bundles on their mounts.

"I think we're quicker each day." He shot Andy a grin.

The boy returned a flash of white teeth. "Yes, sir." He mounted with the ease only a youth could accomplish—one who'd spent many hours in the saddle.

Scaling the cliff proved easier than Seth had feared, as they were able to find a zig-zag pattern that allowed the animals somewhat sturdy footing.

Rachel stayed to the rear of the group as they planned their descent, her uneasy look and white-knuckled grip on the saddle making it clear she loathed this more than the rest of them did.

He gave her what he hoped would pass for an encouraging smile. "Just tuck your horse in behind mine and you'll be fine."

She nodded, but her gaze strayed toward the edge of the mountain. Then downward. Her eyes widened, her face going as pale as the white clouds overhead. She squeezed her eyes tight, and she swayed a bit in the saddle.

Maybe that was his imagination, but it was enough to make him rein his gelding closer and reach for her arm. He kept a steadying grip on her, even after she opened her eyes.

"Just look at me." He kept his voice low and encouraging. She needed something safe to focus on.

She obeyed, although her face hadn't regained its color.

"Do you want to ride down with me? We can tether your gelding to mine." If she lost her balance while in the saddle, a tumble would probably kill her.

She looked like she might accept the offer, but then the steel slipped back into her spine. She raised her chin and focused her gaze. "I'll be fine. I can do it."

He almost grinned at her as he released her arm and straightened in his saddle. "That's my girl."

It took about an hour to descend the mountain, then they traveled through a rocky valley that led them steadily upward, although at a much lower incline.

The easier terrain would give Rachel a chance to unwind from the stress of the mountain they'd just traversed. For her sake, the end of their journey couldn't come fast enough.

Yet when they reached their destination, she expected to part from him. He hadn't even hinted to her yet that he wanted a life with her. She hadn't been ready to hear it, he was fairly certain of that.

The telling of her story—both last night and the other day—seemed a significant step. Monumental. She trusted him with her past, and he knew in every part of him that trust was the biggest gift she could have bestowed. Had she ever told anyone else? He suspected not.

But hearing her history had planted a boulder in his gut that felt like it grew every time he thought of it. Her husband had struggled with a gambling addiction? What were the odds he'd be afflicted with that particular vice? *Lord, why?*

God had completely healed Seth of that obsession. Stripped away all desire not just for the thrill of winning at cards, but also for the taste of alcohol, and the smoky haze of a game room, women moving among them more freely even than drinks.

He could barely stomach the memories, so far had he run from that life. But would Rachel believe it? Drink and gambling had stolen everything good in her world—except her son, of course. When he told her of his past, would she think him just as untrustworthy as her husband had been?

It seemed crazy that God would bring a woman into his life who'd suffered so much at the hands of the same vices the Lord had saved him from. *Father, only You can make this turn out for good. Please.*

A rustle ahead snagged his focus, and he reined his gelding to a stop as he reached for his rifle.

White flashed behind a stubby cedar, drawing his gaze as he positioned his rifle. *White?*

The animal took shape as it stepped forward, but the image still didn't make sense. It looked like a deer, but the coloring was as pale as trampled snow. He'd heard of albino buffalo and how prized they were among Indians and traders. Could this be an albino deer?

He shouldn't miss this chance to claim a valuable trade good, and they did need the meat. Aiming along the barrel, he held his breath and squeezed the trigger.

A clean shot. The animal dropped to the ground in a lump, pressing on his chest at the sight. He'd never get used to taking animal life, even if it was the only way those he loved could live.

Lowering the gun, he glanced back at the group behind him. His gaze swung to Rachel, whose face had paled to almost the shade of the deer. "What's wrong?" He swung down from his horse and moved to her animal's side.

Her hands were shaking as they clutched the reins. "Nothing's wrong." The tendons at her throat worked, and she blinked. "I mean… we're almost out of salt. We don't have enough for this meat and the hide."

The knot in his gut tightened and he rested a hand over her fist. "We'll figure out something. Why are you shaking, though, Rachel? It's not because of the salt."

She turned her gaze on him, her eyes glimmering with enough terror that he had to tighten his jaw to keep from pulling her into his arms to comfort her. "I don't do well with gunshots. It's a weakness."

Her mother. Realization flashed over him like a bucket of water. He brought up his other hand to close over both of hers. "I'm sorry, Rachel. Oh, I'm sorry." He was a lout to not recognize the signs sooner. She'd reacted strongly the time Elias took down a deer while they rode, too. And she'd told him her story.

She shook her head, nudging her horse forward, out of his reach. "I'm fine. Let's do what we need to with this deer."

As he watched the stiff set of her shoulders, he couldn't help the ache in his belly. *Help me help her, Lord. Show me the way.*

~

"What do you make of it?" Seth eyed the smoke curling through the trees ahead.

"Looks like a campfire of some sort. But only one. Maybe a cabin or teepee." Samuel shot a look at the late afternoon sky, and Seth raised his gaze to follow. It had almost reached the time that they would stop to camp for the night. Would these strangers be friend or foe?

"I'll ride ahead and scout it out." Rachel nudged her gelding forward as though she planned to do just that.

"Wait." He didn't even try to hold back the growl from his voice. "You're not going to march in there for those Indians to capture you."

Her spine stiffened, and she turned a glare on him. "I can be quieter than any of you. I've snuck up to Indian camps before and never been noticed. In fact…" Her eyes narrowed and the corner of her mouth tipped upward. "Andy and I spied on your camp the night before we first joined you."

He played her words over in his mind again before they made sense. Even then, they didn't settle well. "You…watched us?" Was she making up this tale to force him into a yes? Surely one of them would have heard or felt her presence. Elias would have, for certain.

Her chin lowered a notch, and some of the confidence slipped from her gaze. "Andy and I both did. I wanted to see what sort of men you were."

A piece that had been missing from the picture in his mind shifted into place. Although…not a complete fit. "Was that after the bear came into your camp or before?"

She ran her tongue over her lips. A nervous gesture. "Before."

He cocked his head as he struggled to make sense of it. "You were thinking of joining us even then?"

A slight shake of her head. "No. Just curious. We saw you riding ahead of us, so later that night, we came nearer to see what you three were about." Her chin rose again. "We did that many times with people we saw on the way from Missouri. Crept up on white men and

Indians alike. One can learn a great deal about a man by watching him at his leisure. How much he drinks. What he speaks of." A shrug, probably meant to be casual, but he could see how much this topic affected her.

"So...what did you learn about us?" They must have passed muster for her to join them after the bear attack, but he still found himself holding his breath as he waited for her reply.

Her gaze slid to Samuel before returning to him. "We saw no sign of whisky. You were easy in each other's company. No vices that were obvious."

He raised his brows. "You approved then?"

A corner of her mouth twitched, but she managed to keep a straight face. "I found nothing to disapprove."

That was probably all he'd get from her, but it was enough. For now. He let a grin slip onto his face as he nodded. "Good. Now"—he turned back toward the smoke—"even though you've proved yourself a capable spy, I'd be a poor excuse for a man if I let you creep closer to that camp without knowing who it is."

He slid her a look, fully expecting the glare that had resurrected on her face. And he was ready for it. "After all, you have a son who needs you. We shouldn't take chances with your life when Samuel and I are around to take the risks."

Her glare slipped, and her mouth formed a thin line. She must see the wisdom in his words. "All right."

Thank you, Lord. Now he could turn his focus back to determining how much threat that thin ribbon of smoke presented. He reached for his rifle. "I'll scout it out and see what we're up against." He slid down from the saddle before his brother had a chance to argue.

After gathering his reins, he handed them up to Rachel. "Hold this boy, will you?"

She took the leathers with a nod, but he closed his hand over hers to get her attention. She stilled, her gaze finding his.

"I'll be back as soon as I can." He wasn't sure what he meant to convey in the look that passed between them. Maybe that he would do everything in his power to keep her and Andy safe. Maybe that he cared more than he'd yet found a way to say. Maybe even that he craved another of her kisses, yet wouldn't attempt it until she showed she was ready.

Her green gaze held a hint of vulnerability, but she seemed to accept what he wanted to express. She gave an almost imperceptible nod. A faint lifting at her mouth.

If he hadn't been watching, he wouldn't have seen the movements. But he did, and her response flooded him with pleasure. "I'll be back." He couldn't help saying it one more time. Then he brushed his thumb across the back of her hand and stepped away.

He sent Andy a nod as he passed, and the boy straightened. "If they're good folks, maybe they have some salt we could use for the deer."

Seth cocked his head. "Maybe so." He should have considered that already.

"Be careful." Samuel's voice was a bit of a growl as he strode by.

"I will." Seth stopped to pat his brother's gelding as he glanced at Samuel's set jaw. "I'll just get my bearings, then come back."

Samuel nodded, but didn't release the clamp of his jaw.

Seth turned to the task before him. Best get this done. *Guide me, Lord.*

CHAPTER 21

All seems well. Yet...is it?
~ Seth

Striding forward into the trees, he kept his tread soft and stayed on a course that avoided the deepest areas of leaves and fallen branches that would sound his approach. The farther he went, the stronger the scent of wood smoke, but the plume stayed in that single stream.

A glimmer of brighter daylight appeared through the trees ahead, like a clearing or open land. He slowed as he neared, straining to see what lay beyond. A large object sat in the clearing, like a building or massive Indian lodge.

He slowed as he reached the edge of the wood, then planted himself behind a thick evergreen.

A cabin sat twenty strides ahead, as ramshackle as any he'd seen in months. The building was about the size of Elias's one-room abode but without the lean-to in the back. A couple of horses grazed on the other side of the structure, not fenced that he could see. Hobbled maybe.

They'd eaten the grass in the clearing to low nubs, which meant they'd been here awhile. Which made him think they were white men. Didn't Indians usually move in a band?

Whoever was inside, hopefully they were friendly and had salt to trade. That white deer hide was too exceptional to let rot because they couldn't cure it properly. And they needed to save the meat.

Should he approach the building alone or come back with Samuel? With two animals, there were likely two men inside. Or maybe one man, and the second horse carried supplies.

Probably these were friendly trappers, just like Elias. And if they meant harm, well…better Samuel stayed alive to get Rachel and her son to safety.

He pushed that thought aside as he stepped out from behind the tree into daylight. Without his horse, he felt only half-dressed, but he held his rifle in both hands.

"Hello in the cabin." He paused for a response, close enough to the trees he could dart back to shelter if needed. Something about this place didn't sit easy with him. Or maybe he was simply picking up on Rachel's shyness of strangers.

A minute or so slipped by before a voice called from in the building. "What be yer business?"

Maybe the wash of relief that swept through him was unfounded, but just the sound of the man's voice seemed to settle his unease. "My name's Seth Grant. I'm with a small group traveling through. We're in need of salt and wondered if you'd have any to trade."

Silence. The thick, rough-cut door at the front shifted, then pushed open just enough for a thick mop of dark hair to stick out. "I suppose we got salt to trade. What you got to give fer it?"

It took a minute for Seth to make out the details of the man. Maybe ten years older than himself, since his hair wasn't taken over by gray yet. He wasn't pointing a gun at Seth, but that didn't mean there wasn't someone else handling that job inside. There were plenty of cracks in between logs that would allow room to sight a rifle barrel.

In his mind, he scanned the dwindling supplies in their packs.

"Fresh deer meat, killed a few hours ago and well drained." They could always find more game if they needed to.

The man spat a stream into the dirt. "Got plenty o' meat. Anythin' else?"

If these were trappers, they likely did have more than enough meat on hand. "Beans then?" Maybe half of their remaining ration would gain them enough salt to prepare the hide. Surely they weren't far from Canada and the end of their journey.

The man nodded. "That'll do." He pushed the door open wider, exposing the rest of his body. "Bring your folks on in an' we'll share a meal with ya. Me an' Hackney here."

Another head stuck out from the interior. This one with a shock of copper-colored hair. "How many ya got?"

Seth hesitated. Should he mention all four of them or just Samuel and himself? He was pretty sure Rachel wouldn't come near these men, even if they did turn out to be a decent sort.

Better leave her out of the conversation. "My brother and I. 'Fraid we won't be able to stop long enough for a meal. Let me go get him and we'll return with the beans for trade."

The dark-haired man nodded. "See you do."

Seth stepped back toward the woods, and as the dimmer light sank around him, he glanced to the cabin again. Both men still stood in the doorway, watching his retreat without apology.

They seemed a little odd, but that should probably be expected with men who lived in this wilderness. He wasn't keen on bringing Rachel and Andy to their knowledge. Maybe he was being too protective, but keeping them back seemed the best way to proceed.

He and Samuel could ride forward to make the trade. Basically, distract the men while Rachel and Andy skirted around the clearing to meet them on the other side.

Then they could all ride a ways farther before making camp for the night.

It wasn't hard to convince all involved that his plan was the best course of action. Yet as Rachel and her son set off to the right to ride around the cabin in a wide circle, he couldn't help a pang in his chest. Nay, more than a pang. A smothering weight.

Just before he nudged his gelding into the trees, Rachel turned for a last look. Their gazes met over the distance. Maybe it was wishful thinking, but it looked like the same longing on her face that yearned inside him.

As soon as they had a chance alone, he would tell her. Tell her of the past God had delivered him from. Then, invite her to join their futures together in their Father's hands.

Purpose soared in his chest as he turned back toward the trees. "Let's go." There was much to be done this night.

When they reined their horses into the clearing, Seth signaled for a stop and called out. "Hello." The men were likely watching for them, but it was always better to give warning in a country like this.

The door swung wide open this time, and the dark-haired man stood in the frame. "Settle yer horses an' come on in. We've a stew that's been simmerin' most of the day."

As much as he knew they wouldn't be staying for a meal, the thought of a thick, warm soup started Seth's mouth watering. He nudged his gelding forward, and Samuel did the same, then they both reined in a few strides from the cabin.

"This is my brother, Samuel." He dismounted and reached behind the saddle to unfasten the sack of beans they had to trade. "I wish we could take you up on that offer, but we need to get another hour or so on the trail before we stop."

"What's yer hurry? I suspect you ain't had comp'ny for a while. Might as well stay fer grub. Hackney here's a decent hand with a spoon, an' you can bed down outta the weather for the night."

Seth shot a glance at the dusky sky. A layer of clouds covered what had been blue earlier. They might see rain tonight, which meant he should pull out the oilcloth and furs when they made camp.

He hoisted the beans and carried them forward. "I'd like to trade this for half a sack of salt, if you can spare it."

The man eyed the bag. "Let's see the beans."

Either he fancied himself a shrewd trader or he wasn't very trusting. Seth unfastened the leather tie and showed the inside. "We've been eating from the same shipment for weeks now and I can confirm they do a good job filling a hungry belly." He offered a grin.

The lightness seemed to have no effect. The man spat a stream onto the ground beside them, then turned to yell back to the cabin. "Hackney, bring a half bag o' salt."

The tall, red-haired Hackney was either partially deaf, or this first man didn't realize his friend was close enough to touch. But the man only tipped his head and shuffled back inside the cabin. Maybe he *was* hard of hearing.

The brown-haired fellow focused on Seth and Samuel again, his look turning curious. "Where you fellas from and where ya headin'?"

Seth glanced at his brother to see if he had any concern about sharing the details. These men seemed harmless enough, if a bit odd. "We've come up from Fort Benton by way of Two Rivers. We're headed to the Canadian territories, near Fort Hamilton."

The man's face finally broke into a grin. "Fort Whoop-up, eh? You don't look like yer bringin' the whiskey, so I guess you'll drink whatever they got."

Seth frowned. "Not planning to drink." What did that have to do with the fort?

The man shook his head and chuckled a dry laugh. "Everyone drinks at Fort Whoop-up. Reds and whites both. The whiskey runs freer there than water in the Marias River. Gamblin', too." A light glimmered in the man's eyes. "Them boys know how ta have fun."

That was the place Rachel planned to start a new life? Did her brother take part in the drink and gambling? She would be furious.

Or heartbroken. Probably both.

He should ask more about the place, but the roiling in his gut kept him from it.

Thankfully, Samuel changed the subject. "Are you aware of any Indians in this area? Maybe camps or hunting parties?"

Good thinking. Maybe these men would know what the braves meant by their strange behavior the day before.

The fellow's heavy brow lowered over his eyes. "There's a band of Kootenai south of here. D'you see 'em?"

Samuel briefly relayed the event as Hackney reappeared in the doorway holding a sack that looked a good bit less than half full. It should be enough for the deer hide, though.

The dark-haired man didn't seem to notice his friend—or ignored him—and as Samuel finished the tale, he crossed his arms in a thoughtful pose. "Strange. We've traded with 'em a couple times an' never had trouble. Maybe they was just tryin' to get you past their camp without you knowin' about it. Sounds like that's about the place where they set up lodges."

That was the only scenario that made even a little sense, although it still seemed odd. He turned his attention to Hackney. "Appreciate the trade. We need to get on the trail."

The tall, red-haired man stepped forward and extended the sack. Out of the corner of his eye, Seth glanced a frown on the face of the front man. What was his name, anyway? He'd never introduced himself.

Seth took the bag with a nod of thanks, then glanced to dark-haired man. "I'm afraid I didn't catch your name."

"Burke. You boys come on back if you don't wanna get wet." The frown was gone from the man's face, and he held a genial look. Almost a smile through his thick beard.

"Thanks for the offer." Seth hooked the satchel of salt behind his saddle, then mounted.

"Take care." Samuel gave a final wave as they turned toward the northbound trail.

Maybe it was his imagination, but the burn of the men's stares seemed to pierce his back until they rode from sight. Had he or Samuel angered the men somehow?

Surely not.

Best put them from his mind and focus on what lay ahead. Find Rachel and Andy. Create some sort of shelter in case of rain.

Find a way to tell Rachel exactly what she meant to him.

CHAPTER 22

This is why I should have let my heart protect itself.
~ Rachel

Rain fell while they slept. A steady patter of drops, not a downpour, and by dawn's first light, the drizzle had ceased. Rachel couldn't help a sigh of relief as she worked through her morning tasks. *Thank you, Lord.*

The muddy ground made it hard to restart the fire, but they had to finish preparing the deer before starting on the trail. At last Samuel nurtured a healthy blaze, and Rachel settled in to roast venison while the men worked on the hide.

Andy's chatter with the two brothers was humorous at times, while they shared stories of hunting or tanning other furs. From their questions and impressed tones, it was easy to tell Andy's experience surprised them. Did they think her neglectful for allowing her son to perform such duties at his young age?

She'd tried to handle the hunting herself, she'd really tried. Yet every time a rifle shot resounded, the acrid burn of powder filling the air, she couldn't seem to still the memories. And images didn't just come immediately after the gunfire. For nights after, they haunted her dreams. Mother's face after she pulled the trigger. Blood spraying in all directions, soiling the yellow of her dress. Her face losing all color. The desperation in her eyes.

No child should see those images. And Rachel would give anything if she'd never seen them herself, even though she'd saved her mother's life.

So Andy had taken over hunting this past year. And each time he left to seek game, guilt pricked her conscience and pressed fear into her chest until he returned. Safely, so far.

"Rachel?"

She jerked at the voice above her, and only the fact that it was Seth's gentle cadence kept her from ducking away. "Yes?"

He crouched beside her. "Smells good over here."

"I'm about half done. How's the hide coming?" She glanced sideways at him as she turned a chunk of meat in the pan.

"Good. They're almost done cleaning, then they'll salt and pack it." His rugged appeal seemed twice as strong this morning, with his short hair accenting the strong lines of his face, and his jaw shadowed by a couple days' growth. No matter how many times she told herself not to fall for this man, she could only pray her heart wasn't too far gone.

She refocused on the venison as she turned another piece. Seth reached for a log from the small stack remaining, then added it to the fire, positioning the wood so the heat would stay about the same under her pan.

"There's something I've been wanting to tell you, Rachel. Two things actually."

Her shoulders tensed. Not that his words should concern, but something in his tone warned her. "Yes?" She kept her focus on the meat, shifting it within the pan.

"When you told me your story the other night, I realized I haven't told you mine. About California."

That wasn't what she'd expected. She raised her gaze to his, searching for a sign of what had put that concern in his voice.

Nothing obvious, but the strain around his eyes matched the shadow of tension in his tone.

"Samuel and I first went west back in '60. I was bored in our little hometown of Yorkville and desperate to get away from the farm. When my brother agreed to go with me, there was nothing left to hold me there. I think he went hoping he could keep me out of trouble, but not even he was able to do that." His voice drifted away at the end, and silence settled over them.

As his words reverberated inside her, what had started as unease tightened into something stronger. How bad was the thing he needed to tell her?

"We started out mining, but most of the gold had already been uncovered. It'd been over a decade since the first discovery. We realized the real money would be made off the miners themselves. I met a man who was scoping locations for a tavern, and we struck a deal. Samuel and I would run the place and Hanks would front the money needed to get things started."

Her stomach churned as realization settled through her. This was worse than bad. Yet it seemed as though he spoke of another man. She couldn't imagine Seth being part of such a venture. Nor Samuel.

"The place did better than any of us dreamed. There were so many people coming to make their fortunes, only to discover the fortunes were already spent. They came to our saloon to drown their sorrows or try to increase their meager findings through games.

"Samuel didn't like it from the get-to. Said we were as bad as thieves and murderers, but all I could see were the profits filling our coffers." His voice grew muffled as his head ducked between his hands. His outline that of despair. Yet she couldn't summon much pity. How many families had he ruined the way hers had been torn apart?

"Samuel left the business, but I couldn't tear myself away. Deep down, I knew he was right. I hated watching men gamble away the money they were supposed to be sending their families. I hated watching lives lost when whiskey ran too freely. It wasn't a good place. And I did more than contribute. I fed the beast that tortured those men.

"It wasn't until I finally came to terms with the damage I was doing and tried to get out that I realized I was as tied to the vices as those men I pitied. The first day away from the saloon, I found myself right back there, receiving cards dealt by another man. This time, I had no control over whether he cheated, and I found myself on the raw end of the game more times than not. I was desperate to recover my losses. Desperate to prove I wasn't a phony, even if only to myself.

"I was mired so deep, I lost everything I could get my hands on. Nearly lost my life more than once. Samuel tried to stop me over and over. Tried to get me hired at the ranch where he'd been working. They all knew who I was. Knew what I'd done. Probably could see my addiction just by looking at me. I wasn't in good shape." His voice cracked on that.

"I thought about ending it all. Knew I had failed in my great adventure away from home. Most of all, I hated the way I still craved the taste of a good hard whiskey, the thrill of the win. Even the feel of the cards in my hands, the clink of the chips, the murky haze of smoke filtering through the room. I never liked the taste or smell of tobacco —at least that's one vice I never took up.

"One afternoon I was near my lowest. I sat in the room I shared with four other men. A room Samuel paid for because I had nothing left. I was there alone and had locked the door to keep myself from going to the saloon."

He gave a hard chuckle. "Locked myself in and slipped the key under the door so I couldn't reach it. I begged for God to intervene. The addiction had become the biggest—the only—thing in my life. I knew I needed someone even more powerful to stop the control I'd given those needs."

He sat for a moment, his hands pressed together as if in prayer. "God took away the power those things had over me. He took away every urge. Every desperate need. Wiped them away. From that moment on, I've never had even a tiny craving for the drink or the gambling."

He raised his head to look her way. She couldn't bring herself to meet his gaze. Couldn't seem to stop the shaking in her hands.

"I knew God gave me a chance to start over. A chance for a new life. Samuel and I left town the very next morning."

"How long ago was that?" The quivering in her voice wouldn't still. As if she had no control over herself. As if the numbness taking over her chest was spreading further. If only it would take her completely. Pull her away from this impossible nightmare.

"About six months. We took the long route northward."

He was quiet, and she couldn't have spoken again if she had to. The only thing she seemed capable of was flipping the meat in the pan. First one way, then the other.

How was it possible Seth had done those things? Not this man she'd come to know and love. For she did love him. She knew that now.

Or at least she had. She wouldn't love another man who was addicted to drink and gambling. She would *not*. What was wrong with her that she was drawn to men like this? Or was it truly all men who suffered from such weakness?

"Rachel, I've never had another urge to enter a saloon, or even take a drink, since that day. God healed me. Completely." His voice held pleading. Quiet desperation. Yet resolve, too.

The combination was almost her undoing. A gut-deep cry sprang up inside her, an urge to escape. To leave this place—this man.

She surged to her feet, her breath coming in short gasps as she spun to get her bearings.

"Ma?"

Andy. She couldn't leave him. Not with these men who were just as untrustworthy as her dead husband. "Come with me, Andy."

"But, Ma—"

"*Now*. Come now." She bit hard on the steel in her tone as she marched toward the thickest part of the woods around them.

His hurried step sounded just behind her. "Yes, ma'am."

At least she could still count on her son to be what she needed.

Now it was time to regain control. Put together a plan for how they would travel the rest of the way to find Henry. Alone.

And she would find a way to put Seth Grant behind her.

~

"I ruined it. Everything. I shouldn't have told her like that." Seth couldn't stop himself from pacing the length of their campsite.

"How would you have told her that would have made the story any different?" Samuel still worked at the deer hide, his efforts marking his words as he scraped the last bits of flesh from the thick leather.

He scrubbed a hand through his hair. "I don't know. Slower. I wouldn't have just spilled it out like that. I should have tried to prepare her."

"What do you think she'll do now?" Samuel's voice was way too calm and steady for the situation.

Seth clamped his fingers on the ends of his hair and pulled. Anything to keep himself from expressing his frustration the way he really wanted to. "I hope she'll think about it a while, then come back and tell me she sees how much I've changed. I hope she'll agree with me that the past is behind us."

"You think that's what she'll do?" Again with the emotionless tone, although maybe this one held a bit of prodding.

He heaved out a frustrated grunt. "Not likely." The knot in his belly hardened. Would she turn her back on him? Why in the rocky hills had he told her? *Because you had to be honest, numbskull.*

But what if he lost her completely? *Oh, God. Let her see reason. Bring her back so I can make this right.*

Samuel shifted from scraping the hide to applying salt. "So, what are you gonna do?"

Should he go after her? Chasing her down might just prove he was still the impetuous man who craved the thrill of winning. She'd left their horses and supplies here, so she'd have to come back. He could wait for her. When she returned, he would prove he was trustworthy. Dependable.

Somehow, he'd prove it.

"I'll wait for her." He spun to face the fire and the pan that now emanated the scent of charred meat. Maybe he could have the remaining venison roasted by the time she came back.

~

Rachel did her best to ignore the glare Andy sent her way as she dropped to her knees beside the tiny creek and splashed water on her face. He didn't understand why they needed to leave Seth and Samuel, and she wouldn't degrade his father or these men by explaining the details to him. She'd always tried to keep him as unaware as she could about his father's sins, although it had been impossible for him not to realize things weren't right.

Now, she couldn't bring herself to tell him the things Seth had done. Couldn't shame the man in her son's eyes. But they had to leave, no matter how much Andy wanted to stay.

She inhaled a sharp breath as the icy water seeped into the pores on her face and dripped down her neck. They'd have to go back and get their things. Maybe she should do it alone.

But Andy would want to say good-bye to these men who had helped him over the past weeks. Even though Seth and Samuel wouldn't want them to leave, she was pretty sure they would be decent about the farewell, for Andy's sake.

She'd have to chance it. Trust them one last time.

Then she would never let another man this close again. No one except Henry. She hadn't seen her brother since she first married Richard, but surely he hadn't changed from the earnest lad she remembered. He had probably been about Andy's age when Mama took him to live with their new stepfather. Henry had been quiet like Andy, sober.

She couldn't wait to reunite.

After wiping her face with her sleeve, she turned to her son, working as much cheer into her face as she could muster. "Soon we'll—"

She broke off when she saw the empty rock where Andy had sat. "Where are you, son?" Spinning, she scanned the woods around her. This area was more verdant than others they'd traveled through, with leaves bushing the trees and shrubs and grass poking up in a few sunny patches. Yet none of the shadows revealed her son.

Her heart surged as she struggled to her feet. "Andy?" Her voice rang high, and her breath came short. She struggled to gather a full inhale to call louder. "Andy!"

She stilled, straining for any sound of his response. Nothing except the pounding of her pulse in her ears.

Had he gone back to the men? He must've.

Raising her skirts, she raced back the way they'd come. She'd only gone a handful of strides before a hand slipped out from behind a tree, clapping tight around her upper arm.

Another hand slammed over her mouth, stilling the scream before it had a chance to escape.

CHAPTER 23

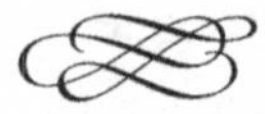

What damage have my sins caused now?
~ Seth

Seth scanned the trees where Rachel and Andy had disappeared. How long would she stay away? It seemed like an hour had passed at least. Was she doing this just to torment him? Or did she really need this much time for her anger to cool?

"I think you should go after her."

He whirled to face his brother, a bit of relief sinking through him with the quiet words. "You don't think that'll make it worse?"

Samuel shrugged. "I wouldn't begin to know what a woman thinks, but maybe she wants you to come find her. Show her you're worried."

He let out a long breath. "I *am* worried."

His brother nodded. "Then go find her. Besides, maybe something happened and she needs help."

A new knot began to form in his middle. If she was in danger out there, and he'd been at camp doing nothing but fretting, he'd never forgive himself. Why hadn't he thought of that earlier?

He reached for his rifle and shot pouch, checked the knife sheathed at his waist, then spun to face the trees. "I'll be back."

"You want me to come?"

Seth paused mid-stride. "No. But I'll send up a shot if there's trouble."

"Fine."

Her trail wasn't easy to follow, as they'd all traipsed this way multiple times going to the creek and back. That was probably where she and Andy had gone, so he headed to the water first.

Neither of them were at the stream, although something about the area didn't seem quite right. Maybe it was his imagination, but the leaves forming the groundcover seemed more disturbed than normal. If that was a sign they'd been here, what would they have done to ruffle the forest floor?

It looked almost as if they'd been playing a game of tag or…maybe struggling.

He fought the wave of bile that churned in his gut. That line of thought was mere speculation that would tie him in knots. Instead, he raised his voice and called out, "Rachel? Andy? I came to make sure you're safe."

Only silence met his words. No twitter of birds, no chatter of squirrels. The quiet pressed hard on his chest. "Please, Rachel. I know you may not want to talk to me. You don't have to, just call out and let me know you're not hurt or in danger."

Utter stillness was his only response.

Something wasn't right. The fine hairs on his neck tingled as the certainty of that fact took hold.

He scanned the mangled leaves for more evidence of what might have happened, then widened his search to see if he could find a trail leading away from the area.

It took a couple minutes, but finally he found it.

Just behind the trunk of a large fir, a small area had been pressed flat, as though someone stood there for a while. Then just beside, the leaves churned with two rows extending farther from the creek. Something had been dragged through there. Or someone.

The drag marks didn't go far, but he was able to pick up a footprint here and there mixed in with freshly snapped twigs, churned leaves, and a recently broken spider's web.

Someone had come through here not long ago. Probably Rachel and Andy. But what had made the drag marks?

He followed the trail of faint signs for at least fifty strides, moving mostly alongside the creek, now out of sight of the fir where he'd first started tracking. Then he came to a place where the leaves were more than ruffled.

Deep hoof marks pressed into the muddy ground, where they mingled with leaves and horse droppings. At least one animal had been tied here for a while.

His chest squeezed hard. Rachel and her son hadn't made these tracks. Their horses were still tied with his and Samuel's. Someone else had been here this morning. These prints had been made after last night's rain.

Had the Indians finally caught up with them? That seemed the most likely. The only people they'd seen for days now were the two mountain men and the band of Indians, and it made no sense that Burke or Hackney would want Rachel or her son. They would have no use for them. Then he thought of Rachel's beautiful face and piercing eyes, and he imagined what the men could want from her.

Fire burned in his belly, spurring him into action.

The path of disturbed leaves was easy to follow from this spot, meaning they'd ridden away from here. He'd need a horse to catch up with them. And maybe he'd need Samuel's help, too.

After a final scan of the area to make sure he hadn't missed a detail, he sprinted back toward camp. Every second mattered.

~

Rachel bit against the rough leather binding her mouth, but if anything, her efforts only tightened the strap. She'd been jostled in front of this man's saddle for what felt like hours, his meaty hold strapping her tight against his chest. With her hands bound in front of her and the leather filling her mouth, she had nothing to fight with except her legs. And kicking would only anger the horse and risk her life.

She turned for a glance at her son, who sat in front of the other man's saddle. Andy met her look, his eyes impossibly wide as the leather covered the lower half of his face.

Anger burned inside her. How could these villains treat a young boy like that? Binding him like a criminal. No child should be forced to experience this much fear.

We'll get out of this. I won't let them hurt you. She willed him to understand the words through her gaze. If only she'd done a better job of protecting him.

The trees around them thinned, and they rode into a clearing where a cabin sat just ahead. She'd suspected these might be the men Seth had traded with for the salt, and this place looked like the cabin he'd described.

This was why she never trusted strangers. Why she avoided towns and other travelers at all costs.

If Seth had never alerted these men to their presence, she and Andy wouldn't be riding with them now, bound and gagged. And what did they want? Other than a few barked commands, neither man had spoken.

It wasn't hard to imagine what they might want from her. And the thought raised bile into her throat that made her want to rip the leather from her mouth and spew all over the beast holding her. But what of Andy? A boy wouldn't be any good to them. He'd be just another mouth to feed.

Surely they didn't plan to kill him. Panic clutched her throat, but she forced her body not to show sign of it. Surely these men weren't killers. Ravishing her would be bad enough. And kidnapping a child.

But surely they weren't the kind of men who could murder an innocent boy.

If they hurt him, she'd spend her every remaining breath ensuring their misery.

The men reined to a stop in front of the cabin, and the one behind her spoke. "Let's get 'em down." He groaned as he dismounted, his large bulk pushing her forward and his arm clamping tighter around her ribs as he pulled her to the ground with him.

As he pushed her forward toward the door, he spoke to his partner. "You sure I can trust ye to keep yer hands off the girl 'til I get back?"

He was leaving? To where? This might be her chance to get them away. Surely she and Andy could overpower the leaner red-haired man.

"Course you can. Long as I get my fair chance at her later."

As she thought. Sickness churned in her middle, but she wasn't done fighting. Not in the least.

The man booted the door open and pushed her inside. "I reckon by the fire's the only place to tie her, but you make sure you keep a rifle on her the whole time. Ye hear?"

"I hear." Red Hair didn't sound like he appreciated being ordered around.

Argue with him, she wanted to say. If the men would fight each other, it would make her job all the easier. Maybe she could help their discord along.

The big man marched her toward the stone hearth, then pushed her down to her knees. His foul breath fanned her face as he tied another leather rope around her hands, strapping her to a bar mounted inside the fireplace for a pot to hang.

"I enjoyed holdin' you all the way here, girlie, but it ain't nothin' to how much I'll enjoy you when I get back. You just wait for ol' Henry." He jerked the knot tight, then before she knew what he was doing, he leaned in and planted a kiss right on her cheek. The scruff from his beard raked across her face, and the awful odor of his breath nearly gagged her.

She jerked back, the leather in her mouth holding in her squeal. The bar wouldn't let her go far, and her effort tightened the strap around her wrists until they cut into her skin.

He cackled as he stood. "We're gonna have some fun, you an' me. I likes 'em feisty."

As his boot thuds marched across the floor, she forced even breaths in through her nose. Her head went light, and she blinked to keep herself in the present.

Andy. Twisting around, she expected to see the tall, red-haired man bringing her son to tie up beside her. Instead, the bigger one grabbed Andy by the arm and pulled him from the other's hold. He kept marching toward the doorway with her boy in tow.

Panic clawed inside her, and she fought against the restraint, trying to scream. *Wait! You can't take him away.* But no sound could break through her gag except a strangled cry.

The men both paused to look at her, and her son turned wide, fearful eyes her way. She wrenched and pulled. They *would not* separate Andy from her. They couldn't.

"You hold tight, missie. Yer boy's goin' to a good place. I think they'll like him just fine." The big man—Henry—sent her a twisted smile, then yanked her son's arm and headed toward the door.

Just before he stepped outside, he turned back and spoke to his cohort. "If those men come lookin', don't hesitate to put a bullet or two in 'em. This far out, won't no one miss 'em, and it'll save us a heap o' trouble."

"I'll take care o' things." The lanky one held up the rifle he clutched in both hands.

Henry's face shriveled in a scowl. "See that you do."

Rachel scraped her leather tie over the metal bar, but it didn't seem to be working. She pulled harder, scrubbing furiously. She couldn't let him ride off with her son. Where would he take him? The Indian camp? Or maybe other people lived in this area.

What would the people he'd spoken of do to Andy?

~

"It must be those brutes we traded with for the salt. The trail's going straight for their cabin." Seth wanted to roar as the frustration welled inside him. Foolish, impulsive idiot. How could he have been so reckless with Rachel and Andy's safety? He never should have approached that cabin. Never should have let Rachel leave camp for so long without going to find her.

"Let's slow up for a second." Samuel's horse dropped back as he reined in, and Seth forced himself to do the same. "Better to find out what's happening at their cabin before announcing our presence."

A dozen strides before reaching the edge of the clearing, they dismounted and crept to trees where they had a clear view of the cabin.

"I don't see any movement." Seth strained as he studied the cracks between the logs for shadows shifting inside. "And no horses."

"They may have hidden the horses. If they're in there, they're probably waiting for us to come looking. I imagine they'll be ready."

"We need some kind of decoy to draw them out. Make them show their presence." Seth gripped the tree tighter to still his urge to charge forward, rifle blazing.

"Any ideas?" Samuel looked to him.

Not an army charge, but maybe a direct approach would be best. "How about if I call out and get them talking?"

Samuel gave him a look. "You think they'll answer you, just like that?"

He shrugged. "Think it'll hurt anything?"

His brother was quiet for a long moment. "What about if one of us sneaks around behind the cabin to look in between the cracks."

"They probably have one watching from the back and one from the front."

Samuel tipped his head. "Maybe. I'll go around back and be ready with a gun while you call out. That way we'll have them covered if they try something."

"Good. Make a whippoorwill cry when you're ready."

"Got it." Samuel moved like a shadow as he shifted from tree to tree toward the position he needed.

He'd disappeared in the shadows of the woods by the time the three-beat bird call sounded. Time to take action.

Seth positioned the rifle in his shoulder and inhaled a breath to call out. "Hello in the cabin."

Quiet filled the air, all animal sounds ceasing. A faint noise drifted from the cabin, like a shuffling. Hopefully he didn't imagine the sound.

When there was still no response, he raised his voice even louder. "Burke. Hackney. We've come for the woman and boy."

"Then come an' get 'em." The voice was muffled but definitely came from inside the building. It didn't sound like Burke's command. It must have been Hackney. Odd, since the other man seemed to prefer leading. Maybe he was occupied with holding Rachel and Andy at gunpoint.

Anger rose in his throat again. "Send them out and we won't hurt you." Although if they injured a hair on the heads of the woman and boy he loved, he'd personally come back and tear these blackguards apart.

Forgive. The thought caught him short, an invisible hand planting on his chest to still him.

He inhaled a breath. *Please, Lord. Help us get Rachel and Andy back safely. Don't let me do anything I'll regret.*

CHAPTER 24

Of all my nightmares, this is the worst.
~ Rachel

"They're right here for you to come an' get."

Seth cringed as Hackney's voice rang through the clearing. The man wasn't offering other options. Which meant the kidnappers had something planned.

If Burke *was* occupied with their prisoners, maybe Samuel could sneak up to the back and find out what was happening inside.

His brother must have had the same idea, for a movement flashed in the woods behind the cabin. Samuel appeared, ducking low as he darted forward, his rifle clutched in both hands.

Fear surged in Seth's chest, especially as his brother disappeared behind the structure. Should he shift over so he could see if Samuel needed help? Maybe he would be more assistance staying in the front, distracting the men inside. That was probably best.

"If I come get them, I'll need your word you're not gonna shoot me the minute I step into the open."

A cackle filled the air. "I doubt you'd take my word for it anyhow."

The man was right. And from the sound of things, he was probably deranged, too.

Samuel appeared again, darting back toward the woods. He must think it safe to maneuver. A minute later, his brother's soft tread sounded among the leaves as he made his way back.

Seth met him partway. "What did you see?"

His brother's shoulders heaved as he worked to catch his breath. "It's just Hackney. He has Rachel tied at the fireplace. There's no sign of Burke or the boy."

A weight pressed hard on Seth's chest. "Where could they be?"

Samuel shook his head, still breathing hard. "I don't know. But I'm sure there's only the two of them in there."

"Think we can take him out easy enough?"

"Yeah. I'll go around to the back again. I can get a clear shot at his arm or something. As soon as you hear my gun, come running and get Rachel out."

Could it be as easy as that? Yet not easy. They may be able to save Rachel, but Andy was even farther out of reach.

He inhaled a steadying breath. First things first. "Let's do it."

After watching Samuel shift through the shadows until he was out of sight again, Seth moved back to his position near the front. He checked his rifle. Everything was ready.

Samuel darted through the open ground at the back of the cabin, disappearing behind the building again.

Seth tensed to spring forward.

The seconds seemed to take hours. Then finally, a blast ripped through the air.

He sprinted into the clearing, charging toward the door. A muffled scream inside the cabin pushed him faster. *Rachel*. If Samuel's shot hadn't disarmed Hackney, he might retaliate against her.

At last he reached the door, ramming his shoulder into the wood. It gave way under his assault, and he stepped inside, raising his rifle to take aim as he struggled to focus in the dim room.

A scrambling sound pulled his gaze down. Hackney sat sprawled on the floor, reaching for a rifle with his left hand. His right arm hung limp, blood marking the shoulder.

"Don't touch that gun." Seth strode forward and kicked the rifle out of his reach. From the corner of his eye, he saw Rachel, her body facing the cold fireplace. She didn't look injured, but he needed to disarm the brigand before he could focus on her.

"I'll tie him up." Samuel stepped into the room, his own rifle in hand.

Seth scanned the area for something to use for a restraint.

Movement from Rachel snagged his attention. A strip of leather tied in her mouth restrained her words, but she was doing something with her bound wrists.

He moved to her and dropped to his knees, working the gag from her mouth.

She puffed out a breath, then pulled in more air. Finally, she turned those fierce eyes on him. "Cut me loose and you can use my ties on him."

He spun to her. Taking her in with his gaze, every brave, beautiful bit of her. In two strides he was by her side, laying aside his gun. Brushing the loose hair from her face, cradling her cheeks in his hands. Filling himself with the sight and touch of her. "Are you hurt?"

She shook her head, red tinging her eyes even as her chin kept its firm resolve. "I'm fine. Cut me free so we can go after Andy."

Her words sliced through the relief flooding him. He pulled out his knife and cut the leather holding her to the metal bar in the fireplace. "Where was Burke taking him?"

"Who's Burke? The man called himself Henry."

Seth shot her a glance before moving to the rope tied around her wrists. "Was he a big man with dark hair?"

"Yes."

He raised his voice for the man moaning on the floor to hear. "Where'd your friend take the boy?"

A louder groan was his only response.

The sound cut short when Samuel kicked him. "Where'd they go?"

Hackney snarled. "You'll never get him back."

They'd have to track the pair. Anything Hackney said probably wouldn't be reliable anyway.

Within another moment, he had Rachel freed. He touched the bright red indentions the leather left on her wrist, his body aching with the pain she'd endured. He couldn't help wrapping an arm around her back and pressing a kiss to the softness of her hair. "Stay put for another minute while we get him tied up."

She nodded, turning her gaze to meet his. He couldn't miss the glimmer of fear there, and it spurred him onward. "We'll find Andy." He stroked his thumb over her wrist. "Don't worry." An impossible request, surely, but he said it anyway.

He took up his rifle again and held the gun on Hackney while Samuel bound him. "Think it's safe to leave him tied here while we ride on, or should we go ahead and put him out of his misery now?" He couldn't help that last part, and Hackney blanched just like he'd expected.

"I'll make sure he won't get loose while we're gone." Samuel finished tying his hands and hoisted the man over to the fireplace. "If you'll please step away, Miz Rachel, I'll give this low-life your spot."

She scrambled backward, then pushed up to her feet.

Seth reached for her elbow, easing her back a little farther. She looked up at him, and he took the chance he'd once thought he might never get. "I'm sorry, Rachel. So sorry."

A frown flicked across her face. "For what?"

Everything. "For approaching these men in the first place. For letting you run into the woods. For not coming to find you sooner."

She looked away, a muscle in her jaw flexing. "Let's just find my boy."

The knot in his chest tightened. She held him responsible. As he did, too. *Lord, forgive me, please. Help Rachel forgive me, too.*

And more than anything, help us get Andy back.

~

Burke didn't seem to be trying to disguise his trail. Not that it would be easy to hide hoof prints in the woods after a rain, but when they opened out on the rocky area that descended gradually, it sure didn't seem to Seth that the man kept to places where his tracks wouldn't show.

Which meant he must have expected Hackney to stop them at the cabin. Burke was probably moving quickly so he could get back to do whatever he had planned for Rachel.

The thought churned the bile in Seth's belly, and he pressed a hand to Rachel's arms where they wrapped around his waist. She sat behind him in the saddle, and their headlong ride through the rocky terrain kept her clinging to him. He was pretty sure she wouldn't sit so close otherwise, but the feel of her gave him strength to keep moving.

His gelding was breathing hard, so Seth reined in at the base of the mountain they'd traversed the day before. "Let's let the horses rest before the climb."

"Where do you think he's heading?" Rachel's breath brushed his neck as she spoke.

"My instinct says he's going to the Indians we met with a couple days ago, but I can't for the life of me figure why. You think he's planning to trade him as a captive?" Samuel sat with his arms crossed in front of him, wrists resting on the saddle.

Rachel's body tensed, her arms tightening around him. "Why would he do that? What would they do with him?"

"I don't know." He hated to start a new round of fears churning in her mind. "Let's just keep following and see where he goes."

He looked to his brother. "Ready to move on?"

Samuel nodded and nudged his horse up the incline.

They made it over the rocky peak without mishap, passing their campsite at the base of the other side. He couldn't help but remember sitting under the stars with Rachel as they watched for signs of Indians. She'd shared a huge part of herself with him—her story. He could only pray they could find that same openness again.

Except this time, there would be no secrets between them. No past hovering over their shoulders. Lord willing, they'd be able to move forward in a new life together with Andy.

But they had a long way to go before they reached that happy future. *Help us, Lord. Please.*

Finally, they reached the woods where the Indians had forced their escort two days before.

The dim light under the trees gave the place an unnerving feel. Or maybe that was his memories. Rachel, too, tightened her grip around his waist. He closed his hand over hers, a silent reminder that they would face this together.

They had to slow the horses to a walk as the trees drew closer together. They followed the game trail, yet they needed to watch both sides of the path to see if Burke rode away from the more traveled route.

He pointed to the right edge and turned to Samuel. "You watch the ground on this side and I'll watch the left."

"Got it."

Now he could push his gelding into a faster walk, and he kept his ears tuned to any noise that might signal someone around them. He'd never forget how soundlessly the Indians had faded from the trees before.

After what felt like half an hour, Samuel called in a low tone, "There. Are those tracks?"

Seth jerked his gaze to the right side of the trail. "I see it." He scanned the stirred leaves for sign that it was definitely a horse that made the marks. Even if it was a horse, how could they know for sure whether it was Burke or the Indians?

He glanced up at Samuel. "Think we should follow it?"

His brother's brow drew low as he studied the area. "It's hard to know for sure. The leaves have definitely been turned today, and the animal was going the same direction we are. That makes me think there's a good chance it's him."

Seth nudged his gelding forward. "Let's see where it leads."

They seemed to be going deeper into the darkness, and the hairs on the back of his neck tingled the farther they went. *Lord, should I do something different? Show me how to find Andy. How to keep Rachel safe.*

He shouldn't have brought her into danger like this. He had a feeling she wouldn't have been happy to stay in safety, but he should have at least tried.

Through the trees far ahead, a lighter area appeared, like that of a clearing. Was that the open land the Indians had led them across before? Unless his senses were off, they were on the wrong side of the game trail for this to be the same area.

What then?

As they neared, something about the opening seemed odd. He slowed his gelding as he strained to see. Were those Indian lodges out there? They sure looked like it. This must be the camp those braves were leading them away from. And Burke's trail led straight to this place.

"Why would he take my son to the Indians?" Rachel's voice came out in a harsh whisper.

"That's a good question. Maybe in trade for something? Or maybe to get in their good graces." He reined in his gelding, as did Samuel. They needed to develop a plan before going farther.

"What would they do with him?" This time he could hear a bit of fear in her whispered tone.

That fear pulsed through him, too. He'd heard stories of what Indians did with their white captives, but they'd always seemed far too outlandish to be possible. Surely, they wouldn't—couldn't—do those heinous acts to a boy like Andy. *God, let us be in time.*

Seth made a decision. "I'm gonna move closer on foot and try to see what's going on."

Before he could shift to get off the saddle without disturbing Rachel, she slid down. "I'm going with you."

He dismounted and handed his reins to her. "The Indians may be watching for us. I'll have a better chance of staying out of sight by myself."

She took the reins and handed them to Samuel, who had also dismounted. "I'm going too, Seth."

Her tone—although spoken low—left no doubt of her determination.

He let out a sigh as he met her gaze. "Stay close."

"I'll be your shadow." Her moss-colored eyes held such purpose, such...he couldn't even define it. Intelligence maybe. But more than that. The special quality that was Rachel herself.

His sudden urge to take her in his arms was too much to ignore. He wrapped a hand around her arm and brushed a kiss across her forehead.

He expected her to pull away, maybe even jump back and slap him. But she didn't, and when he did ease back, her eyes had drifted shut, but slowly raised to look at him.

It made him love her all the more.

He stroked her arm once with his thumb. "Let's go get our boy."

Then he turned and headed toward the clearing before he could see her reaction to the words.

CHAPTER 25

God, for once, let my instincts follow Your guidance.
~ Seth

This man had the power to shake Rachel to her core. Knocking her off guard and making her want more, even when she should keep him farther than arm's length away.

As they moved to a better scouting position, she struggled to focus, to hone her attention on stealing forward. Being soundless required shifting into a deep awareness. An intense concentration.

They each took up position behind a sturdy tree where they had a view of the cluster of teepees. All seemed quiet inside, as though the entire camp was empty. Had the Indians left for some reason? Gone on a hunt? A few animal skins were stretched on frames in various stages of the tanning process.

A movement flicked on the far side of the group. A horse's tail? Yes. A chestnut rump similar to the horse Burke had ridden. Although, half the horses in this country may also share a similar look from this distance.

An Indian brave appeared in the midst of the camp, striding from one lodge to another. He ducked through the leather flap and disappeared inside.

All settled into quiet until the sound of voices drifted toward them. They were the deep baritone of men and seemed to grow louder, yet the words were spoken in a foreign tongue.

Then another voice sounded, one impossible to mistake. Burke's lazy drawl held an angry bite.

Rachel's body tensed at the sound of him, the man who'd bound her. Placed his vile hands on her. Pressed his foul lips against her. His voice rose above the others, but she couldn't make out his words.

Another tone spoke, quieter than Burke's, yet forceful.

A second later, the door flap where the Indian had entered was thrust aside. Henry Burke charged through it, his face contorted in anger. Behind him, he yanked another form.

Her heart clutched. *Andy.* She gripped the tree for support. Strained to see her son's face. Every muscle within her wanted to run to him. Jerk him away from that knave and take him far, far away from here.

"Don't, Rachel. Wait until the right time." Seth's words barely penetrated the pain inside her. Andy looked so scared as that worthless kidnapper jerked him forward, marching toward the chestnut horse.

Indians surged out of the teepee behind them—braves, every one. Some carried rifles and none looked happy. They tracked behind Burke, an unfriendly escort out of their camp.

But he was leaving with her son.

If he got the boy mounted, they could disappear again before she and Seth could remount. She couldn't let them get away.

"Easy." Seth's calming tone brushed against her as his strong hands closed around her upper arms. When had he moved behind her tree?

"We can't let them get away. We have to go *now.*" She shifted her shoulders to wiggle out of his hold.

His grip tightened. "If we charge out there now, the Indians might take us all captive. That could make it impossible to get Andy away."

She tried to let the words penetrate. Tried to see the wisdom he seemed to believe so firmly. But as she watched Burke position his horse to mount, one hand still clutching Andy like a shield, her chest ached as though it was being sliced open.

Seth's arms wrapped around her, and all she could do was hold onto them, a sob building in her chest.

The sound of Burke's voice drifted toward them again, rising in anger as he paused to look back at the Indians. It was still impossible to understand the words—he spoke their language—but the venom in his stance was clear.

He leaned forward as though spitting toward the Indians, and Rachel sucked in a breath. Surely he hadn't.

The braves charged forward, swarming Burke with a surge of enraged passion. She struggled to keep her gaze on Andy. Not to lose him in the melee.

The natives seemed not to notice the boy at all, twisting Burke's grasp from the boy as they clutched the man from all sides.

Andy ducked away from them, disappearing among the buckskin-clad bodies. Her heart surged into her throat, and she screamed a desperate cry as she jerked out of Seth's arms, sprinting with every bit of strength she had to reach her boy. She had to get him out before the Indians trampled him.

But then Andy appeared, crouched in a ball as he rolled out of the crowd. He lay still for a heartbeat—a horrible moment when it seemed he might be truly hurt. Then he sprang to his feet.

"Andy!" She screamed his name as she closed the distance between them.

A shout sounded above the din of Indian voices. She was two lengths away from her son when the men reached him.

One brave grabbed Andy's arm, yanking him to a stop. Andy fought against the man's grip, but with his hands still tied in front of him, he was no match for the massive Indian.

Two more braves sprinted past the man and boy, both with their rifles raised to fire—pointed at her.

She jerked to a halt, not two strides from one of the men. Painfully aware of how empty her hands were, she raised them away from her sides to show she wouldn't resist. At least, not yet. Not until her odds were better.

The second gunman paused to the side, his rifle pointed beyond her.

Seth. Had he followed her out into the open? Were they both now useless to Andy? All three of them captives? How foolish she'd been to dart out like this. Seth was right. If only she'd waited, not let her fear overpower her good sense. Hopefully Samuel was watching so he could look for a chance to get them out.

Another Indian called from the camp. The group swarming Burke had quieted some, so it was easier to hear this man's voice. He spoke in the Indian tongue and must have been talking to the one holding Andy, for the man pushed her son forward—toward her.

She studied the brave's face for a sign of what he intended, but his tanned skin and sharp features held no expression.

He and Andy reached her, and the man pushed her son into her chest. It took everything in her not to wrap her boy in her arms and cling to him.

"Ma." Andy's voice met her ear, filling her with warmth that was almost crippling.

"Hold on, son."

She had to figure out what these Indians were doing so she didn't get Seth, her son, or herself shot. With gradual movements, she eased her hands around her son's shoulders, keeping her eyes on the two Indians in front of her. The one still held his rifle pointed at them, but the man who'd brought Andy to her had released the boy and stepped back. Something softened in his eyes as he watched her. Was he truly allowing the reunion she craved?

She closed her hands around her son, pulling him close. Breathing him in. "Oh, Andy." Tears burned up her throat, stinging her eyes. If the Indians weren't watching so closely, she would have let herself cry. Her son was safe and back in her arms.

"I'm all right, Ma." He must have realized how close she was to breaking down.

She sniffed back the tears and straightened, only loosing her hold enough to allow him to straighten as well. A quick sideways glance showed the Indian to her right did have his rifle pointed at Seth.

What would happen to them now? No matter what, she'd not allow her son to be parted from her again.

~

Seth raised his gaze from the reunion of mother and son across the clearing to the place where the Indians had swarmed Burke. The group was disseminating now, with one man leading away the horse. Two more bent over Burke's limp body.

The sight tightened the knot in Seth's gut. The man had been evil, a fact made clear by his kidnapping and what he'd planned for Rachel. He wasn't sure what he thought about this method of demise, though. At least Rachel and Andy were safe from him forever.

Now they had another obstacle to face. His fingers itched to reach for the knife at his waist, but he kept his hands out where the brave holding the rifle on him could see them both.

An older Indian who'd been standing back from the fray strode toward them. Feathers hung from both his braids, and his buckskin tunic was heavily beaded. Maybe he was a leader among the band. He walked with a bit of hunch, as though he was older than he looked, or maybe sick.

He drew near and stopped where he could see them all clearly. He spoke to Seth, but pointed to Rachel. "This boy mother?" His words were heavily accented and had that languid quality of a man not quite in his full strength.

Seth nodded. "Yes. She is his mother."

The man pointed to Seth. "You father?"

He wanted with everything in him to be able to nod and confirm the question, but he didn't have that right. Not yet. He shook his head and pointed to himself. "Friend."

The man nodded, then turned to look at the Indians still bent over Burke's lifeless form. "Henry Burke not friend." He turned back to meet Seth's gaze with a glare. "Not friend to Indian. Not friend to boy and mother." He motioned toward Rachel and Andy with a dramatic wave.

"He make bad trade before, but this more bad. Want trade boy for much furs." The Indian looked back at Andy, and his gaze seemed to roam over the lad. "Want boy to take place of my son who dies."

He looked back at Seth and touched his own chest. "Standing Horse no want boy from other mother. No want trade much furs. Give boy back to you." He extended both arms with a flourish, as though presenting a gift. "You ride in peace."

Seth struggled to take in the words, struggled to fill in the gaps with something that made sense. The man was sending them on their way?

The Indian motioned for the two braves to lower their guns, which they did, although both still held their weapons in both hands, ready to aim again should the situation require.

Seth needed to say something to the man. Express his gratitude so they could leave this place.

Rachel beat him to it. "Thank you, Standing Horse, for returning my son to me." Her voice rang clear as she stood with her back straight and her chin high, her arms still around Andy. This woman was a match for any man, white skin or red.

The brave nodded, accepting her gratitude as though he understood the words.

Seth raised a hand. "We leave you in peace." He met the Indian's gaze, receiving a nod of his own. Then Seth looked to each of the other Indians, letting his eyes speak his peaceful intentions. The last thing he wanted was to anger one of them now.

The older man raised a hand in farewell, then stepped backward.

Seth reached for Rachel's arm and tugged her toward him. She followed his lead, turning away from the Indians. She kept Andy tucked firmly under her arm as they walked back toward the trees.

The burn of a dozen stares heated the skin on his back, but he forced himself to take measured steps. Not to look over his shoulder.

You've done it, Lord. How is it you've brought us through this mess completely unscathed?

After stepping into the shadow of the woods, he pulled Rachel closer, slipping his arm around her back. "You hurt at all, Andy?"

"No, sir. Just ready to have my hands free." The boy spoke in a low tone to match the one Seth had used.

"We'll take care of that as soon as we're—"

A movement shifted ahead of them, and Seth lunged forward, blocking Rachel and Andy from this new threat. A man stepped from behind a tree, and Seth had a hand on his knife before his mind registered Samuel's form.

He growled as he struggled to slow his racing heart. "You almost had a blade through your gullet, little brother."

Samuel's chuckle drifted nearer as he strode forward. "I figured you heard me. You must be getting sloppy, big brother."

"I didn't think you'd be hiding behind a tree when we could have used an extra rifle out there." He took his brother's proffered hand and pulled him into a quick hug. Now that his heart rate was settling, the relief of having all four of them together—and safe—was making his legs shaky.

While Samuel greeted Rachel and Andy, Seth cut the boy's bonds loose, then gathered his and Rachel's rifles from where they'd dropped them behind the tree.

"Let's get the horses and head out of here." He handed Rachel's gun to his brother, since she looked like she wasn't turning loose of her son any time soon.

Not that he could blame her.

Within minutes they were mounted again. Rachel snugged behind him and Andy behind Samuel.

"The horses have had a few minutes to rest, so we can move faster now." He motioned for Samuel to take the lead and fell in behind him.

Within minutes they'd found the game trail and were moving at a swift trot. Afternoon had passed through the last few hours, and the dusky light of evening was settling in the air as they finally exited the trees.

Samuel reined down to a walk and motioned for Seth to guide his horse alongside. "You wanna camp at the base of the mountain where we did before?"

They'd traversed this cliff a couple of times now, so it would be a little easier to do in the dark, but still not safe. He rested his hand on Rachel's where she held his middle, then looked over his shoulder to catch her at the edge of his vision. "What do you think?"

She didn't answer right away, a sure sign she wasn't eager to stop. He'd like to get farther away from the awful ordeal, too. But he also didn't want to risk their lives or their animals on that steep, rocky terrain.

"I guess we'd better make camp." Her tone sounded resigned, not at all eager.

He stroked the back of her hand with his thumb. "We'll take turns on a watch."

"All right." Her voice was closer to his ear, her tone softer. The words meant for him, and they slid another thread of longing through him.

If she came to sit with him again tonight, he'd tell her how he truly felt. Hopefully, she wouldn't run away again. But if she did, this time he'd go with her.

CHAPTER 26

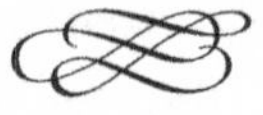

This purging...who would have thought that I'd be stronger for it?
~ Rachel

It was hard to believe Rachel had lain in this exact spot, staring up at these same stars, just days before. And once again, she couldn't sleep for the day's events whirling through her mind.

Seth had taken the first watch tonight, with Samuel planning to spell him partway through. She'd not even volunteered to take a shift. Her nerves were still so raw from almost losing her son. But lying beside him now, listening to the steady in and out of his breathing, was slowly calming her spirit.

Thank you for protecting him, Lord. For protecting us both. And thank you for Seth. Samuel, too, of course. But Seth had been her rock through the entire ordeal. From the moment he crashed through the door to take control of Hackney to the one where he'd jumped in front of her and Andy to protect them as his brother stepped from behind a tree. She'd never thought she could trust a man again, especially not someone as impetuous and emotional as Seth, but her heart wanted so badly to believe in him.

Could she? Even if he had left his vices behind, only a short time had passed. Not even *he* could say for sure that he'd never succumb to temptation again. One time so easily slid into two, and the fangs of addiction took control again.

Still, her arms longed for his touch, her spirit his nearness, if only just for tonight. Creeping from the makeshift bedroll they'd created from the scant supplies Seth and Samuel had brought, she crawled toward where Seth sat.

He extended a hand to her, as she somehow knew he would, and she settled against his arm, allowing him to pull her against his side. The awful events of the day had wiped away her ire, and now she owed him an apology.

Before she could work up the words, his husky vibrato warmed the air between them. "Can't sleep?"

"I can't seem to stop listening for Andy's breathing."

Seth eased out a breath. "I know what you mean. I've never been so scared in my life. I don't think I'll ever forgive myself for letting you stay out in the woods so long. Or for approaching that cabin in the first place."

There was the perfect lead-in. She should take it before she lost her nerve. "I'm sorry about leaving camp like that. For getting so angry and stalking out. I should have had more control."

He didn't answer right away, and the warmth of his breath heated her cheek as he looked at her. "I thought it might be more than anger that made you leave like that. Maybe a little fear."

How was he able to look into her like that? This man knew her better than any other person. Maybe even better than she knew herself. She would have never expected that to be a comfortable feeling—being so vulnerable before him—but he didn't abuse his knowledge. And it made her want to be honest with him. To open up a little more.

"You're right. I was afraid." She inhaled a steadying breath. "Richard stopped gambling and drinking once. It lasted three months.

He started helping in the fields again, and even tried to get to know his son better. I thought maybe that awful mess was behind us.

"Then one day he disappeared again. He didn't come home for two days, and when he did, he had a black eye and sutures closing a cut across the back of his hand. He was drunk and angry. I'd never seen him that furious. I made the foolish mistake of confronting him." The memories flooded back in a wave, catching her almost before she had a chance to shore herself up against them. A sob slipped through, as she thought of the little bundle she never had the chance to hold. Even now, her hands ached from the loss. Her heart squeezing so much she could barely draw breath.

Seth pulled her closer, and another sob pushed out. The tears burning her eyes threatened to break through. She couldn't let them. Not now of all times.

But for once, they wouldn't be stopped.

A hot drop plunged down her cheek, opening the trail for another. More tears slid down her other cheek. The sobs wouldn't be held back now.

Seth had both hands around her, one stroking her arm, the other brushing the hair from her face. "Cry, honey. It's good to cry."

His words made no sense, but her body seemed to believe him, for she couldn't make herself stop. She did her best to keep the sobs quiet. The last thing she wanted was to wake Andy so he could witness her emotional collapse.

As her body purged itself, her mind replayed the awful day she'd lost the baby. She'd not even let herself cry then, even when her heart was being wrenched in two, the separation of the child that should have been hers to love.

By the time the tears waned, Seth's sleeve was a soggy mess where she leaned against him. Her own cuffs weren't much better from wiping away her blubber. A final sob slipped through as she lifted from his shoulder. "I'm sorry." Her whisper came out hoarse, still choked with emotion. "I don't usually let myself cry."

He reached up to finger a strand of her hair. "My mama always said tears were healing for a woman. She was a strong lady, but when she needed to cry, she did. I hated to see her red nose and puffy eyes when I was little, but by the time I was about Andy's age, I realized she was always better for it afterward."

An image of him as a twelve-year-old boy skittered through her mind, tugging a smile even though her face felt tight from emotion. She wiped the rest of the moisture from under her eyes, then eased out a long breath. With the spent air, she let go of the tensions from the day. And maybe some of the tensions from past years. Her shoulders sagged from the loss, as if she'd been using the strain to prop herself up.

She finally worked up the nerve to look at Seth, and the sweet expression shimmering in his eyes made her want to crawl into his embrace again.

"Feel any better?" One corner of his mouth tugged upward.

"I do actually. Your mama must be a smart woman." And strong, too. Stronger than her own mother.

He nodded, his gaze wandering off into the distance. "I'm not sure any of us appreciated her enough until we moved away. At least, that's the way it was for me."

Then he turned his focus back to her, all trace of sweet reminiscence slipping from his expression. "Rachel, I don't think I can ever quite put into words how sorry I am for how hard things were for you. And Andy. I need you to know something, though."

His gaze was more earnest than she'd ever seen it. "I'm not the same man your husband was. We've made some of the same mistakes, but there's one very big difference with me." When he paused, she drew only a tiny breath so she wouldn't miss his next words.

"God healed me. He took away the addiction—the cravings for drink and the urge to win. He wiped it all away. I can't even stomach the thought of those things now."

He took her hand with his free one, and determination marked the change in his tone. "I understand you're not sure if you can trust me. You've been hurt, maybe even worse than I know. You *should* be careful before trusting another man with your heart. With your and Andy's safety.

"But, Rachel, with God's help, I *will* prove trustworthy. I will grow into the man you need. I may not always get things right, but you can have faith that I'll be striving to do what's best for you and Andy. You have my word."

Tears sprang to her eyes again, and she sniffed them back. Yet her defenses were so weak now. "Seth…" What could she even say to him? He was right that she couldn't trust again, even though she wanted to believe him more than she wanted her next breath.

He released her hand and moved his fingers up to cradle her cheek. "It's all right, Rachel. Take as much time as you need. Just know that when we reach Canada and find your brother, I'll not be walking away from you. I'll be there every time you need me. Whenever you're ready, all you have to do is look up, and you'll see me waiting." As his mouth tugged into a grin, his teeth glimmered in the moonlight.

He wore that rogue's smile, the one that made her heart flutter. She laid her hand over his on her cheek, then turned her face to plant a kiss on his palm. "Thank you."

And she meant the words from the bottom of her heart. The future looked hazy just now, but having Seth to lean on—even if just for tonight—was a gift from God.

Thank you, Lord.

~

"What should we do with Hackney?" Seth finally spoke the question he knew his brother had been brooding over as much as he had.

They were nearing the cabin. Again. The feeling of returning to this place of dread had been hovering over him for the last hour or so. Probably, they all felt the same way.

"I don't think the kidnapping was his idea." Rachel's soft voice drifted over his shoulder from where she was tucked behind him.

Could she possibly harbor anything but hatred for the man? He'd held her at gunpoint while her son was taken away. The abduction may not have been Hackney's idea, but he'd sure gone along with the plan.

"He's injured." Samuel's voice held its usual low tenor, but a bit of regret laced the words. Pulling a trigger aimed at flesh and blood had to have been hard. Yet without that injury, there may have been a lot more bloodshed before they could get Rachel away.

"He wasn't as rough with me as the big man was." Andy spoke up from behind Samuel's saddle.

Seth forced himself not to show his body's response to the words. Even the boy was going to champion this despoiler? "So you think we should find him a doctor and turn him loose?" There may have been too much anger in his tone, but had they all forgotten what the man had done?

"That's not what I said." Samuel's tone held a warning. "He might need a doctor. And then I guess we should see if there's any law in this area."

Seth sighed. He didn't want to be vengeful, but the man had taken part in kidnapping Rachel and Andy, then planned to assault Rachel in the worst way. There was no chance Seth would let him walk away with no recourse. "How far away do you think we are from Simeon's place? Have we crossed into Canada yet?"

"Based on the map Elias drew, I think we will soon. Maybe another week to Simeon's, possibly less, depending on the terrain."

"Good." It would be a relief to be among friends again. Not only for the reunion with their brother and sister, but also to have Rachel and Andy in safety and among people who would help nurture and care for them. Maybe Rachel would get a chance to see how a loving family could interact. Because he was pretty sure from their letters that both Simeon and Noelle had healthy, loving families there in the Canadian mountains.

Light through the trees ahead showed the clearing approaching quickly. Seth reined in his horse. "Think we should check things out before we ride in there? We tied him pretty well, but anything could happen."

"I'll take a look through the back like I did before." Samuel stopped beside them and tapped Andy's leg. "Can you hold this gelding for me?"

"Yes, sir." Andy slid down and took the reins while Samuel dismounted.

As his brother crept around to the rear of the cabin to peek through the cracks between logs, Seth helped Rachel dismount, then climbed down and positioned himself where he'd have a clear shot should the need arise.

Samuel appeared from the trees behind the building, leaning low as he darted forward, rifle braced in both hands. He disappeared in the shadows behind the structure.

Seth barely breathed as he held his body rigid, gun poised, finger hovering over the trigger.

Then Samuel appeared around the side of the cabin, walking upright and looking their way with a grim expression. "Seth, come take a look."

The knot in his belly jerked tight as foreboding slid over him. Had the man gotten himself loose? How could that be possible?

CHAPTER 27

~ SETH

This wasn't the way I had planned, yet I lean on Your leading, Lord.
~ Seth

"Stay here with the horses." Seth sent Rachel a meaningful look, and she nodded, wrapping her arm around her son's shoulders. A possessive hold.

He used long strides to cover the ground to the cabin, and his brother waited for him by the closed door. Samuel's mouth held a tight line as he watched Seth approach.

"Is he gone?" Seth studied his brother's eyes for an answer.

"Dead. Looks like he had a knife we didn't find."

Dead? Seth blinked, trying to catch up with the unexpected turn. "If he had a knife, why wouldn't he have just cut himself loose?"

Samuel shook his head. "I don't know. Not sure if you wanna go in, but this is definitely not something the others should see."

He followed his brother inside, and a single look at the man slumped over his bound arms, sitting in a pool of his own blood, was all Seth needed. He turned away, his heart aching. He'd wanted

Hackney punished, but not like this. Not at his own hand, sitting in his blood, far from anyone who might care about him.

"I suppose we should bury him. And maybe see if there's any correspondence that might tell us of family we should notify." A glance around the room didn't reveal much.

Darkness was falling in earnest by the time they'd dug a decent grave and piled rocks over the freshly churned ground. They stood in front of the plot, and Samuel prayed for God to have mercy on this man's soul. It was all they could do.

A numbness had fallen over the group, but they all agreed they'd rather push on to their previous camp before stopping for the night. This place held too many memories—some that may turn into nightmares. Besides, they needed to see if Rachel and Andy's horses were still in the area.

They found Hackney's horse tied in the woods, then loaded the animal with food they'd garnered from the cabin. Finally, they were off again, winding their way through the trees. Rachel's cheek rested on his shoulder for much of the way, and he could only be thankful for the trust she placed in him with that act.

By the time they reached the camp, her steady breathing in his ear proved she must have given in to her exhaustion. After the strain of the day before, then being up so long into the night, she had every right to be weary.

Samuel's gelding raised a nicker as they reined in, and when a responding whinny sounded through the woods, Rachel lifted her head from his shoulder.

"Where are we?" Her voice held a sleepy scratch that tightened a longing inside him.

"We're back at camp. I'll slide off, then help you down."

She straightened, pulling her warmth away from his back, a loss that went deeper than a mere layer of his skin.

He dismounted, then reached up for her. Part of him didn't expect she'd allow him to help her down, but she rested her hands on his shoulders and let him lift her by the waist.

She must have been weak from sleep, for when her feet touched the ground, she kept sinking.

"Whoa, there." He gripped her waist tighter, pulling her back up and toward him.

She sank against his chest, utterly spent. "I'm sorry, Seth." Her soft voice, muffled in the cloth of his shirt, was almost too light to hear.

"Nothing to be sorry about." He kept a sturdy arm around her, then used his other hand to stroke her back. "Nothing at all."

Holding her here, soft and completely pliant, was like nothing he'd ever felt. Strength normally resonated from her, even in her moments of exhaustion. Yet now, the primary feeling he sensed in her was trust. And exhaustion.

The former caused a burn in his throat that he wouldn't deny even if he wanted to. Only God could make him into the man she needed, and maybe the Father above was doing just that.

~

The next few days on the trail seemed rather dull after the turmoil of the kidnapping, but Seth would prefer boring and safe any day—at least, when it came to Rachel and her son. Andy had been quiet for the first day but was working back out of his shell much quicker than when they'd first met him, and Rachel seemed to have shed a few defensive layers, too. He couldn't get enough of this new openness about her. This lightness.

She didn't seem immune to his touch either, which was better news still. Maybe soon she would be ready for another kiss. But he'd committed himself not to rush it. Only when she was ready to trust him fully.

"I think we may be getting close." Samuel studied the map as they paused for a quick midday meal during the fifth day back on the trail.

"Really? What should we be watching for?" Andy peered over his arm as he munched a bite of cold cheese and hamsteak. The supplies they'd brought from the kidnapper's cabin were nothing short of delicious.

"This map doesn't give landmarks for where we turn, but the letter from our brother says we'll come to a cabin tucked in a little valley surrounded by mountains on three sides. That cabin belongs to his wife's brother."

"Does your brother live near there?"

"A few hours' away in a big valley. Simeon's cabin sits on one corner, and my sister, Noelle, and her family live near them. There're some other people nearby, too. The aunt and uncle of Simeon's wife, I think."

"Are they close to town?" Rachel's question might have sounded innocent to anyone else, but he didn't even have to glance at her to know she was worried. How would she ever live near a fort as she planned, with all manner of men coming and going?

Hopefully she'd find Simeon's little valley more to her liking, but if she didn't, he'd go where she wanted to. He'd not completely made up his mind to live permanently where his brother and sister had settled anyway. But it'd be nice to stay a while and get reacquainted.

Samuel straightened and folded the map. "You folks ready to mount up? I think our path will level out for a while."

Back on the trail, travel was much easier than the rocky path around the mountain they'd ridden that morning. A peak rose up on their right, so steep and rocky it looked almost like a wall had grown up in the midst of the flatland they traveled.

"Aren't you glad we don't have to climb that?" He sent Rachel a grin.

She raised her gaze to the top of the precipice. "Quite." Then she brought her focus back to him. "I'm getting better at heights, though."

"Ho, there." Samuel threw out a hand to stop them as he jerked his reins tight. "Move back."

Seth jerked his focus to see what had alerted his brother even as he reined his horse backward to get out of Samuel's way.

A cabin.

When they'd all backed out of view of the structure, Seth looked to his brother. "Do you think that's the one Simeon wrote about? His brother-in-law's place?"

Samuel glanced up at the cliff wall as if he could see the cabin beyond. "It could be. One of us should check to make sure before we all make our presence known."

"I'll go see." Seth nudged his horse toward the path they'd been traveling.

"Wait, Seth." Rachel's voice held enough fear, he reined in his gelding.

Turning to meet her troubled gaze, he let her see his earnestness. "I'll be careful, Rachel. If this isn't the man we're looking for, I'll come back straightaway, and we'll move on."

Her lower lip slid between her teeth for a moment. Finally, she nodded. "Be careful."

A noise drifted through the air, calling his attention back toward the cabin. It sounded like the steady *thwak* of an ax on wood. He guided his gelding forward, watching for the first glimpse of activity ahead.

The man came into view first, lean and sinewy with his shirt sleeves rolled up as he heaved an ax into a log. The cabin appeared next, a sturdy structure, bigger than Burke's had been. At least two rooms by his guess.

Another movement snagged Seth's gaze. A small figure shifted near the cabin's door. A child? The dark head lifted, revealing...yes, a child. But older than he'd thought. Maybe ten or eleven.

The man saw him then and spun to face him. Seth rode forward, keeping his posture relaxed to show he was no threat. About twenty strides away from the building, he reined in.

"Howdy." The man wiped his brow on his sleeve and settled an arm around the shoulder of the girl who'd come to stand by him. "We don't get much company. Are you headed toward one of the forts?" He looked about Seth's age, maybe a couple years older. Just right for the man they sought. And his expression seemed pleasant enough.

Seth offered a friendly smile. "Actually, I'm looking for my brother who lives in this area. Do you know Simeon Grant?"

The man's look changed in an instant, splitting in a wide grin. "I do. Are you Seth or Samuel?"

Relief washed through Seth's chest like a river breaking through a dam. They'd made it. "Seth. Does that mean you're Joseph Malcom?"

"Sure am." The man tucked the girl against him with an affectionate squeeze. "And this is Amelie, our oldest." His gaze moved past Seth. "Where's your brother?" Worry creased his brow.

Seth sent a glance over his shoulder. "Coming behind me. I rode in first to see if we'd found the right place."

Malcom started for the cabin door. "Bring him on. My wife will be eager to feed you both."

Seth turned and nudged his gelding into a jog back toward the others. Hopefully Rachel would be glad for female company.

Within minutes, he led the entire weary party toward the cabin. It was almost too much to fathom that they'd reached the end of their journey. Simeon and Noelle both lived less than half a day's ride from here. They could possibly be there tonight.

Thank you, Lord. Only God could be credited for bringing them through the harrowing journey unscathed.

The door flung wide, and Joseph stood in the frame, a young boy in his arms. "We'll put your horses in the corral. I can tie mine outside if you think they'll be a bother." He set the boy on the floor and stepped outside.

They dismounted and followed him around the side of the house, and the man continued talking. "Your brother and sister live a few hours away, so we'd be glad to offer shelter for the night." He turned to them with a grin. "I'm sure we'll have time later to get acquainted, but my wife would love the company as long as you'll stay."

Seth glanced at Rachel to see if she was uneasy at the thought of sleeping here. She met his gaze with a tiny shrug. Did that mean she trusted Joseph Malcom? Or maybe she was placing her trust in Seth's decision. A weighty charge.

He looked to his brother, who gave a faint nod. All right then.

He turned back to Joseph. "We appreciate the offer. We'll happily sleep on the floor if you have the space. Otherwise, we can camp on the trail."

They reached the corral and Joseph stepped to the gate. "We've one extra bed and plenty of open floor. My wife happens to be the best cook in the Canadian territory, so I hope you're hungry."

The words tightened the empty places in Seth's belly. A real dinner and a sleep under a real roof. It sounded like heaven for his weary bones.

~

It had been so long since Rachel had spoken with a woman, it appeared she'd completely lost the ability. Each time Mrs. Malcom sent her a smile or asked a question in her lovely French accent, Rachel's tongue tied itself in knots, stumbling over answers so much she ended up cutting her responses short.

Monti—as she insisted on being called—was graceful about Rachel's lack, but it didn't make the episodes less embarrassing. The couple's daughter turned out to be only a year younger than Andy, and the two watched each other with curious gazes as they all lingered over the meal Monti had laid out within minutes of their arrival.

As quiet as the girl was, their three-year-old son was vivacious. He babbled on through the meal and while they lingered around the table, keeping Samuel on one side and his father on the other occupied during every spare second.

In short, the meal was lively. Not something she could remember experiencing since she was a girl visiting her friend Emily's home. The conversation and easy laughter flowed so freely, they almost made her want to join in. But for now, she was content to watch the others.

Seth was beside her, and as he finished his meal and sat back in his chair to answer a question about the length of their journey, his hand found hers under the table. Warm and strong, his fingers wove between hers, infusing her with a sturdiness that grounded her.

If he minded her silence, he didn't let on, just glanced at her with a smile every so often. Once or twice he pulled her into the conversation, but he must have sensed her chaotic emotions. And she was more grateful than she could say that he didn't push.

She'd get there in time.

After the meal, Monti led her to the bed chamber she and Andy would share. "I hope this will be comfortable for you." She pushed open the door, revealing a lovely room. The quilt across the bed brightened the chamber with spring colors arranged in the form of flowers.

"This is beautiful." Rachel stepped closer for a better look, although she didn't dare touch. Such fine stitching, although not without the occasional variation, made it clear the crafter had labored over the detail. "Did you sew it?" She looked back at Monti.

Her delicate features pinkened, and she dipped a nod. "*Oui*. It was my project during the cold days last winter."

"I've stitched one quilt, but it was nothing so nice as this one." The blanket had covered their bed after she was married, but Richard wretched on it so often during his drunken stupors, she'd eventually burned the thing. It hadn't seemed worth the effort to make another, so she settled for a store-bought woolen blanket.

"The time will come again when you will want to work with your hands, you think?" Monti rested a gentle hand on her shoulder, her eyes offering encouragement.

Rachel inhaled a breath. "I hope so."

The farther she traveled into this new life, the more buried dreams seemed to be resurrecting themselves. If only she could dare to follow them.

CHAPTER 28

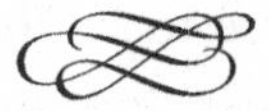

This isn't the journey's end I'd planned, yet could this be the one intended for me?
~ Rachel

The day smelled fresh, like hope and new beginnings.

Seth couldn't help a whistle as they rode the next morning. *Home*. He could feel it in the air. Taste it in the sunshine.

Rachel sent him a sidelong look, a smile quirking the corners of her mouth. "I wish a warm breakfast always made you so happy."

Monti's fresh-from-the-oven baguette had been an excellent start to the day, especially smothered in jam. But that wasn't the only reason for his smile.

He shot her a raised-brow grin. "This is nothing. Wait 'til I'm filled up with your fresh made bread. You won't be able to keep me quiet."

She dipped her chin, and her cheeks appled. Was that a blush? He just barely bit back a chuckle. The sweet warmth on her face made her absolutely beautiful.

Radiant. He'd have to bring on that look more often.

Within another hour, the tension seemed to ripple among them. They all felt how near they were to Simeon's valley, even Andy, as was plain by the questions he asked.

"Do you think there'll be any boys my age?" The lad peered around his mother to look at Seth as they rode four abreast through the open rolling hills.

"Well…" He scanned his memory for ages. "I think my nephew Robert will be eleven, or close to it. His sister Hannah is two years older, so she'd be about thirteen, give or take a few months. I'm sure they'll keep you busy."

A light shone in Andy's eyes, and he sent a hesitant look to his mother. Seth couldn't see her response, but it must have been encouraging, for Andy's hesitation turned to anticipation.

Had he ever played with others his own age? Hopefully Simeon's young'uns would help draw him out.

They crested a gentle hill, and the sight that spread before them caught Seth unaware. A wide valley stretched across the landscape, flanked by mountains on all four sides. The flat area was wider than any they'd seen on their travels, and three groups of buildings clustered in different parts of the spread.

"This must be it." Samuel's voice held a low reverence. They'd all stopped their horses to take in the view, for there was so much to see.

"It's more than I imagined." Seth studied the buildings. "I guess these might be Simeon and Noelle's homes." He motioned to the two cabins on the right side of the valley, both of which looked of newer construction than the buildings on the far left. In that distant cluster, mature trees shaded the house, barn, and other structures, although it was hard to make out details so far away.

"We ready?" Samuel's words nudged him from his studying.

"Let's go meet our family." He sent a smile to Rachel. Hopefully she would know he meant them to be her family too. Someday. As soon as she was ready.

She met his look, a hesitant smile playing on her lips.

With a nod, he moved his horse forward.

The first cabin they came to seemed quiet except for three horses dozing in the corral. Andy's mare nickered, and a bay gelding answered.

Seconds later, the cabin door flew wide, and a blur of blonde hair ran across the front porch and down the stairs. "Seth. Samuel."

Seth slid from his mount as a rush of joy pressed through him. He barely turned in time to catch the woman flinging herself in his arms. "Noelle."

The warmth of his sister's hug was like coming home, coiling all the good times and the homey smells and the feeling of security into a warm ball in his chest. He breathed in the scent that had always been Noelle's—their second mother. "I've missed you." He hadn't known how much until this moment.

She pulled back enough to raise her face to his, then sniffed, smiling through red-rimmed eyes. "It's about time you came to see me." Then she turned to Samuel and wrapped him in the same, all-encompassing hug.

Samuel pressed his face into Noelle's hair, and Seth could feel those same emotions coursing through him again as he watched the embrace. There was nothing quite as wonderful as family. Truly, this was coming home.

He turned his attention to Rachel and Andy, who had dismounted and stood back to watch them. He stepped to Rachel's side and slipped an arm around her waist, then leaned close to her ear. "I think you'll like her. She's a bit exuberant now, but when things settle down, you can get to know her. You actually remind me of her."

She turned a skeptical gaze on him.

He let his grin slip out as he nodded.

Motion in the doorway caught his eye. Two children stood there, close in age, maybe six or seven, both with Noelle's fair hair.

She pulled back from Samuel and motioned for the young ones. "Come, Lena and Eli. Meet your uncles." She turned to find Seth with her gaze, and that seemed to be the first time she noticed Rachel and Andy.

Her eyes lit, and she moved toward them. "I'm so sorry. Once I saw these boys of mine, I lost all manners." She pressed a hand to her chest. "I'm Noelle Abrams, the one who used to keep these two in line."

She gave Seth's arm a smack with the back of her fingers. Not hard, but he winced to make it seem worse. "Ow."

Noelle rolled her eyes as she'd done a thousand times before, then refocused on Rachel.

Seth's turn then. "Noelle, this is Rachel and her son, Andy. They've been riding with us since Fort Benton." He kept his arm around Rachel, both so she would feel the strength of his presence, and so Noelle would clearly know what this woman meant to him.

From the sparkle in his sister's eyes, she read everything he'd intended—and probably a great deal more. He fought to keep the heat from rising to his ears, but he'd never been good at hiding his emotions.

"Well." Noelle reached forward to take Rachel's hand. Her body tensed under his arm, but she allowed the action.

"I'm happier to meet you than you could possibly imagine." Noelle released Rachel and turned with a wave for them all to follow. "Bring yourselves in and meet my little ones. My husband's out hunting this morning, but he'll be back in a couple hours."

"Have you been to see Simeon yet?" This question she directed to Samuel, as she slipped her hand through the crook of his arm and walked with him toward the porch.

"Not yet. We stopped at the first cabin we came to. Stayed with Joseph and Monti last night."

"Oh, aren't they wonderful? I wish they lived closer so we could visit more." Noelle motioned toward her own little ones. "Eli is our oldest. He's eight. And Lena is six. Short for Evelena."

Noelle kept the conversation lively as they settled inside. Within a few minutes, she'd sent her children back out to spread the word that they'd arrived. Just like Noelle to be so efficient. When he was little, he called that trait bossy, but either way, she knew how to take charge and get things done.

Rachel was just starting to lose some of her tension when noise sounded from the yard.

"That must be Simeon." Noelle stepped to the door and opened it wide. "There you are. I'm so glad you could all come."

When Noelle shifted to the side, the man silhouetted just outside the door frame seemed larger than life. This broad-shouldered giant of a man couldn't possibly be his brother.

Simeon stepped inside, light from the lanterns giving expression to his features. He was tall, broad, and cut from this wilderness as though he'd been raised here. Yet underneath the fully grown exterior was a bit of the boy Seth remembered. Or at least, thought he remembered. He and Samuel had been so young when Simeon married and struck out to make his fortunes in the west.

Simeon's gaze slipped over him first, then Samuel, and his mouth twitched in a grin as he extended a hand. "Welcome home, boys. It's good to see you."

Seth couldn't help feeling like a lad in the presence of their big brother, but there was also the feeling of camaraderie. This man was family, even if it had been almost a score of years since they'd seen him.

While he introduced Rachel and Andy to their brother, more people entered the house. He could feel Rachel press into him, and he kept an arm around her waist. Simeon introduced his wife, Emma, and their three children, Hannah, Robert, and little Will, who'd just turned two.

The place was a cacophony of noise, and Robert soon snagged Andy to go see the horses. They needed to unsaddle their own mounts, so maybe that would be a good way for Seth to get Rachel out of the melee, too.

Before he could slip out with her, Noelle announced that she wanted Rachel and Andy to stay with her for at least the first night. Probably best, so his bossy sister could help them settle in. He'd be staying close, too.

Just yet, he didn't feel comfortable leaving Rachel. The last thing he wanted was for her to feel abandoned with the mass of his family.

~

The day they arrived at Noelle's house was a blur for Rachel. A sea of faces and names, eager children and adults just as excited about the reunion.

She'd never been part of a family like this. Each person seemed genuinely thrilled to see the others, the love evident in their faces and hugs and nudges. Surely this was a result of so many years apart, but it made her wonder just how magical their childhood must have been.

The stories Papa told of families like these had seemed make-believe, for she'd never really thought it possible for love to flow so freely.

Seth stuck close to her, for which she was grateful. Yet, she didn't like how it sometimes kept him from visiting with the other men. She'd been through events much harder than this and managed them on her own. She could handle this too.

Except she wasn't on her own. God would provide the strength she needed. He'd already done so much for her. He'd brought her and Andy from a farm in Missouri all the way to Canada, through Indian territory, past forts filled with raucous men, over mountains and across rivers. He'd protected them from danger by bringing them under the watchful eyes of two of the kindest, most upstanding men she'd ever known.

And He'd given her a man to love, a man she'd never have believed existed until this journey's end.

And all the while, she'd worried and fretted and second guessed Her Father.

I'm sorry, Lord. Sorry for not looking to You first.

As they sat around the table the next morning and finished the breakfast meal, the day seemed to hold an expectant feel.

"What say you, boys?" Daniel, Noelle's husband, relaxed in his chair, a mug of coffee in one hand. "Would you like a day to settle in, or do you wanna see the area?"

Samuel pushed his empty plate away. "I'd like to see the place. Emma said something about her uncle having herds of horses and cattle. Do they pasture nearby?"

Daniel nodded. "We can ride out there." He turned to Seth. "You coming, too?"

Seth shook his head. "I think I'll stay around here for now." His gaze slid to Rachel for a half second before returning to his brother-in-law. "I'd like to see it, but maybe there'll be a chance later."

Should she tell him now that he needn't stay on her part, or wait until they were alone? Richard had hated when she contradicted him in front of others, even if Andy was the only one watching. She'd do better to tell Seth in privacy as soon as she could secure a moment with him.

About an hour after they finished the morning meal, she found the opportunity. Samuel had ridden off with Noelle's husband, and Andy was occupying the younger children with a ball and stick. It seemed Noelle was expecting another babe and had retreated to her room for a few minutes of rest.

"I think I'll go for a walk." She sent Seth a bright look. "Would you like to join me?"

He'd just stretched out in the oversize chair by the hearth—perhaps not good timing on her part—but he pushed up to his feet. "Sure."

They started toward the nearest mountain, walking among the low cedar and pine that lined its base. The sun shone brightly, but the glow didn't seem to carry the same strength here as it had in Missouri. Certainly there wasn't the same muggy feeling in the air.

Now, how should she broach the topic? Thankfully, he was the first to speak.

"I hope my family hasn't been too much for you."

She meant to let out a soft chuckle, but it came out more like a half-laugh, half-huff. "They were a little overwhelming at first. But very…interesting. I've never seen people who share so much. Who love so much."

He chuckled. "I guess that comes from having so many kids among us. The house was always loud. Whether we were laughing or fighting or just eating the evening meal." His gaze shifted to her. "Do you think you can get used to it? At least for a little while?"

She knew what he was asking. But she needed to say her part first.

She stopped and turned so he would have no doubt of her earnestness. "I can get used to it. I know you've witnessed my weak moments, but I'm strong. Truly. I can manage a few eager family members. You don't need to linger around the house just to protect me from your sister." She said the last bit with hint of a smile so he would know she meant the words in the kindest possible way.

He studied her, his intense gaze not just reading her words and expression, but pressing deeper, seeing the emotions she was trying not to show.

One corner of his mouth tipped, but his eyes didn't give credit to his attempt at a grin. "I guess I'm afraid you'll decide I'm not worth all the chaos and run."

The vulnerability in his words, in his gaze, speared her. "I guess I've run away before, haven't I?" She slipped her hand into his. She wasn't usually the one to initiate a touch, but this seemed right.

He rubbed his thumb across the back of her hand. "This time, I'll go after you straightway. You won't get far." Now the grin did touch his eyes.

She inhaled a strengthening breath. Now was the moment. "You know, it's possible for a person to change. If God steps in, takes away any desire for that old habit."

He stilled, searching her gaze.

She let him see the truth in her eyes, spread across her face.

"Do you mean it?" The yearning in his expression made her chest ache.

"I do." The next words spilled out, not nearly as frightening as she expected them to be. "I may have the urge to run every now and then, but I'm going to have to trust God to keep me strong. We both will."

His gaze glimmered, the depth of his feeling pressing harder on her chest. He stepped closer, bringing him near enough that the warmth of his breath brushed her face. "I won't gamble with your heart, Rachel. I'll work hard to be the man you and Andy need. The man God's called me to be."

He took her other hand and lifted their joined fingers to his chest.

"I won't always get it right. I might disappoint you." One corner of his mouth tipped. "I'm pretty sure I will disappoint you, every so often. Hopefully not where it really matters, though." His face turned serious again. "With God working with us, we can be *stronger together.*"

The beat of his heart thumped against her fingers, matching the racing of her own pulse. *Lord, let me not choose blindly. Give me wisdom.*

This decision should frighten her more than it did. The thought of giving herself again to a man. Yes, that did scare her. But the thought of giving herself to this man? To Seth in a marriage interwoven with faith in every part?

She could summon no panic at the thought.

So she raised her gaze to meet his, locking with those intense eyes that made her want to lose herself in him. "I believe you're right. We *can* be stronger together."

His Adam's apple bobbed. "I thought I'd have to wait longer before I could ask this." He raised one of her hands to his lips and pressed a kiss to her knuckles. "Rachel Gray, will you do me the honor of marrying me, allowing me to become a father to Andy, to point him to the Heavenly Father?"

His words were perfect, capturing her heart's desire for all three of them. She had to swallow the lump of emotion clogging her throat. "Yes, Seth. Please."

His gaze was hungry, searching hers, perhaps to be sure he'd heard right. Hopefully her smile would be proof enough, for she couldn't seem to hold in the giddiness sliding through her.

Bit by bit, one side of his mouth tipped in that roguish grin that always started a flutter in her middle. He eased forward, lingering an extra second with their foreheads not quite touching. As though savoring even the thought of a kiss.

Then he tipped his head and brought his mouth to hers.

The sensation was everything she'd imagined, and warmth settled through her. This was what it felt like to be home.

CHAPTER 29

Where these people I love abide will always be home to me.
~ Seth

This day had been unlike anything Seth expected. So much better. So much fuller.

He stood by the fence in the dim light of the moonless sky, taking a minute to enjoy his gelding's company before going inside for the night. In truth, he needed a moment to clear his head.

It still seemed almost too wonderful that Rachel had accepted his proposal. After spending more time than they should have on their walk, she'd slipped her hand in his as they meandered back to Noelle's cabin.

The request she made of him on that return trek was what now had his mind churning. She wanted to find her brother before they wed. Wanted him to be there for the ceremony.

Of course she did. She needed her own family here, especially the one relation she still seemed to hold affection for. He couldn't deny her—*wouldn't* deny her.

But he also couldn't deny the fact that finding one man in the midst of this vast wilderness could be nearly impossible. *Lead me to him, Lord. Please.*

Maybe Henry would still be at Fort Hamilton as he'd been the last time he wrote to Rachel. About a year ago, she'd said.

At least she agreed to let Seth ride on to find him alone, leaving her and Andy at Noelle's home. With both his brothers and his brother-in-law here to protect them, he didn't worry about their safety. And time with Noelle might be good for Rachel. A chance to play with all the youngsters would surely be fun for Andy. Like having cousins he'd never known about.

And these would truly become his cousins.

A grin tugged his face. *You've given so much more than I deserve, Lord. Thank you.*

With the prayer on his lips, he gave the horse a final pat and turned toward the cabin. Light filtered through the window, drawing him toward the warmth of family—both those who'd been connected to him since birth and those who would soon be his to claim in truth.

When he pushed the door open, little Eli sprung toward him. "Guess what, Uncle Seth. Ma says we can go swimming tomorrow with Andy if you'll take us. Will you? Please?"

He raised his gaze to the adults in the room, mainly his sister, whose mouth pursed in that look she always wore when things were playing out just as she planned.

"Where do you swim? Is there a lake I haven't seen yet?" He turned the question to Eli, shooting a glance up at Samuel, who would hopefully be his partner in this excursion. Three exuberant bodies might be more than he could take on alone.

Samuel didn't wear the grin he expected. Instead, he had had a serious look that struck a chord of dread in Seth's chest.

Eli was already answering, though, so he forced himself to listen. "...it's a creek but there's a spot perfect for swimming. We take our lines an' try to catch Mama fish to cook after we swim."

The words called up memories of his own childhood, so clear they could have been memories of the week before. Again, he lifted his gaze to Samuel as he answered the boy. "That sounds like the perfect thing. Maybe your Uncle Samuel will come along. He's always been the better fisherman."

"Yeah." Eli turned his blond head and pleading eyes to his other uncle. "You'll come, too, won't you? I'm not too good at the fishing part."

Samuel reached out and tousled the boy's head. "'Fraid I can't this time, but I'll take you fishing sometime soon." He raised his gaze to Seth, all hint of mirth slipping from his eyes. "Rachel said you're going on to Fort Hamilton to look for her brother. I'd like to go instead."

The words struck Seth like a blow, though he couldn't say exactly why. "What do you mean? You want to go with me?"

Samuel shook his head. "Your place is here. I want to see the fort, so I'll go without you."

The idea made sense, but something about the proposition didn't sit right. "Are you sure? Maybe it is best we go together."

Samuel shook his head, determination locking his jaw. "Your place is here."

Seth shot a look at Rachel, who sat beside Noelle. She raised her brows and gave a slight shrug, a message that clearly said, *Do what you think is best. I support your decision.* A trust that should warm him to the core.

Except this didn't feel right.

He turned back to Samuel. "Why don't we sleep on it and decide tomorrow."

"I was planning to head out tomorrow. I'll leave after I break my fast."

"Tomorrow?" He wanted to grunt in frustration. "Why the rush?"

Samuel raised a brow, a grin tickling his mouth for the first time. "You want her brother here for the wedding, right?"

In other words, the sooner he went, the sooner they could be married. He couldn't disagree with that line of thinking. And it gave him a bit of relief to see that Samuel didn't seem reticent about him being the first to marry.

He let out a breath and scrubbed a hand through his hair. "All right. If that's what you think should happen." He sent a final look to Rachel to make sure she didn't have thoughts to add. Her eyes showed simple agreement.

Easing out a breath, he finally met his brother's gaze. "I appreciate it. Be careful, though." *Please.* He may be adding another important piece to his family, but he couldn't bear to lose this part of him. His brother. His twin.

~

"You're going to love it, Ma. I promise."

Rachel couldn't help a smile at her son, especially since this was the fourth time he'd said the words since she agreed to go swimming with them. "I hope so."

But *love* might be too much to hope for. She'd settle for *tolerate.*

She followed her son out of the cabin and down the porch steps. Noelle's husband and children were hitching the wagon she and Seth would take to the swimming hole.

Just then, Seth and Samuel stepped from the barn, Samuel's horse ambling behind him.

Saddled and ready to leave.

A pang pressed her chest at the sight. She hated to make him leave again after they'd just arrived here. Maybe she should go herself instead of asking either of the brothers to attend her errand. Seth would surely hate the idea, and she wasn't fond of it herself. Not with the reputation for drinking and carousing Fort Hamilton had gained.

Samuel shook his brother's hand, then turned and climbed astride his big red gelding in a fluid motion. Both men turned toward her and Andy.

Samuel offered a grin as he neared. "Enjoy the swim. I'll be back in a week or so with your brother."

She raised a hand to shield her eyes from the sun. "You have the letter I wrote to him?"

He patted his pack. "Tucked in oilcloth so nothing can hurt it."

She smiled her thanks. "I'm sorry to ask this of you, but you have my thanks."

His grin tipped more on one side than the other, that same look Seth could accomplish. "I'm glad to see the country." With a final glance around, he raised his hand in farewell. "See you soon."

As his horse found its traveling stride, Rachel turned her gaze to Seth. The man looked almost lost standing alone in the yard, staring out after his brother. She moved to his side and slipped her hand in his. He wove their fingers together and pressed her hand against his leg, as though he needed all the contact he could get just now.

She studied his profile, the tight line of his jaw. The worry creases at the edge of his eyes. "Are you concerned?"

He let out a long breath and turned to her. "I don't know if I am or not. He should be fine, but something doesn't feel quite right." Then his face eased into a smile. Not his wide grin, but a real smile, nonetheless. "Now I'm placing him in God's hands. And we're all going swimming, right?"

He turned to Andy. "Did you tell your ma she's gonna love this? 'Cause we'll make sure she does."

"I did." Andy nodded in full agreement.

She couldn't help but laugh. "I hope this is half as good as you're both building it up to be."

A twinkle lit Seth's gaze as he slipped an arm around her waist and turned her toward the barn where the sound of children's voices called to them. "It'll be better than good."

And as she strolled to the barn nestled in Seth's hold, her son whistling a cheery tune beside her, she couldn't help sending a silent prayer upward. *Thank you, Lord, for bringing me home.*

THE END

There is no fear in love; but perfect love casteth out fear:
1 John 4:18 (KJV)

Did you enjoy Seth and Rachel's story? I hope so!
Would you take a quick minute to leave a review?
It doesn't have to be long. Just a sentence or two telling what you liked about the story!

~

And would you like to receive a **free short story about a special moment in Gideon and Leah's happily-ever after**?
Get the free short story and sign-up for insider email updates at https://mistymbeller.com/free-short-story

And here's a peek at the next book in the series, *This Daring Journey,* (Samuel's story):

CHAPTER ONE

"What hornet's nest have I stepped into now?"
~ Samuel

LATE AUGUST, 1869
NEAR FORT HAMILTON, ALBERTA, CANADA

A shot ripped through the air, and Samuel Grant ducked down in his saddle. A reflexive action, because the rifle hadn't been aimed at him.

At least, he didn't think so.

Still, the thud of his pulse accelerated. He must be nearing Henry Clark's cabin along the Belly River. The man he'd been sent to find. Maybe Clark was hunting.

Samuel straightened and cupped a hand around his mouth to sound his presence. But another voice broke through before he could call out.

"Woman, quit yer fire and we'll not hurt you." A deep, tobacco-roughened tone yelled somewhere in the woods ahead.

The men at the fort had said Clark built a cabin out here by the river for his wife. Was she being accosted by intruders? Where was Clark?

Reaching for his Hawken rifle, Samuel slid from his gelding as soundlessly as he could. If Henry Clark or his family were in trouble, surely they'd appreciate help. Another blast echoed as he fastened his horse to a tree. This shot sounded nearer. Maybe it had come from where the man's voice had originated.

He gave the animal a pat, then turned his focus to the danger, creeping from tree to tree.

Another boom. This one's reverberation was more like the first gunshot he'd heard. Not only had it come from the same location, but it sounded like the same model of gun. "I said leave." The woman's voice was muffled by trees and distance, but he noticed something of an accent. Slight. "You do not hear English?" Her tone held a mocking quality now. "How about French." She let loose a melodic string of words Samuel couldn't comprehend. That must be her native tongue, as easily as it flowed.

The man hiding in the woods started to speak again, but the woman's voice rang out, growing in pitch and covering whatever he meant to say.

"Or perhaps you don't understand French either. Must I speak the language of the *dirty redskin* for you to hear me?" The way she spat the label made it clear she disliked the ugly moniker.

Then she spoke in a high-low cadence that caught Samuel's breath. He couldn't understand a word—if they were meant to be words—but each syllable rang with fluid motion. Only a native speaker could be so comfortable piecing those sounds together. Was she Indian then?

He crept closer, moving toward her instead of to the right where the man had to be standing. Another rifle shot brought him up short.

"Did that help you understand, dirty white man? None of my people would act as you have. And now I say again, *leave this place*."

This woman had more spunk than a starving dog fighting for fresh meat. Could she be Clark's wife? How far had the man gone to hunt? Surely, he'd come to his woman's defense if he were close by.

"You can spout your fancy language all day. It won't change what we came to do." The gravelly voice again. It held just enough leer to make Samuel's gut churn. *We* meant there was more than one man trying to advance on her. "We've got enough fellas to quiet you down for a long time, but things'll go better if you put your gun on the ground."

Samuel shifted his direction toward the men again, tuning his senses to pick-up on any sound they made. As he crept forward, both warring parties fell silent.

He kept his steps as noiseless as possible, walking on the balls of his feet and straining for any sign of movement through the trees. When he caught a flash of brown, approximately the color of the buckskins most of the men at the fort had worn, he ducked behind a sturdy tree. He needed to get closer so he'd have a good shot, but he'd have to wait until the men were thoroughly distracted.

A faint rustle sounded from the direction of the attackers, then half a second later, another shot exploded. A man screamed, filling the air with curses and names no woman should hear, much less be called.

When his screaming settled to muttering, she called, "There's more where that came from."

Samuel peeked around the tree. The men were shifting, maybe bringing back the injured man. This was Samuel's chance.

He darted forward to hide behind another tree. He was closer with fewer branches encumbering his view. He could see four men. Rangy mountain men, just like all the others he'd seen at the fort. Crimson smeared the shoulder of one, whom the others gathered around.

They were talking in low murmurs so Samuel couldn't make out the words. But they must have reached a consensus, for the three uninjured men straightened and raised their rifles. They looked to be planning an attack. If he didn't act now, he might lose his opportunity.

Positioning his gun, he aimed down the sight at the tree just above one man's head. *Lord, let this do the trick.*

He squeezed the trigger, and the bullet surged toward its target in a deafening blast and a cloud of gunpowder.

Another shout. More cursing as the men turned to find this new source of danger.

"Get down." The one with the most gray in his full beard motioned the others toward a fallen log. The wounded man limped slower than the others, clutching his shoulder.

"That won't help you any." Samuel filled his voice with as much confidence as he could muster. "I have half a dozen men hiding with rifles aimed at you. And five more circling around to your rear."

As he motioned toward the trees behind the attackers, he could see the tops of their heads spinning to search.

He pushed his advantage. "You'll obey the lady's orders and leave here, or I'll tell my men to pick you off one by one. It won't take more than four shots, you can be sure."

The older fellow spoke. "We've got no trouble with you. That woman's husband sold us this place. We've come to collect."

Samuel barely bit back a growl. "By running her out of her house? Or did you plan to make her part of the bargain? Either way, you're not collecting today. We'll let you get your horses and ride away, but if one of you so much as looks back, I'll give the sign for my men to let loose. Clear?"

Gray Beard raised his head a little, scanning the area. Samuel worked hard not to flinch, not to show his hand.

Just then his gelding whinnied from the trees behind him. Other horses answered, probably those belonging to these men. The cacophony filled the woods.

The ruckus must have appeared to give truth to his bluff, for Gray Beard raised his hands, then eased up from behind the log. "Don't shoot. We'll leave. Like I said, we've no fight with you and your men."

"All four of you stand up, then drop your rifles right there." He aimed his gun at their leader, but kept his gaze circling all four of them. He wasn't naïve enough to think these were the only weapons the villains possessed, but he was counting on their fear of his greater numbers to keep them from circling back with other guns.

When they'd laid their rifles down, he said, "Now march toward your horses and mount up. Once you're on, I'll give you to the count of twenty before I give my men the nod to start shooting. I suggest you be out of range by then."

"We'll be gone." The men marched toward the shifting animals he could just see through the branches. Gray Beard had a stiff set to his shoulders, as though not a bit happy with being forced to leave his prize. The injured man stumbled, unsteady. Thankfully, one of the others helped him mount.

When they were all in the saddle, he gave them one last reminder. "I start counting now."

Gray Beard sent an annoyed scowl back his direction, then signaled his horse forward, the others following close on his animal's tail.

In less than a minute, the crashing of the animals' hooves through the woods died away. Eerie silence took over the area.

Samuel eased out a breath. Now he had to figure out where Henry Clark was, and why his wife had been left alone to defend herself.

And he had to make sure he didn't get himself shot in the process.

Moriah Clark angled her face so she could see better through the peephole between cabin logs, straining to catch any motion in the trees at the edge of the clearing. She could hear the occasional hum of male voices, but no movement. Were they spreading out to approach her from all sides? That's what she would have done from the start if she'd been planning the attack. Thankfully these men weren't so strategic.

And thankfully, she'd sensed something was wrong before the first man stepped from the trees. Before she met Henry, she would have assumed that instinct was her ancestors' spirits warning her. Now, she could direct her thanks to the proper source.

Thank you, Lord. And please give me wisdom to know how to fend them off.

A rustling in the cradle behind her spread tension through her shoulders. Then a soft murmur. *Not now, Lord. Please.*

She sent a glance back as the blanket shifted, and a tiny hand rose up from the cloth. Another mew sounded. Cherry wouldn't be put off much longer. Moriah's own body told her how long it had been since her daughter's last meal.

She turned back to the peephole to scan the woods again. The crash of steps sounded in the trees, too heavy for men. Horses? Were more strangers coming? Surely these intruders weren't leaving of their own accord. Maybe she should send another shot their way.

Her daughter let out a cry, the warning kind that always preceded a full-blown wail. If she didn't at least pick-up the babe, the men would hear and know she was more vulnerable than she pretended. She couldn't shoot attackers and nurse an infant at the same time. So far, she'd been able to keep Cherry a secret from the rest of the world, and she couldn't let that change now. Both their lives would be in even greater danger.

With a final scan revealing no more motion in the trees, she turned from the lookout position and laid her gun on the table, then strode toward her baby girl. She slid her hands under the bundle of blankets swaddling the little body, then scooped Cherry up and tucked her close. "It's all right, honey. We're safe."

Cherry nuzzled Moriah's neck, seeking out her long-awaited meal. The feel of her tiny, trusting daughter was almost enough to distract her from the danger outside. Or at least make her want to hide away and pretend everything in the world was as sweet and innocent as this new life.

But she couldn't let her guard down. Cherry depended on her mother to be strong, to protect her from evil men. Her daughter had no idea yet about the ways of the world. Especially in this territory where half-Peigan women who married white men were considered nothing more than a commodity. Worth a handful of horses, if she kept her mouth shut and filled her husband's belly.

Turning, she held her daughter close and moved back toward the peephole. She couldn't shoot the rifle with Cherry in her arms, but it was quiet outside. Maybe the men had left. Was that too much to hope for? God could perform miracles, so maybe He'd answered this prayer. *Finally.*

Cherry's nuzzling became insistent as Moriah peered through the hole to the world outside. The baby banged her little mouth against Moriah's neck to show her frustration. "It's all right, sweet one. Wait a minute longer." She bounced to soothe the babe even as she tried to focus on the trees.

Something moved out there. A blue cloth shifted among the branches, then a man stepped from the woods.

Her body tensed. Should she lay Cherry down so she could shoot at him? She had to. If he advanced much closer, he could charge the cabin and barge in before she could react.

But he stopped. Only a few yards away from the trees, he halted, his gun held loosely in both hands.

"Ma'am. I ran those good-for-nothings off, and I'm not here to hurt you." His voice rang loud in the clearing, deep and commanding. It held a civilized edge, unlike the men who'd made three attempts now to take over her cabin. Was this another of their tactics?

He spoke again. "My name is Samuel Grant. I've come to see your husband, Henry Clark. I assume this is his place. I'm a friend of his sister, Rachel. She sent me with a letter for him."

The words seemed foreign as she tried to draw them in. Henry's sister? Had Rachel heard of her brother's death?

Moriah's heart thudded hard in her chest. That wasn't possible, since she'd been careful not to let anyone know of his passing these last six months. She'd known the harassment would start as soon as men from the fort realized a woman lived alone in this well-built cabin.

Cherry shifted again in her arms, rooting into Moriah's neck as she renewed her search for nourishment. She grunted her dissatisfaction at being thwarted for so long.

"Ma'am. Are you kin to Henry Clark?" The man outside shifted and seemed to be growing impatient.

If he really was a friend of Henry's sister, she owed it to Rachel to let her know of her brother's death. Henry had been so fond of the sister he hadn't seen in over a dozen years. He'd read her letters for weeks after receiving each one. In fact, he'd been using those missives to teach Moriah to read English.

Before the hunting trip that changed everything. Her heart squeezed at the reminder.

"Ma'am?" The man was peering toward the cabin as though he thought maybe she'd slipped out the back door. He might come investigate if she didn't say something soon.

Cherry let out a complaint, the kind of cry that came just before the true wails. She wouldn't be silenced much longer.

Moriah had to get rid of this man.

Get THIS DARING JOURNEY at your favorite retailer.

ABOUT THE AUTHOR

Misty M. Beller is a *USA Today* bestselling author of romantic mountain stories, set on the 1800s frontier and woven with the truth of God's love.

Raised on a farm and surrounded by family, Misty developed her love for horses, history, and adventure. These days, her husband and children provide fresh adventure every day, keeping her both grounded and crazy.

Misty's passion is to create inspiring Christian fiction infused with the grandeur of the mountains, writing historical romance that displays God's abundant love through the twists and turns in the lives of her characters.

Sharing her stories with readers is a dream come true for Misty. She writes from her country home in South Carolina and escapes to the mountains any chance she gets.

Connect with Misty at www.MistyMBeller.com

ALSO BY MISTY M. BELLER

Call of the Rockies

Freedom in the Mountain Wind

Hope in the Mountain River

Light in the Mountain Sky

Courage in the Mountain Wilderness

Faith in the Mountain Valley

Honor in the Mountain Refuge

Peace in the Mountain Haven

Calm in the Mountain Storm

Brides of Laurent

A Warrior's Heart

A Healer's Promise

A Daughter's Courage

Hearts of Montana

Hope's Highest Mountain

Love's Mountain Quest

Faith's Mountain Home

Texas Rancher Trilogy

The Rancher Takes a Cook

The Ranger Takes a Bride

The Rancher Takes a Cowgirl

Wyoming Mountain Tales

A Pony Express Romance

A Rocky Mountain Romance

A Sweetwater River Romance

A Mountain Christmas Romance

The Mountain Series

The Lady and the Mountain Man

The Lady and the Mountain Doctor

The Lady and the Mountain Fire

The Lady and the Mountain Promise

The Lady and the Mountain Call

This Treacherous Journey

This Wilderness Journey

This Freedom Journey (novella)

This Courageous Journey

This Homeward Journey

This Daring Journey

This Healing Journey

Made in the USA
Las Vegas, NV
07 December 2023